MORE NOVELS BY GARY D. SCHMIDT

Straw into Gold

Lizzie Bright and the Buckminster Boy

The Wednesday Wars

Trouble

What Came from the Stars

Orbiting Jupiter

Pay Attention, Carter Jones

OKAY for NOW

GARY D. SCHMIDT

HOUGHTON MIFFLIN HARCOURT
BOSTON   NEW YORK

All rights reserved. Originally published in hardcover in the United States by
Clarion Books, an imprint of Houghton Mifflin Harcourt Publishing Company, 2011.

For information about permission to reproduce selections from this book, write to
trade.permissions@hmhco.com or to Permissions, Houghton Mifflin Harcourt
Publishing Company, 3 Park Avenue, 19th floor, New York, New York 10016.

hmhbooks.com

The text of this book is set in 13-point Garamond No. 3.

Library of Congress Cataloging-in-Publication Data is available.
Library of Congress Control Number: 2010942981

ISBN: 978-0-547-15260-8 hardcover
ISBN: 978-0-544-02280-5 paperback

Manufactured in the United States of America
DOC 11
4500792433

My dear Anne,

all of these pages are for you —

except a few of them.

Those are for Mark Hutchins, of New Portland Hill, Maine.

You'll know which ones are his.

But the rest are all yours,

because I love you.

CHAPTER ONE

The Arctic Tern
Plate CCL

JOE PEPITONE once gave me his New York Yankees baseball cap.

I'm not lying.

He gave it to me. To me, Doug Swieteck. To me.

Joe Pepitone and Horace Clarke came all the way out on the Island to Camillo Junior High and I threw with them. Me and Danny Hupfer and Holling Hood-hood, who were good guys. We all threw with Joe Pepitone and Horace Clarke, and we batted too. They sang to us while we swung away: "He's a batta, he's a batta-batta-batta, he's a batta . . ." That was their song.

And afterward, Horace Clarke gave Danny his cap,

and Joe Pepitone gave Holling his jacket (probably because he felt sorry for him on account of his dumb name), and then Joe Pepitone handed me his cap. He reached out and took it off his head and handed it to me. Just like that. It was signed on the inside, so anyone could tell that it was really his. Joe Pepitone's.

It was the only thing I ever owned that hadn't belonged to some other Swieteck before me.

I hid it for four and a half months. Then my stupid brother found out about it. He came in at night when I was asleep and whipped my arm up behind my back so high I couldn't even scream it hurt so bad and he told me to decide if I wanted a broken arm or if I wanted to give him Joe Pepitone's baseball cap. I decided on the broken arm. Then he stuck his knee in the center of my spine and asked if I wanted a broken back along with the broken arm, and so I told him Joe Pepitone's cap was in the basement behind the oil furnace.

It wasn't, but he went downstairs anyway. That's what a chump he is.

So I threw on a T-shirt and shorts and Joe Pepitone's cap—which was under my pillow the whole time, the jerk—and got outside. Except he caught me. Dragged me behind the garage. Took Joe Pepitone's baseball cap. Pummeled me in places where the bruises wouldn't show.

A strategy that my... is none of your business.

I think he kept the cap for ten hours — just long enough for me to see him with it at school. Then he traded it to Link Vitelli for cigarettes, and Link Vitelli kept it for a day — just long enough for me to see him with it at school. Then Link traded it to Glenn Dillard for a comb. A comb! And Glenn Dillard kept it for a day — just long enough for me to see him with it at school. Then Glenn lost it while driving his brother's Mustang without a license and with the top down, the jerk. It blew off somewhere on Jerusalem Avenue. I looked for it for a week.

I guess now it's in a gutter, getting rained on or something. Probably anyone who walks by looks down and thinks it's a piece of junk.

They're right. That's all it is. Now.

But once, it was the only thing I ever owned that hadn't belonged to some other Swieteck before me.

I know. That means a big fat zero to anyone else.

I tried to talk to my father about it. But it was a wrong day. Most days are wrong days. Most days he comes home red-faced with his eyes half closed and with that deadly silence that lets you know he'd have a whole lot to say if he ever let himself get started and no one better get him started because there's no telling when he'll stop and if he ever did get started then pretty Mr. Culross at freaking Culross Lumber better not be the one to get him started because he'd punch pretty

Mr. Culross's freaking lights out and he didn't care if he did lose his job over it because it's a lousy job anyway.

That was my father not letting himself get started.

But I had a plan.

All I had to do was get my father to take me to Yankee Stadium. That's all. If I could just see Joe Pepitone one more time. If I could just tell him what happened to my baseball cap. He'd look at me, and he'd laugh and rough up my hair, and then he'd take off his cap and he'd put it on my head. "Here, Doug," Joe Pepitone would say. Like that. "Here, Doug. You look a whole lot better in it than I do." That's what Joe Pepitone would say. Because that's the kind of guy he is.

That was the plan. And all I had to do was get my father to listen.

But I picked a wrong day. Because there aren't any right days.

And my father said, "Are you crazy? Are you freaking crazy? I work forty-five hours a week to put food on the table for you, and you want me to take you to Yankee Stadium because you lost some lousy baseball cap?"

"It's not just some lousy—"

That's all I got out. My father's hands are quick. That's the kind of guy *he* is.

Who knows how much my father got out the day he finally let himself get started saying what he wanted to say to pretty Mr. Culross and didn't even try to stop himself from saying it. But whatever he said, he came home with a pretty good shiner, because pretty Mr. Culross turned out to have hands even quicker than my father's.

And pretty Mr. Culross had one other advantage: he could fire my father if he wanted to.

So my father came home with his lunch pail in his hand and a bandage on his face and the last check he would ever see from Culross Lumber, Inc., and he looked at my mother and said, "Don't you say a thing," and he looked at me and said, "Still worried about a lousy baseball cap?" and he went upstairs and started making phone calls.

Mom kept us in the kitchen.

He came down when we were finishing supper, and Mom jumped up from the table and brought over the plate she'd been keeping warm in the oven. She set it down in front of him.

"It's not all dried out, is it?" he said.

"I don't think so," Mom said.

"You don't think so," he said, then took off the aluminum foil, sighed, and reached for the ketchup. He smeared it all over his meat loaf. Thick.

Took a red bite.

"We're moving," he said.

Chewed.

"Moving?" said my mother.

"To Marysville. Upstate." Another red bite. Chewing. "Ballard Paper Mill has a job, and Ernie Eco says he can get me in."

"Ernie Eco," said my mother quietly.

"Don't you start about him," said my father.

"So it will begin all over again."

"I said —"

"The bars, being gone all night, coming back home when you're —"

My father stood up.

"Which of your sons will it be this time?" my mother said.

My father looked at me.

I put my eyes down and worked at what was left of my meat loaf.

It took us three days to pack. My mother didn't talk much the whole time. The first morning, she asked only two questions.

"How are we going to let Lucas know where we've gone?"

Lucas is my oldest brother who stopped beating me up a year and a half ago when the United States Army drafted him to beat up Vietcong instead. He's in a delta somewhere but we don't know any more than that because he isn't allowed to tell us and he doesn't write home much anyway. Fine by me.

My father looked up from his two fried eggs. "How are we going to let Lucas know where we've gone? The U.S. Postal Service," he said in that kind of voice that makes you feel like you are the dope of the world. "And didn't I tell you over easy?" He pushed the plate of eggs away, picked up his mug of coffee, and looked out the window. "I'm not going to miss this freaking place," he said.

Then, "Are you going to rent a truck?" my mother asked, real quiet.

My father sipped his coffee. Sipped again.

"Ernie Eco will be down with a truck from the mill," he said.

My mother didn't ask anything else.

My father brought home boxes from the A&P on one of those summer days when the sky is too hot to be blue and all it can work up is a hazy white. Everything is sweating, and you're thinking that if you were up in the top—I mean, the really top—stands in Yankee Stadium, there might be a breeze, but probably there isn't one anywhere else. My father gave me a box that still smelled like the bananas it brought up from somewhere that speaks Spanish and told me to put in whatever I had and I should throw out anything I couldn't get in it. I did—except for Joe Pepitone's cap because it's lying in a gutter getting rained on, which you might remember if you cared.

So what? So what? I'm glad we're going.

After the first day of packing, the house was a wreck. Open boxes everywhere, with all sorts of stuff thrown in. My mother tried to stick on labels and keep everything organized—like all the kitchen stuff in the boxes in the kitchen, and all the sheets and pillowcases and towels in the boxes by the linen closet upstairs, and all the sturdiest boxes by the downstairs door for my father's tools and junk. But after he filled the boxes by the downstairs door, he started to load stuff in with the dishes, stuff like screwdrivers and wrenches and a vise that he dropped on a stack of plates, and he didn't even turn around to look when he heard them shatter. But my mother did. She lifted out the pieces she had wrapped in newspaper, and for a moment she held them close to her. Then she dropped them back in the box like they were garbage, because that's all they were now. Garbage.

Like Joe Pepitone's cap.

On the third day, Ernie Eco came down with the truck, and me and my brother and Ernie Eco and my father loaded the beds and the couch and the table and chairs—the stove and the refrigerator belonged to the guy we rented the house from. After that we loaded all the boxes. My mother had dug up the garden she'd worked on and put the plants into pots and watered them for the trip, but Ernie Eco said there wasn't any room for them and even if there were he might have to make a quick turn and they'd flip over and get the truck all dirty and so my father said to leave them and we should all get in the car since we were ready to go.

"Not yet," my mother said.

We all looked at her, kind of startled.

She went back to the pots, all lined up on the front porch, and she took three in her arms and carried them to the McCall house next door. Then she came back, took up another three, and carried them across the street to the Petronis. When she came back again, I started up to the porch to help but my father smacked me on the shoulder. "If she wants to do it, let her do it herself," he said. Ernie Eco laughed, the jerk.

So my mother carried all the pots, three by three, and put them by houses up and down the street. People started coming out on their stoops and they'd take the pots from her and put them down and they'd hug my mother and then she'd turn away.

So that's what I was doing — watching my mother give away her plants — when Holling Hoodhood came up the street carrying a brown paper bag. I'd never seen him on this side of town before.

He waved. "Hey, Doug," he said.

"Hey," I said.

"Mr. Swieteck."

My father nodded. He watched my mother. He wanted to get going.

A minute passed. My mother was back up on the porch, gathering another armload.

"I heard you were moving," said Holling.

"You heard right," I said.

He nodded. "No eighth grade at Camillo Junior High."

"I guess not."

He nodded again.

Another minute passing.

"So," he said, "I brought you something to remember us by." He held up the bag and I took it. It wasn't heavy.

"Thanks," I said.

Another minute.

"Where are you moving?"

"Marysville."

"Oh," said Holling. He nodded like he'd heard of it, which he hadn't since no one has ever heard of it unless he lives there, which hardly anyone does. "Marysville."

"In the Catskills," I said.

He nodded. "It'll be cooler up in the mountains."

I nodded. "Maybe."

He rubbed his hands together.

"You take care of yourself, Doug," he said.

"Say hi to everyone for me," I said.

"I will."

He held out his hand. I took it. We shook.

"So long, Doug."

"So long."

And he turned, walked across the street, said hi to my mother. She handed him one of her plants. He took it, and then he was gone. Like that.

"Go get in the car," said my father.

I went over to the car, but before I got in, I opened up Holling's brown paper bag and took out what was inside. A jacket. A New York Yankees jacket. I looked at the signature on the inside of the collar. You know whose jacket this was, right?

I put it on. I didn't care how white the sky was, or how much the whole world was sweating. It felt like the breezes on the top stands of Yankee Stadium.

"What a stupid thing to give you in the summer," said my father.

I zipped up the jacket.

"Get in the freaking car!"

Didn't I tell you that Holling Hoodhood is a good guy?

When we got to Marysville, around noon, we found the house that Ernie Eco had set up for us past the Ballard Paper Mill, past the railroad yard, and past the back of a bunch of stores and an old bar that looked like no one who went in there went in happy. The house was smaller than the one we'd had, so I had to room with my brother still—and there wasn't a bedroom for Lucas if he came home. My brother said he'd sleep on a couch in the living room at night so he didn't have to room with a puke, but my father said he didn't want him hanging around like he owned the place or something. So he moved his stuff up with me.

Terrific.

The first thing I had to do was find a place to hide the jacket, which my brother didn't know was Joe Pepitone's. If he had known, he'd have ripped it off me before we'd crossed the Throgs Neck Bridge. But he would find out. He always found out. So I kept it on, even though Holling Hoodhood was wrong and it was just as hot in Marysville as on Long Island and I was melting inside so bad that I was afraid I'd sweat Joe Pepitone's signature off.

My father said he was going with Ernie Eco to the Ballard Paper Mill to sign some forms so he could begin work on Monday, and my mother said she didn't think the Ballard Paper Mill would be open today, on a Saturday, and my father said what did she know about anything and left with Ernie Eco. So my brother and I carried all the furniture in, and I carried all the boxes in, except my mother told me to leave the kitchen boxes on the truck until she got the kitchen clean enough so a human being could eat in there without getting sick—which she hadn't finished doing by the time my father got home.

It turned out to be one of the wrong days. Again. Of course. My father couldn't figure out why my mother hadn't gotten the kitchen ready. He couldn't figure out why we hadn't gotten the kitchen boxes off the truck. He couldn't figure out why my mother hadn't gotten groceries yet. All she had to do was walk over to Spicer's Deli! He couldn't figure out why there wasn't food on the table for lunch. She had time enough to get the crucifix up in the hall, but she didn't have time enough to make a couple of sandwiches? It was already two o'clock! And he really couldn't figure out why Mr. Big Bucks Ballard was only going to give him a salary that was barely half of what Ernie Eco had promised.

I told him we didn't have lunch yet because how were we supposed to know where Spicer's Deli was and he had taken the car anyway and Mom had to clean up the kitchen because he sure wouldn't have wanted to eat in this dump before she did that.

My father turned to look at me, and then his hand flashed out.

He has quick hands, like I told you.

"Why don't you just stay here in your new jacket and get those boxes off the truck and into the nice, clean kitchen while we go out to find a diner?" he said. He told my mother to go get in the car, and my brother too — who smirked and swung like he was going to hit my other eye — and then they were gone, and I was left alone in The Dump.

I went down to the basement and looked around. There was only a single light bulb hanging, and it shone maybe fifteen watts. Maybe ten. A huge octopus of a furnace reached across most of the ceiling, and cobwebs hung on its tentacles, drifting up when I walked beneath them. Under the stairs it was open and dry and dark — a few old paint cans piled on top of each other, a couple of broken window frames, something dead that once had fur. I looked around and found a nail — you can always find a nail in an old basement — and hammered it in behind one of the stairs. That's where I hung Joe Pepitone's jacket.

Then I got those boxes off the truck.

And after that, I went out to explore the great metropolis of Marysville, New York.

Terrific.

Here are the stats for stupid Marysville:

> *Eight beat-up stores and a bar out front of where we were living.*
> *Four blocks of houses as tiny and beat up as ours.*
> *Twelve blocks of houses that had grass out front, a lot with bikes lying on their lawns like their kids were too stupid to know that anyone could walk off with them.*
> *Big trees along all the streets.*
> *Eighteen houses with flags outside.*

Twenty-four sprinklers going.

Fourteen people out on the stoops, sitting around because there wasn't any boring thing else to do in boring Marysville. Two who waved at me. One with a transistor radio on — except it was the stupid Mets and not the Yankees.

Two dogs asleep on their porches. One barked. One looked like it was too hot to think of chasing me, even though he knew I didn't belong.

A girl rode by on a bike with a basket on the handlebars. She looked at me like the dogs did, and then went on. Probably she knew I didn't belong too.

I hate this town.

I hate that we had to come here.

I decided to take a left, then go back to The Dump along another block so people didn't think I was lost or something. And so I turned the corner and looked down the street. There was the girl again, putting her bike in a rack and getting ready to head up into this brick building that was trying to look a whole lot more important than it should because no matter how important it looked it was still in stupid Marysville.

I crossed the street like I'd done it a million times before. It was shadowy under the maples in front of the building.

The girl saw me coming. She reached into the basket and pulled out a chain with pink plastic all around it. She looped it around the bike and the rack and clicked it all together and spun the combination lock before I had crossed the curb. Then she looked up.

I pointed to the chain. "Is that because of me?" I said.

"Should it be?" she said.

I looked over the bike. "Not for this piece of junk," I said. "And if it wasn't a piece of junk and I did want it, a pink chain wouldn't stop me."

She turned and picked up the books from the basket. "Is there something you do want?"

"Not in this town."

Her eyes narrowed. She held her books close to her—like my mother with her plants. And then I knew something.

This is what I knew: I was sounding like Lucas when he was being the biggest jerk he could be, which was usually just before he beat me up.

I was sounding like Lucas.

"You must have just moved here," she said.

I decided I wouldn't be Lucas.

"A few hours ago," I said. I put my hands in my pockets and sort of leaned back into the air. Cool and casual.

But I was too late.

"That's a shame," she said. "But maybe you'll get run over and I won't have to chain my bike anymore.

Now I'm going up into the library." She started to talk really slow. "A library is a place where they keep books. You probably have never been in one." She pointed to the street. "Go over there and walk down the broken white line with your eyes closed, and we'll see what happens."

"I've been in plenty of libraries before," I said.

She smiled—and it wasn't the kind of smile that said *I love you*—and she skipped up the six marble steps toward the marble entrance. You know how much I was hoping she would trip on the top step and scatter her books everywhere and she'd look at me like I had to come help her and I wouldn't but maybe I would?

But she didn't trip. She went in.

And so what if I've never been in a library before? So what? I could have gone into any library I wanted to, if I wanted to. But I never did, because I didn't want to. You think she's been to Yankee Stadium like I have? You think Joe Pepitone's jacket is hanging up in her basement?

I climbed the six steps—and she didn't see me trip on the top one, so it didn't matter. I pushed open the glass door and went in.

It was dark inside. And cool. And quiet. And maybe stupid Marysville was a dump, but this place wasn't. The marble outside led to marble inside, and when you walked, your footsteps echoed, even if you had sneakers on. People were sitting around long tables with green-shaded lamps, reading newspapers and magazines. Past the tables was a desk where a woman with her glasses on a chain looped around her neck was working as if she didn't know how dumb glasses look when you've got them on a chain looped around your neck. And past her started the shelves, where I figured the stuck-up girl with the bike was, picking out a new stack of books to put into her basket and take back to her pretty little Marysville house.

Suddenly I wasn't sure I wanted her to see me.

So when I saw another staircase — marble again — circling up to the next floor, I took it. Its steps were smooth and worn, as if lots of people like the girl with the bike had been climbing up here for lots of years. Even the brass banister shone bright from all the hands that had run along it.

So what if everyone in stupid Marysville comes into the stupid library every stupid day? So what?

I got to the top and into this big open room with not much. There was a painting on the wall, a guy with a rifle across his chest looking as if he was having a vision or something. And in the middle of the room, there was this square table with a glass case on top. And that was it. All that space, and that was it. If my father had this space, he'd fill it with tools and boards and a drill press and a lathe and cans and stuff before you could spit twice. There'd be sawdust on the floor, cobwebs on the ceiling, and the smell of iron and machine oil everywhere.

I went over to the table to see how come it was the only lousy thing in the whole lousy room.

And right away, I knew why.

Underneath the glass was this book. A huge book. A huge, huge book. Its pages were longer than a good-size baseball bat. I'm not lying. And on the whole page, there was only one picture. Of a bird.

I couldn't take my eyes off it.

He was all alone, and he looked like he was falling out of the sky and into this cold green sea. His wings were back, his tail feathers were back, and his neck was pulled around as if he was trying to turn but couldn't. His eye was round and bright and afraid, and his beak was open a little bit, probably because he was trying to suck in some air before he crashed into the water. The sky around him was dark, like the air was too heavy to fly in.

This bird was falling and there wasn't a single thing in the world that cared at all.

It was the most terrifying picture I had ever seen.

The most beautiful.

I leaned down onto the glass, close to the bird. I think I started to breathe a little bit more quickly, since the glass fogged up and I had to wipe the wet away. But I couldn't help it. Dang, he was so alone. He was so scared.

The wings were wide and white, and they swooped back into sharp rays. And between these, the tail feathers were even sharper, and they narrowed and narrowed, like scissors. All the layers of his feathers trembled, and I could almost see the air rushing past them. I held my hand as if I had a pencil in it and drew on the glass case, over the tail feathers. They were so sharp. If my hand had shaken even a tiny bit, it would have ruined the whole picture. I drew over the ridges of the wings, and the neck, and the long beak. And then, at the end, I drew the round and terrified eye.

On the table beside the display case was a printed card. I put it in my back pocket.

When I got home, Mom had brought two hot dogs back from the diner, wrapped in aluminum foil and filled with ketchup and mustard and pickle relish and sauerkraut like in Yankee Stadium, and I know because I've been to Yankee Stadium, which you might remember. She was moving around the boxes and still cleaning in the kitchen, and we could hear my father downstairs clanking away at his tools and swearing that Mr. Big Bucks Ballard wasn't going to get away with being such a freaking cheapskate and what did they take him for? Some kind of a jerk?

Well, he wasn't some kind of a jerk, he said when he came back upstairs.

He wasn't some kind of a jerk, he said when he told

me and my brother to carry all our stuff upstairs and sort it out, which I ended up doing by myself because my brother wouldn't.

He wasn't some kind of a jerk, he said when he hollered up at us to cut out the wrestling and turn out the light and go to sleep — which hadn't really been wrestling but my brother trying to find out where I'd put the jacket, which he still didn't know belonged to Joe Pepitone and which he didn't really want anyway so he wasn't half trying.

That night, I lay in the dark and drew the falling bird in the air: the wings, the tail feathers, the long beak. The eye. I drew them all again and again and again, trying to feel the wind through the feathers, wondering how whoever drew it had made it feel that way.

I fell asleep.

The terrified eye.

On Sunday, as soon as I woke up, I could tell it was going to be one of those days where the temperature is so high that you wonder how anything can still be alive. It was hardly morning, but already the room was sweating hot. If there had been curtains, they would have hung like they were dead.

When I came downstairs, Mom was already in the kitchen, sweating, trying to keep the pancakes warm in an oven that only kind of worked, and sizzling bacon in the frying pan over the one burner that lit, and scrambling eggs in the bowl next to the frying pan, and timing it all so that when Dad came down he could eat the pancakes and bacon, and then the scrambled eggs cooked in the bacon grease and he wouldn't have anything to complain about. I guess Mom figured it was worth the sweat.

I went outside so that I wouldn't throw off the timing. Everything was white and glarey. The sun wasn't up that far, but you still had to squint, and the light gave everything that kind of droopy feeling that lets you know this is going to be a long and slow and drippy day and you better think about finding a pool someplace and how that first cold plunge is going to feel great.

Not that stupid Marysville would even think of having a pool.

I waited by the back door as the sun got hotter, staring at the hard-packed dirt of the backyard, wondering how even the few patches of crabgrass were still alive. I waited until after my father had eaten and gone off somewhere with Ernie Eco. I waited until after my brother came down and ate the rest of the pancakes and then went off somewhere, probably with whoever he could find who had a police record. Then I went inside. My mother was folding a wad of newspaper and putting it under the wobbly kitchen table.

"You've been in the sun," she said.

I nodded. "It's already pretty hot out."

"Can I scramble you some eggs?"

I shook my head. "I can do it." I broke two eggs into the frying pan. The bacon grease was still hot, and the eggs began frying up pretty quick.

"Do you think you're going to be happy here?" she said.

I watched the eggs start to turn white. "I guess," I said. "Here as anywhere. How about you?"

"Me?" she said. "Here as anywhere." She got up from underneath the kitchen table.

I'm not lying when I say that Hollywood actresses would kill for my mother's smile. You think Elizabeth Taylor can smile? If you saw my mother's smile, you wouldn't even let Elizabeth Taylor in the same room.

If Joe Pepitone saw my mother's smile, he would give up baseball for her. That's how beautiful her smile is.

She put some toast on for the two of us, and I searched through all the boxes still stacked in the kitchen until I found some strawberry jam, and by then the egg yolks were too hard but who cares and we each had one and split the toast and we sat there quiet in the heat, me looking up to watch her smile and wondering how I could ever draw it, it was that beautiful.

I felt my hand trying to figure out how to do it. But it was like trying to draw the feathers of the bird. It didn't feel like my fingers were going the way they should. I *knew* my fingers weren't going the way they should.

We finished breakfast, then cleaned up together. Afterward we unpacked all the dishes and pots and dry food and stuff and put everything away. (I carried out the box of broken dishes without unwrapping them.) By then, it was almost 150 degrees in the kitchen, but when we looked around, everything was settled just the way she wanted it, and when I said, "I don't think I've ever been in a room where you could fry eggs while holding them in your hand," she went over to the sink, filled a glass full of cold water, turned, and—I'm not lying—threw the whole thing all over me.

She did.

Then she smiled again and started to laugh, and I started to laugh, and I took another glass and filled it up and she said "Douggie, you better not—" and then I threw the water over her and she laughed even louder until she started to snort and then we both laughed even harder and she filled her glass again and I filled my glass again and before long everything was dripping and it wasn't because of the humidity.

Then my father came home with Ernie Eco. Walked into the wet kitchen.

My mother looked at him, then opened a cabinet door and pulled down the Change Jar. She handed me four quarters and told me that we needed a gallon of milk—which we really didn't need but I'm not stupid. I left through the back door, crossed the hard-packed dirt, and was gone before whatever happened happened.

* * *

That night, I heard everything through the cardboard walls. The Dump wasn't a wreck like he said. And so what if Ernie Eco saw it? So what?

I lay in the dark, the criminal snores of my brother honking in the bunk beneath me, and I thought of my mother's sweet smile. Maybe she could take me to Yankee Stadium.

I felt my fingers moving again, trying to get that smile right.

I went back to the library on Monday, a little while after my father swore himself out of the house and headed off to the Ballard Paper Mill, where he was going to let Mr. Big Bucks Ballard know he wasn't some kind of a jerk. When my mother told him that maybe he shouldn't say anything and he should be happy to have a job, he said something to her that you don't need to hear but that I heard fine, since the walls in The Dump are, like I said, cardboard.

So I got to the library way too early because it was still dark inside, and I sat on the marble steps to wait, since what else do you think I'm going to do in stupid Marysville, New York? I mean, it wasn't like Horace Clarke was around to bat with.

So I guess I waited most of the morning. When people walked by, they'd look at me like I didn't belong there. You know what that feels like after a while?

I'm not lying, if Joe Pepitone had walked by, he would have stopped. He would have sat down next to me on the stupid steps and we would have talked about the season, like pals. Just talking. How maybe the season wasn't going as good as he wanted. How maybe he'd only had thirteen home runs last year, but so what? He had thirty-one the year before that. And even though he wasn't playing as many games this year, he'd probably get way past thirteen. Stuff like that.

And then someone would notice that Joe Pepitone was sitting on the steps of the library with me, and the news would spread all around stupid Marysville, and people like the girl with the stupid pink chain would start to gather and they'd all look at me and wish they were sitting on the steps with Joe Pepitone. And then Joe Pepitone would say, "Hey, Doug, it's getting crowded around here. What say we go someplace and throw a few?" And we'd get up and walk through the crowd, and the girl with the stupid bike would have to back away and everyone would look at us and they'd wish they were the ones walking someplace with Joe Pepitone to throw a few.

So I waited on the library steps.

But Joe Pepitone didn't come.

The girl with the bike did.

I looked at her. "You going to the library again?" I said.

"No," she said, "I'm not going to the library again. What are you doing here?"

"What does it look like?"

"It looks like you're waiting for the library to open."

"That's right." I leaned back against the stairs. Pretty cool, like before.

She got off the bike and flipped down the kickstand. "Do you think I can trust you?" she said.

I wondered if this was supposed to be a trick.

"Sure," I said. Kind of slowly. Probably not so cool.

"Then watch this for me."

She walked down the block. I leaned forward and saw her turn into a store. After a minute, she came out with two Cokes in her hand. She walked back and handed me one. It was so cold, there was still ice on the outside of the bottle, and frozen air came out of the open top like fog.

She sat down next to me. "You didn't steal my bike," she said.

"This piece of junk?"

"You know, you might have to wait a long time," she said.

"Where did you get these?"

"My father owns Spicer's Deli."

"So you just went in and told him to give you two Cokes and he gave them to you?"

"No, I didn't just go in and tell him to give me two Cokes. I asked for a Coke for me and a Coke for the skinny thug sitting on the library steps."

"The skinny thug?" I looked around. "Is someone else here?"

"The library is only open on Saturdays," she said. "And since today is Monday, you're going to be here for a while. So I felt sorry for you and got you a Coke."

"How do you know it's only open on Saturdays?"

She looked at me like I was visiting from Planet ZX-15. "Most people can tell when they read the sign posted on the door that says the library is open only on Saturdays."

I took a sip of the Coke. "I didn't see the sign," I said. "And what kind of a library is only open on Saturdays?"

"Why do you care?" she said.

I pulled the card from the display case out of my pocket and showed her.

"'Arctic Tern,'" she read aloud. "You want to see an Arctic tern? Wouldn't it be a whole lot more likely to find one in, say, a zoo?"

"A painting of one," I said, and took another sip of the Coke.

"That's not how you drink a really cold Coke," she said.

"What?"

"That's not how you drink a really cold Coke."

"So how do you drink a really cold Coke?"

She smiled, raised the Coke to her lips, and tipped the bottle up.

She gulped, and gulped, and gulped, and gulped, and gulped. The ice on the bottle's sides melted down toward her—and she gulped, and gulped, and gulped.

When she finished, she took the bottle away from her lips—she was still smiling—and she sighed, and then she squared her shoulders and kind of adjusted herself like she was in a batter's box, and then she let out a belch that even my brother couldn't match, not on his very best day.

It was amazing. It made birds fly out of the maples in front of the library. Dogs asleep on porches a couple of blocks away probably woke up.

She put the bottle down and wiped her lips. "That's how you drink a really cold Coke," she said. "Now you."

So what would you do? I lifted the Coke to my lips, tipped the bottle up, and gulped, and gulped, and gulped. It was fizzing and bubbling and sparkling, like little fireworks in my mouth.

"You know," she said, "it's a little scary to see your Adam's apple going like that."

The fireworks exploded—and I mean exploded.

Everything that was fizzing and bubbling and sparkling went straight up my nose and Coke started to come out all over the library steps and it wasn't just coming out of my mouth. I'm not lying. By the time the Coke was done coming out of both places, my eyes were all watered up like I was about to bawl—which I wasn't, but it probably looked like I was—and there was this puddle of still fizzing Coke and snot on the steps, and what hadn't landed on the steps had landed on my sneakers, which, if they had been new, I would have been upset about, but since they had been my brother's, it didn't matter.

"If you—"

"Don't get mad," she said. "It's not my fault that you don't know how to drink a really cold Coke."

I stood up. I tried shaking the Coke and other stuff off my sneakers.

"Are you going to keep waiting for the library to open?" she said.

"No, I'm not going to keep waiting for the library to open."

"Good," she said. "Then do you want a job?"

I looked down at her. There was still a little Coke up my nose, and I was worried that it was going to start dribbling out, which would make me look like a chump.

"A job?" I said.

"Yes. A job for a skinny thug."

"What kind of a job?"

"A Saturday delivery boy for my father."

"A delivery boy?"

She put her hands on her hips and tilted her head. "Fortunately, you don't have to be too smart to do this."

"Why me? I mean, there's got to be a hundred kids in this town you could have asked."

"Because you have to deliver stuff out to the Windermere place and everyone's afraid of her and no one wants to go. But you're new and you don't know anything about that so you seem like the perfect guy. What's your name?"

"Thug," I said.

She tilted her head back again.

"Doug," I said.

"I'm Lil, short for Lily, short for Lillian. So finish your Coke—but don't let your Adam's apple do that thing."

And that's how I got the job as the Saturday delivery boy for Spicer's Deli—five dollars a Saturday, plus tips—which, if you ask me, is pretty impressive for having been in stupid Marysville for only two days. Even my father said I'd done good. Then he added that it was about time I earned my keep around the place. When did I start?

"A week from Saturday," I said.

"If they thought you were any good, they would have started you *this* Saturday," he said.

Terrific.

CHAPTER TWO

The Red-Throated Diver
Plate CCII

THE NEXT SATURDAY—the Saturday before I was going to begin my new job at Spicer's Deli, which if they thought I was any good I would have been starting now—I was waiting on the library steps.

Again.

People who passed by looked at me like I didn't belong.

Again.

I hate stupid Marysville.

Every few minutes I went up the six steps to the library doors and tried them and they were, of course, still locked, so I'd go sit down. I waited for what must have been an hour, until finally the woman with her glasses on a chain looped around her neck — she already had them looped around her neck even though she wasn't even in the library yet — she came walking up the block and climbed the steps and looked back down at me like I was trespassing.

"The Marysville Free Public Library does not open until ten o'clock," she said.

"I know," I said.

"These steps were not made for people to sit on," she said, "especially since you might get in the way of others who would wish to use them."

I looked up and down the block, then moved way over to the edge of the steps. "Dang," I said. "I didn't see all the people jamming to get inside. Don't they all know that the Marysville Free Public Library does not open until ten o'clock?"

She sniffed. I'm not lying. She sniffed. "Go find some other place to be rude," she said.

"Is this one reserved for you?" I said.

I know. I was sounding like Lucas.

She took out a key from her purse, put it into the door and opened it, and went inside. She clanged the door shut behind her. She turned the bolt in the lock hard enough for me to hear.

I hate this stupid town. I hate it.

I waited on the steps. Right in the middle of them. My legs all spread out as far as I could spread them.

It wasn't too much longer before an old guy came from the other direction. He had glasses on a chain looped around his neck too, and I almost told him what a jerk he looked like with glasses looped around his neck, except I figured it wouldn't make any difference. He probably wouldn't even care that he looked like a jerk.

"You're an eager one," he said. "But the library doesn't open until ten o'clock."

"That's what I've been told," I said.

And he laughed, like there was something funny about that.

"I see you've met Mrs. Merriam. Is that why you're sitting like that?"

I looked at him. He had hair coming out of funny places — like his ears, his nose, between his eyes. He didn't need the looped glasses to look like a jerk.

"I guess," I said.

"You should be glad she hasn't called a policeman to have you removed." He pulled out a pocket watch — I'm not lying, a pocket watch — and flipped it open. "It's already past nine thirty," he said. "I don't think we'll undermine all law and order in the state of New York if I let you in early."

He put his pocket watch back and then took the steps kind of slowly. He puffed his breath out when he reached the top. "There seems to be more of these every time I climb them," he said, and took a key from his pocket.

The library was even cooler than it had been a week ago, and darker, since the only light came through windows that were stained yellow and didn't let in all that much.

Mrs. Merriam glanced up from the desk, and when she saw me, the look on her face was the look she probably gave to the bottom of her shoe when she stepped in something that she didn't want to step in.

"The library does not open until ten o'clock," she said.

"Exactly right," said the man, who was still puffing a little.

"Mr. Powell," she began.

"Just this once," he said.

"You don't know the meaning of *just this once*. How many times have you let the Spicer girl in early *just this once?*"

"For which she will one day thank us when she dedicates her first book to the Marysville Free Public Library." Mr. Powell turned to me. "Perhaps you will do the same. Now, is there anything I can point you toward?"

I shook my head. "I'll look around."

He nodded. "If I were you," he said, "I'd start in the nine hundreds, over there—but that's because I've always been partial to biography."

I didn't go over to the 900s. First I tried the 500s, which looked pretty dull if you ask me, and then over to the 600s, which looked a whole lot duller, and I'm not lying. The 700s were better, and I looked through a bunch of them to see if I could find a picture of the Arctic Tern. But I couldn't.

I guess you're wondering why I didn't go up to the book on the second floor right away. I mean, that's what I was there for, not for some stupid biographies in the 900s. But I think it was because I didn't want Mrs. The-Library-Isn't-Open Merriam's eyes looking at me like I was something on the bottom of her shoe when I went up there. I just didn't.

So I messed around in the 700s looking for the tern until I saw Mr. Powell head over to the front doors to unlock them so the bezillion people who had been waiting outside and probably spreading themselves all over the six steps could come in, and some did, and the library began to hum with talk that carried because of the marble, and Mrs. Merriam adjusted her looped glasses and started checking in returned books and telling people to keep their voices low, and I crossed the hall and went up the stairs.

No one had come up here yet, so the lights hadn't been turned on. But the Arctic Tern was still there, falling. The morning sun that slanted through the windows — they were stained yellow up here too — the sun showed the water darker, and rougher. And the terrified eye.

I put my pretend pencil over the glass case again, and I started drawing the wings. I drew the lines down from the wingtips, and then sharply back up into the body. I tried to fill in the six rows of feathers, keeping them all the same in each row until I came in close, where the feathers faded into the body—dang, they looked like fur. I could feel the wind rush over their tightness. Then, following the line down the bird toward the water, curving it up around his neck a little—no, a little less, and then back down again toward the water, ending at the perfect point of his lower beak, where it stopped being beak and became air.

And then the light snapped on.

Mr. Powell.

Puffing. A lot.

He looked at me, a little surprised. (He had his glasses on, instead of looped across his chest, so he didn't look like too much of a jerk.) "I'm sorry," he said. "I should have turned these lights on sooner."

"It doesn't matter," I said.

He walked over to the glass case and looked down into it. *"Sterna arctica,"* he said.

I looked at him. "Arctic Tern," I said. I didn't want him to think I was a chump, like I didn't know the bird.

"That's right," he said. "There used to be a little card around here somewhere. Isn't it a beauty? You can feel it plummeting through the air."

I didn't say anything.

"I came up to turn the page. I do it once a week. But I can wait, if you want."

I shrugged.

He looked down again at the Sterna bird. "I think I'll wait," he said.

"Who drew this?"

He turned and pointed to the picture on the wall. "He did. John James Audubon. Almost a hundred and fifty years ago." He looked into the glass case. "You want to try drawing it yourself?"

I shook my head. "I don't draw."

"Ever try?"

"I said, 'I don't draw.'"

"So you did. I'll leave the book open to this page, and if you change your mind or want to read about the artist, I'll—"

I turned and left before he could finish. What a jerk. Didn't he hear me say I don't draw? Chumps draw. Girls with pink bicycle chains draw. I don't draw. Was he old *and* deaf?

I hate this town.

A week later, I wasn't at the library when it opened at ten o'clock, and if you've been paying attention, you should know why. I was over at Spicer's Deli before nine, still tasting the salt-and-peppery fried eggs that my mother had made for me before I left. Mr. Spicer and Lil were standing by two wagons, and one was already packed with filled brown bags. "Lil will have the second one waiting for you by the time you get back from this first run," Mr. Spicer said. He handed me a drawn map with the houses of the customers marked and told me the order I should go in, which depended on how far away the houses were and how much ice cream was in the brown bags—which made a lot of sense, since it was already somewhere up in the eighties probably, and the white haze in the air said it was going to be a whole lot hotter.

"Do you want to warn him about Mrs. Windermere now or later?" said Lil.

Mr. Spicer looked at her. "He doesn't have anything to worry about," he said.

Lil looked at me and mouthed, *Yes, you do.*

"All the houses on this first run are within a couple of blocks of the deli," Mr. Spicer said, "so it shouldn't take long if you put your mind to it. You better get going before the ice cream starts to melt."

So I got going. But I'm not lying, it wasn't so easy to match Mr. Spicer's hand-drawn letters to the letters on the street signs, and so it probably did take a little longer than it would have for someone who had lived all his life in stupid Marysville, which Mr. Spicer didn't seem to understand as well as he should. "You'll have to pick up the pace if we're going to get all these orders delivered," he said when I got back.

I nodded.

"Lil's got the next wagon all set. Right? Here's the map. You'll get to know all of these by heart, but you have to keep your mind on it this time."

Terrific.

"Are you going to warn him about Mrs. Windermere yet?" said Lil.

I set out again, dragging the wagon behind me. After ten minutes, I had no idea how to find any of the streets on the map, and so I had to stop and ask someone who was edging the lawn in front of her house, like it really mattered to anyone if her grass was cut in a straight line. I held out the map and asked if she knew where the street was for the first house.

She put down her edger, took off her garden gloves, and looked at the map. "That's Gardiner. That's this street," she said. She pointed up at the sign on the corner. "Didn't you see it?"

No, I didn't see it, jerk. I wouldn't have asked you if I had seen it, would I? That's what I wanted to say.

"So number nineteen would be..." I said.

"A few houses down on the other side. Evelyn Mason's place." She pointed. "It's the bright yellow one with the white impatiens under the porch."

I headed down to Evelyn Mason's place with the stupid white impatiens under the stupid porch, knocked on the stupid door, handed over the stupid bags of groceries, showed her the stupid map and said, "I have to get over to...," and she pointed the way.

That's how I got by the rest of that Saturday morning. I showed the customers the map, and they pointed the way. It worked pretty well—until Ernie Eco drove by and he said what was I doing and I told him and he asked if I needed help finding the houses and I said I did and he looked at the map and told me the way to the house after the one I was already heading to, but he told me to go in completely the wrong direction and by the time I got that figured out and turned around and found the last house, their ice cream had mostly melted inside the foil bag and they wouldn't pay for it. So I took it back. Mr. Spicer said it could happen on anyone's first day but I shouldn't let it happen again and next time he'd have to take it out of my salary.

Ernie Eco probably thought he was a barrel of laughs.

He probably thought I was a chump.

Then Mr. Spicer nodded to the last wagon. "It's for Mrs. Windermere," he said.

Lil whistled kind of low, like something out of *The Twilight Zone.*

"Mrs. Windermere," I said.

"This one's got ice cream too. Lemon ice cream, which is expensive. So pay attention."

I nodded. I wondered if he might hand me a cold Coke before I left. The mercury must have left ninety behind a long time ago. And I sure did know what to do with a really cold Coke.

"Mrs. Windermere is supposed to pay you," Mr. Spicer said. "Cash on delivery. Sometimes she tries to charge it, but then she forgets, and I have to drive over and she's forgotten that she didn't pay and we have a really unhappy scene. So make sure you come away with" — he looked down at her bill — "twenty-two dollars and seventy-eight cents."

"Okay," I said. Waiting for a cold Coke. Waiting for a cold Coke. Waiting for a cold Coke.

"And you won't even need a map for this one," Mr. Spicer said. "Go over to the library, take the street that runs into it — that's Green Street — and head out until the houses stop and there's a big field. Go across that, and you'll see this huge brick house. That's where she lives. Got it?"

"Twenty-two seventy-eight," I said.

Mr. Spicer nodded. "In hand," he said.

A Coke, I thought. *A really cold Coke with ice coming down the sides.*

He looked at me. "You waiting for something?"

"I wouldn't be in a hurry either if I was him," Lil said.

I set off on the last run of the Saturday deliveries. I decided that if I found any sprinklers going, I'd jump through them, since everything I was wearing was already dripping wet anyway.

But there weren't any sprinklers the whole way. Are you surprised? There never are.

Do you know how many blocks there were before the houses started thinning out after the library?

Fourteen.

Do you know how many trees there are along the road once the houses started to give out?

Six.

Do you know how much shade they gave?

Maybe a tiny bit more than zero.

Do you know how big that field before Mrs. Windermere's house was?

Big. And the path that I had to drag the wagon on wasn't exactly mowed.

By the time I got there, I couldn't believe I was still sweating, since it felt like anything liquid must have baked out of me. I couldn't believe there was still frost on the metal foil around the expensive lemon ice cream.

Mrs. Windermere's house spread out at the end of a long brick path—and the bricks were baking hot—that led up from the road through gardens on either side that had just been sprinkled with sprinklers, which were turned off now, of course, and then past some tall evergreens and then into some high trees that, finally, spread some shade down onto the world and then through some more gardens with flowers that I would have died to bring home to my mother and finally more baked bricks right up to the house. It was the biggest house I'd ever seen that one person owned. I mean, there were pillars in the front. Pillars! More windows than Camillo Junior High. This green and white ivy climbing up everywhere. And a doorway with a round window over it. That's right. Over it. No one could even look out of it, it was that high up.

It was quiet under the trees. No wind. The only thing I heard was someone pecking at a typewriter and then the little bell dinging when whoever was typing reached the end of a line. But nothing else. It was like even the birds knew they had to be quiet, because I guess no one was supposed to disturb the great Mrs. Windermere.

I left the wagon at the foot of the steps that led up to the door, and I rang the doorbell and stepped back.

Typing not stopping. Little bell still dinging.

I waited for a while.

Typing not stopping. Little bell still dinging.

I went up and rang the doorbell again. Twice. Knocked. Twice.

Typing stopping.

I took a step back, which turned out to be a really good thing, because the door suddenly swung open and there was Mrs. Windermere—at least, I figured it had to be her.

She had hair as white as clouds, and about as wispy too, and big. It was all gathered like one of those huge thunderheads that rises on hot summer days. The top was in sort of a bun and tied tight with red rubber bands. And in that top bun — I'm not lying — there were three bright yellow pencils stabbing through. She wore a bluish kind of gown that shimmered — it looked like something that someone about to go to an opera would wear (not that I've ever been to an opera, or would ever be caught dead at one. Can you imagine Joe Pepitone ever going to an opera?). With the cloud on top and the shimmering blue beneath, she looked like a rainstorm that could walk around all by itself. Which wouldn't have been so bad on a day that wanted to be a hundred degrees.

All this, by the way, took about half a second to see, because she hadn't even finished opening the door when she said, "Who are you?"

That's not really what she said. She used a word that I'd never heard a lady use before. It came pretty close after *Who*. You can figure it out for yourself.

"Who do you think I am?" I said. I know: sounding like Lucas. But you have to remember that she started it. And it was hot. And Mr. Spicer had never given me that really cold Coke. Ice coming down the sides.

She looked behind me at the wagon. "I think you are a very skinny and very rude delivery boy, and you are a very skinny and very rude delivery boy whom I have no time for right now. Go away and come back later this afternoon."

She closed the door. Hard.

Typing starting up again. Little bell dinging.

I could almost hear Lil snorting, back at the deli.

I stood out there for a couple of minutes. To be as thirsty as I was, you'd have to be in the French Foreign Legion and lost somewhere out in the Sahara for a week. I thought about dragging that wagon back down the baking brick walk and through the field to the road. I thought about dragging that wagon down all of those fourteen blocks back to Spicer's Deli. And then I thought about doing it *all over again* in the afternoon.

I rang the doorbell.

Typing not stopping. Little bell still dinging.

I rang the doorbell again. Twice. Knocked. Twice. Stepped back.

Typing stopping, and this time the door opened even more quickly.

"Do you know what Creativity is?" Mrs. Windermere said.

You have to admit: this is not something you expect a normal person to say.

"I'm not sure," I said.

"I'm sure that you do not know, or you would not be ringing this doorbell. Creativity is a god who comes only when he pleases, and it isn't very often. But when he does come, he sits beside my desk and folds his wings and I offer him whatever he wants and in exchange he lets me type all sorts of things that get turned into plays for which people who own New York stages are waiting. And right now, he is sitting by my desk, and he is being very kind. So if you would go away and —"

"Suppose you offer him some ice cream," I said. "Would he stay longer?"

She looked behind me again, at the wagon. "Ice cream?" she said.

I nodded.

"What kind did I order?"

"Lemon."

She considered this. "Lemon?" she said.

I nodded again.

She looked at the wagon once more.

"Go around back. There's a door into the kitchen. Put everything away where it's supposed to go. If you cannot figure out where something is supposed to go, for heaven's sake, don't come and ask me. Leave it on the kitchen table. You better start with the ice cream. And do not make any noise."

She closed the door, again. Hard, again.

I followed the brick path around the house to the back. I should tell you that there was no shade around this side of the house, so things were getting sort of desperate in the Thirsty Department. The kitchen door was up three steps, so I grabbed the ice cream and headed up.

The door was locked. Of course. Of course it was locked.

I thought about going around and ringing the doorbell again.

I thought about walking away and leaving the whole thing right there. Melted lemon ice cream all over the back steps.

Instead, I looked under the mat by the door, and there it was: the key! Pretty sneaky of Mrs. Windermere. No one would ever think to look there if he wanted to break in while she was away at the opera.

Here are the stats for Mrs. Windermere's kitchen:

The floor was white and yellow tile — twenty-four tiles wide, eighteen tiles long.
One rack with sixteen copper pots and pans hanging over a woodblock table.
Four yellow stools around the woodblock table.
Twelve glass cupboards — all white inside. You could have put my mother's dishes into any one of these and you would have had plenty of room left over.
And the dishes! All white and yellow. And the glasses! Who knows how many? All matching. Not a single one chipped.

You know who deserved this kitchen, right?

Before I did anything, I drank about a gallon and a half from the faucet. I put my head under and let the water run. I didn't even care if Mrs. Windermere came in and saw me doing it. It wasn't like I was using one of her glasses. And it tasted so good. Even better than a really cold Coke.

Then I put all the groceries away, starting with the lemon ice cream into the freezer. I left the fresh beans and carrots and onions on the woodblock table, but everything else got put away in cupboards that, if you asked me, were pretty full already. But no one was asking me.

I took another long drink for the road. Another gallon and a half, I'd say.

Then I started out the back door—and remembered: $22.78.

I could hear the typing and the dinging through the house. They were going pretty steady. Probably the god Creativity was still being good to her.

But I needed the $22.78.

I swung open the door out of the kitchen and went into a dining room. It was cool and dark and full of roses—big red ones on black wallpaper, and big red ones in a vase in the middle of a dark table that looked like it should be in a museum or something.

I followed the sound of the typing and the dinging. Down a long, long hall with walls hung with framed photographs of actors and actresses—Richard Burton and Elizabeth Taylor and Yul Brynner with his bald head and Telly Savalas with his bald head and Danny Kaye and Lucille Ball even, all posing on stages. Then the hall let into a bright sitting room, all yellow and white again. And then down another short hall there was a glass door with diamond panes and behind that I could see Mrs. Windermere typing wildly—sometimes her hands went high above her shoulders before they dropped down to smack at the keys. And by the way, there wasn't any god sitting on the chair by her desk with his wings folded. He couldn't have sat there if he wanted to. The chair was filled with books, most of them lying open, one on top of another.

I waited before knocking at the glass door. I'm not lying, her typing was a sight to see.

But I couldn't stand there forever. So I knocked.

Typing not stopping. Little bell still dinging.

I knocked again. Twice.

Without turning around, she waved her hand to shoo me away.

So I knocked again.

Both hands up above her shoulders this time. Both hands dropping down to the typewriter. She turned around. Slowly. There was this look on her face that . . . well, if she had reached for one of the sharp pencils stabbed through her bun, I would have been gone.

"What is it now?" she said.

"I have the bill," I said. "Twenty-two seventy-eight."

You have to remember that we were talking through

the door here, which made the whole thing kind of weird. It was like I was talking through glass to some sort of prison inmate.

"Put it on my account," she said. She turned back to the typewriter to sort out all the keys that were jammed together now.

"I can't," I said. "Mr. Spicer wants me to bring the cash back to him."

She was working over her typewriter.

"Mrs. Windermere?" I said.

"Arrrgghh," she said. I'm not lying. "Arrrgghh." Just like that. Then she stood up and grabbed the door handle—which was glass too, by the way—and threw the door open. "You fix the typewriter keys," she said. "I'll get the money."

I went into the room. It was bigger than I had thought. Its walls kept going back and back, and every wall had dark wood bookshelves to the ceiling, and every bookshelf was crammed. Out on the floor there was a round table heaped with books. Beside that was a dark couch covered with rows of books. Everywhere on the floor, piles of books leaned into each other. On the sides of her desk and in front of her desk, more piles leaning. I never thought that one person could own so many books. I picked one up off the desk and smelled its pages. The smell of old paper.

I worked at separating the keys in her typewriter.

I found out pretty quickly that the trick is to take one key at a time and just let the ink get all over your hands, and I got most of them done by the time Mrs. Windermere got back. She threw twenty-five dollars at me.

"I don't think I have any change," I said.

"Keep it," she said. "Splurge. Go on a shopping spree. Book a trip to Monte Carlo. Do whatever you want. But do it away from me. Here, stop fussing with that. You'll just get everything all inky."

She took over the typewriter keys, and I think by the time I backed out of the room with the twenty-five dollars, she had forgotten I was there.

Two dollars and twenty-two cents. It was the only tip I had gotten all day, but it was a good one: $2.22. Do you know what you can do with $2.22? I had never had that much money all my own. $2.22.

So maybe it was because I was thinking about the $2.22 that I turned the wrong way in the short hall and got into a room I hadn't been in before. It was all light blues with white furniture and a white fireplace with small stone lions on either side and another vase on a dark table filled with pink roses.

And over the fireplace, a huge picture of birds. The same size as the one of the Arctic Tern. And by John James Audubon again. You could tell.

But this one was different. One bird was the mother. Two were swimming away, doing what they felt like doing, not even looking at her. And there was this small bird, pretty young. It was looking like maybe it wanted to swim where the other two birds were, but maybe not. And anyway, he was afraid to try. And the mother? Her neck was turned all around about as far as it could possibly go, and she was looking far away, at something a long way out from the picture. She was looking at a place she wanted to go but couldn't, because she didn't know how to get away.

There were flowers beside her.

I stood there looking at that picture for a long time — even after the typing and dinging started up again. The little one didn't know what he wanted to do at all. I reached up and touched the glass over it.

Cold.

Then I found the kitchen again, went out, locked the door behind me, and hid the key in its so-secret spot that no one would ever think to look in. I wiped my inky hands on the grass and dragged the wagon back to Spicer's Deli.

When I pulled the wagon inside, Mr. Spicer looked at his watch, then at me, like I hadn't been paying attention.

"Did you see Mrs. Windermere?" said Lil.

"Yup," I said. I handed Mr. Spicer the twenty-five dollars. He counted it, took it to the register, and paid out my tip. "Pretty nice," he said.

I nodded.

"Well?" said Lil.

"Well what?" I said.

"I pay salary every other Saturday," Mr. Spicer said.

"Okay," I said. I still had my $2.22 in hand. "That's fine."

I know. I'm a chump.

"So what happened?" said Lil.

Then Mr. Spicer handed me a Coke.

You remember, right, that I know what to do with a really cold Coke?

I did it. Except the burp, since Mr. Spicer was right there.

"Not a thing," I said when I finished.

"You skinny thug," said Lil.

I handed her the bottle.

I burped when I got out onto the street. I'm not lying, it was a pretty good one. Birds flew out of the maples.

I put the $2.22 in my pocket and went up to the library. Mrs. Merriam looked at me, then went back to whatever she'd been working at to let me know that I wasn't worthy of Her Majesty's attention.

So what? So what? It wasn't like I needed her attention. I just came to the library to see if I could get that beak right, which I probably couldn't on account of how I don't draw. Like I told Mr. Powell.

So what?

I went upstairs. The lights were on. Mr. Powell hadn't turned the page of the book; it was still open to the Arctic Tern.

But there was one thing that was different. There were three large blank sheets of paper on the glass display case. And there were five colored pencils: gray, black, green, blue, and orange. Dark orange. They were all sharp. There was an eraser too. Waiting like I had ordered them.

I ran my hand over the glass on top of the Arctic Tern. Then I left. I didn't touch anything, since I don't draw. Remember?

That night at supper, my father asked if I started the job.

I nodded.

Did I get paid?

Tips.

Tips? That's all? Tips? Didn't I get paid for the day?

I told him I got paid every other Saturday.

He told me I was a chump, and he and my brother laughed at me like I was the jerk of the world. Like I was never going to see any of that money. Like I was about as useless as a rubber crutch.

My mother turned and looked out the window, at something far away.

* * *

That next week, I ran into Lil Spicer three times. The first two times, I looked like a chump.

The first time, I had finally jumped under a sprinkler because it was so hot the sidewalks were white and shimmering, and if there was any place within ten miles to go swimming, I didn't know about it. I guess I got desperate. So I jumped under a sprinkler not so far from the library, and it was perfect, and I had just come out from under it when, of course, Lil Spicer turned the corner on her bike, looking as cool as if she had been in Monte Carlo or something.

As soon as she saw me, she started to laugh.

"Did you fall into a pool?" she said. It took her a while to say this, since she was mostly snorting.

"No, I didn't fall into a pool," I said.

"Did you—you did! You went under a sprinkler!"

I didn't say anything. What would you have said?

"You're trying to stay cool by running under sprinklers. Just like when you were a cute little boy instead of a skinny thug."

"Yes, I'm trying to stay cool."

"I suppose that's one way to do it."

"Yes, it's one way to do it."

Lil Spicer started to laugh again.

"It's a pretty dumb way," she said.

"Thanks for pointing that out," I said, and went

on down the white-hot sidewalk, wishing that I wasn't squishing so much.

"You're leaving...you're leaving footprints," she pointed out. She was laughing so hard, she was almost crying.

I hate this town.

The second time was on Friday. I was heading toward the library—and yes, I know it's not open on Friday but who knows if a miracle might happen and it would be open after all? So I was heading to the library, and when I turned the corner, there, two blocks away, was my brother, with a new group of criminals. It hadn't taken him long. They were in front of Spicer's Deli, probably figuring out how to rob it. My brother sat on a Sting-Ray that wasn't his—I guess it belonged to some weaker member of the pack—and he was probably talking about how hard life was where we had come from, and how he'd been in knife fights that were for real, and how he'd even seen a teacher get knifed—which was all a lie, but when he pulled up his shirt and showed the long scar he had gotten from climbing over a fence—which was what he was doing right now, pulling up his shirt—who could tell it wasn't a scar from a blade?

I moved back into the shadows beneath the tall maples in front of the library. I didn't move. That's how packs detect you. You move, they see you out of the corners of their beady yellow eyes, and then they swarm for the kill.

Which was why I did not move when I felt a large, wet, sloppy plop drop down from the branches overhead. *Large* isn't the right word, and *drop* isn't either. Think *pour down* for *drop down* and you have it about right. There was a rustle, and a crow flew away, grinning. I did not move. The plop slimed down my hair, over my ear, and then along my neck and into the collar of my T-shirt, and still I didn't move. I waited. I could feel the bird poop starting to crust over in the heat, and still I didn't move. I waited. Until finally, finally Mr. Spicer came out and hollered, and my brother hollered back and stood up on his Sting-Ray—he was really pretty good at balancing on the thing—and then he looked my way. I think my heart stopped. I almost panicked and moved. But someone must have said something—probably God—and so he turned and headed the other way on his bike, hollering once more at Mr. Spicer before he left, the jerk.

My heart started up again.

I waited in the shadows until he biked around the corner with the rest of the pack, and then I reached up to wipe off the bird poop.

Except before I got to it, I heard Lil's voice.

"Did you know that half of your head is covered in bird droppings?" she said.

"It's not bird droppings," I said.

"It's not?"

"Dropping. It's one dropping. Not droppings. It's not like I stood here and let this army of birds poop on me."

"So you stood there and let only one bird poop on you. Good for you."

"I didn't *let* it poop on me."

"Oh," she said.

Do you know how she said *Oh*? It wasn't like she was figuring something out and had just gotten it. It was like she was saying that I was the jerk of the world, which I had been hearing a lot lately.

"It sure is a mess," she said. "When you have hair as black as yours, it really shows well."

"Thanks," I said.

"Do you need some help cleaning it up?" she said.

By the way, and not that I think you're not too smart or anything, but I just want to make sure: You do know that she wasn't really offering to help, right?

"No," I said. "I don't need any help."

"If you ask me," she said, pushing her bike past, "you are someone who needs a lot of help." She turned and looked back at me. "Maybe you should try going under a sprinkler," she said, and smiled helpfully.

I smiled back and watched her ride away.

Then I reached up and felt the bird poop in my hair.

It was crusty all right, but it was still sticky enough to smear. I rubbed as much as I could out of my hair and onto my fingers and then onto the grass. I didn't get much out before it all hardened.

So I did go under a sprinkler on the way home. It wasn't a bad idea.

The third time, I didn't look like a chump—at first. I was spading up a place for a garden in front of The Dump, and I'm not lying, this was hard work, since no one had spaded up this ground since forever. It took all morning, but I had almost finished when Lil Spicer came riding up on her bike. In her basket, she's got these plants.

It was the eeriest thing. It was like we'd had the same dream or something.

"Hi," she said.

"Hi," I said.

"My mother sent these over," she said.

"How did you know I was digging up a garden?"

Lil got off her bike and put down the kickstand. "My mother is weird like that when it comes to plants. She knows." She reached into her basket and held them up. "Daisies," she said.

They were long, and bright white blossoms fell out of the damp newspaper.

We planted them together. And watered them. And then tightened the soil around them. It means something, you know, when people plant things together. By the time we were done, these daisies were strutting their white hearts out in front of The Dump — which didn't look quite so much like a dump anymore.

"My hands are all dirty," Lil said.

I almost reached out to hold them. I think she would have let me.

How come when you're feeling good like this, something always happens to wreck it all? How come?

So we're standing there, Lil and me, Lil holding her hands out, and my brother, my jerk brother, comes riding up on his Sting-Ray. He gets off and looks at the daisies. Then he looks at us. "Nice," he says.

"Thanks," says Lil, because she doesn't know yet that he's a jerk and she doesn't know like you know that he's not really saying they're nice.

"Looks like they need some water," he says.

My stomach starts to twist up.

"They're fine," I say.

"We've already watered them," says Lil.

"Not enough," says my jerk brother, and he walks over and stands next to them.

He leans down over the first flower and lets fall a glob of spit — about as big as the bird poop. It falls right into the flower, and its head bobs down with the weight.

Then my jerk brother leans over to the next flower. He lets fall another glob of spit.

Lil gets on her bike and rides away.

My brother spits on every one of the flowers. Big globs that he hacks up from deep in his lungs somewhere.

"Looks a lot better now, don't you think, Douggo?"

I stood there like a chump.

You see how things never go right when you're feeling good?

"You see how things never go right when you're feeling good?" said my father that night. "You work like a freaking dog and get ahead in production because you've been doing a good — no, a great — job, and so you take a few more minutes for lunch to relax a little. Who cares? You're still making your quota. So who freaking cares? But it turns out that Mr. Big Bucks Ballard cares, and he lays into you for coming back late — like it's going to cost him a whole dollar and a half. 'We don't get things done around here by coming back late,' he says to me when I come in. 'Try not to make it a habit.' *I'll make it a freaking habit if I feel like making it a habit,* I almost said to him."

And stuff like that, through the meat loaf and green beans and canned peaches.

"Who does he think he is?" said my father.

I almost said that maybe Mr. Big Bucks Ballard thinks he's my father's boss, but I'm not an idiot. My father's hands were twitching like they wanted to flash out, and I didn't want them to flash out my way. So I shut up and ate, which is what he would have told me to do if I had said anything anyway. My mother mostly looked out the window.

"Things never go right when you're feeling good," my father said again.

After my father and my brother left, I helped my mother bring the dishes into the kitchen. "Thanks for the meat loaf, Mom," I said.

"Thanks for the daisies," she said.

"I'll dry," I said.

That smile.

The next Saturday's deliveries went better, mostly because I remembered the routes.

Evelyn Mason on Gardiner was waiting for me at the back door, which she held open as I carried her bags of groceries in and put them on the kitchen counter. "You're so skinny," she said.

"I think that's everything," I said.

"I want you to sit right down there and pour yourself a glass of milk," she said. Then she opened up the box of cinnamon doughnuts I had delivered.

You don't know how much I love cinnamon doughnuts.

I had two with a glass of milk. Evelyn Mason looked

as happy as I probably looked. "I'll order some chocolate doughnuts for next week," she promised. I didn't tell her not to.

On the next run, I got turned around and had to ask a mailman where the Loeffler house was. I showed him my map. "You need to be on Washington Street," he said. "It's parallel to this one, but two blocks that way." When I got there, Mr. Loeffler was sitting on his front porch with a light bulb in his hand. He stood up when he saw me turn the corner. "Exactly who I've been waiting to see," he said.

"I'm not late," I said.

"No, no. I just need someone to change the bulb over the back door. I'm a little shaky on ladders, you know."

I changed the light bulb while he held the ladder.

I climbed down and looked at him. He looked a little shaky on the ground too.

"Anything else?" I said.

We went all over his house and changed six light bulbs. He must have spent a lot of time in the dark.

"That's just great," he said. He was pleased as all get-out, you could tell. He handed me a dollar bill. "For services rendered," he said.

On the last run in town, I went to the Daughertys' first — they were the people whose ice cream had melted last Saturday.

Mrs. Daugherty met me at the back door. Five kids watched through the screen while she inspected the ice cream straight off.

"Did the ice cream melt again?" the littlest one asked her mother.

"No, Phronsie. Not this time."

"That's good," Phronsie said to me. "Because if it was melted, then Ben and Joel and Davie said they were going to have to kill you."

I looked at the three boys.

They smiled at me.

"Not really," they said.

"Don't be too sure," Mrs. Daugherty said to me.

And when all that was done, I had to head out to Mrs. Windermere's.

It was a load pretty much like last week's — a little more, at $23.65. "Don't forget the money," said Mr. Spicer, and I promised I wouldn't.

"Don't ever turn your back," said Lil.

"Lillian," said Mr. Spicer.

"I warned you," she said.

It was a day more than hot enough to make you work up a sweat. But the blue of the air went forever, and when the houses gave out and the road passed into the open field and there was just the sound of cicadas, Marysville didn't seem so bad.

Except it would have been a whole lot better with a really cold Coke.

Or if Joe Pepitone and I were walking side by side trading stories, and then we stopped for a while and threw in the field with the cicadas. That would have been even better. That would have been a whole lot better.

So I was looking out into the field, thinking about throwing with Joe Pepitone, and then this thing happened. Maybe the god of Creativity flew by and brushed me with his wing. I don't know. But suddenly, out in the field, it wasn't Joe Pepitone I was throwing with. It was Lucas — which, just so you know, would never have happened. But I could see us, Lucas back from Vietnam and me, throwing out in the field on a blue summer day. Like that. Throwing back and forth, and the sound of cicadas and bees and high-up birds and the leather smell of our gloves and the ball smacking into them. Lucas laughing in the sun.

It was almost like seeing a ghost.

I got to Mrs. Windermere's and I could hear her typing and dinging, so I went around to the back door and found the Cleverly Hidden Key and brought in her groceries and put them away, starting with the ice cream. Then I swung open the kitchen door and headed into the house to get the $23.65. I followed the sound of her typing and dinging until I could see her through the glass door, typing madly in another opera dress. Pencils still stabbed through her hair. Hands flying like birds in a panic.

But before I knocked, I went into the blue room.

I don't know how long I stood there, staring at the picture. I didn't even hear the typing and dinging stop or Mrs. Windermere coming into the room.

"Aren't they beautiful?" she said.

I nodded.

"What kind of ice cream did I order this week?"

"Peppermint. What kind of birds are they?"

"Audubon called them Red-Throated Divers. They're a sort of loon. It's a lovely family group, I think. Peppermint?"

"Some family," I said. "No one's paying attention to the mother. Who could blame her if she took off? Look at them."

A minute or so went by, and then Mrs. Windermere said, in a voice as soft as summer blue air, "Skinny Delivery Boy, you have it all wrong. Look how she's standing close to her little one. She's looking around to watch for the next spectacular thing that's going to come into his life."

And I'm not lying, she was right.

After dropping off the wagon and pocketing ten dollars for my pay plus Mr. Loeffler's dollar plus a $1.35 tip from Mrs. Windermere and drinking a really cold Coke with Lil and not telling her a thing about Mrs. Windermere no matter how hard she tried to make me and not burping until I got out on the street, I went to the library. Mrs. Merriam glanced up when I came in. "Oh, it's you," she said, in that Disgusting-Thing-on-the-Bottom-of-My-Shoe kind of voice.

I went upstairs. The lights were on and Mr. Powell was standing by the glass case. He looked up at me as I came over. The three blank sheets of paper were still there, and there was another pencil. A light blue.

I moved the sheets over and looked down at the Arctic Tern. Those sharp wings. The neck. The beak. Everything dropping toward the cold, cold sea.

The terrified eye.

I let my hand follow the lines over the glass. I stopped over the eye. My fingers moved.

"I don't think I know your name yet," said Mr. Powell.

"Doug Swieteck."

Mr. Powell held up the black pencil. "Mr. Swieteck, would you like to try to draw it?" he asked.

"I don't know how," I said.

"Then let's begin," said Mr. Powell, and I'm not lying, when I took the black pencil in my fingers, it felt . . . spectacular.

CHAPTER THREE

The Large-Billed Puffin
Plate CCXCIII

OKAY. So I was going to the library every Saturday. So what? So what? It's not like I was reading books or anything.

I went every Saturday because I had a lot to get in. There were only three weeks left in August and then a few days in September before stupid Washington Irving Junior High School of stupid Marysville, New York, was scheduled to open its stupid doors and suck us away from summer. Only three weeks. And there was a lot to learn.

"We'll start with contour lines," Mr. Powell said that first Saturday. "Put your hand up on the paper — no, higher up — the paper is the same size as the page in Audubon's book, so you want to try for the same proportions. Look at the tern. Good. Now draw the outline of the bird. You don't need to look at your paper. Bring your line down from that first tip. Not quite so slowly. Bring it all the way down to the beak."

I brought the line all the way down to the beak.

"Now, start on the right side and let's do the same thing: bring the line all the way down to the beak. Don't look at the paper. That's it."

"How am I going to make the lines meet if I don't look at the paper?"

"You're not."

I finished the right side of the bird, then looked at the paper.

"That doesn't look like much of a bird," I said.

"Not yet it doesn't."

"It looks more like I'm showing what isn't the bird."

Mr. Powell put his hand over mine and stopped it. I looked up at him, and he had this smile. It wasn't like my mother's smile, but it was okay.

"That's right, Mr. Swieteck," he said. "That's exactly what you're doing. Most young artists take a long time to understand that. Let's try it again. Turn the sheet over. This time, let's go a little faster with the lines. And as you start — that's it, right there — as you start, think about how the line is sending out information about the bird. How is the air moving over the feathers? How are the feathers stirring? How fast is the bird traveling?"

"Fast," I said.

"Keep that in mind as you bring the line down."

I brought the line down.

"Stop," Mr. Powell whispered. "You're about to come to the front edge of the wing, right?"

I nodded.

"Think about how the air is hitting that edge."

Okay, you're probably not going to believe this, but when I did think about it, I really could feel the air right on my shoulders. I'm not lying.

"Press down harder on your pencil to show how it feels."

I did.

"Harder. You won't break the point."

Harder.

"The right side, same thing."

I did it again.

Mr. Powell nodded. "Now, Mr. Swieteck, let's bring in the neck and the head and beak. We'll let this white space here between the wing lines be the body. So imagine the neck extending out of that space. Put your pencil where you're going to begin. Very good. Now, bring your line down. A little faster. Audubon worked with curves on this bird, so that's what you're going to want to work with. Let it come around—yes, just so. Now bring your pencil to where you're going to start on the right side. No, look at the picture. You see how Audubon started this wing down a little lower? Why do you think he did that?"

"Because if the wings were at the same height, he'd look like he was hanging stuffed in a museum somewhere."

Mr. Powell smiled again. "You're talking about something called composition. But let's not get ahead of ourselves. Draw the right line. A little faster."

We filled all three sheets of paper, front and back. And I think we could have filled a whole bunch more if Mrs. Merriam hadn't come up and reminded Mr. Powell that there were other patrons of the Marysville Free Public Library, not to mention all the cataloging for those new books from Houghton Mifflin, and she couldn't do that by herself and check books in and out also, could she?

"Of course not," said Mr. Powell, even though she probably could if she just put her looped glasses on and got to it.

"End of your first lesson," said Mr. Powell. He looked over the drawings. "Take this one home," he said. "Here's something a little advanced for you, but I'm curious. See if you can figure out how to draw in the feathers. Think of it as a problem to be solved." He rolled the paper up into a scroll and handed it to me. "Take the pencils. I'll clean the rest up later. Right now, I've got to go catalog."

When I came down into the cool of the library that afternoon, it was only three thirty and no one else was in the whole place as far as I could see, so I don't know what Mrs. Everything-Has-to-Be-Cataloged-This-Second Merriam was all fussed up about. Along the line of my thumb there was a dark streak from the pencil. I decided I wouldn't wash my hands for a while to see if I could make it last.

By the way, in case you weren't paying attention or something, did you catch what Mr. Powell called me? "Young artist." I bet you missed that.

That night, I worked on the feathers before my brother came up to bed, which wasn't easy, because I didn't have a desk so I had to use the floor. And I didn't have much time, because my brother could come up any second—like, during some Marlboro commercial—and he'd find me on the floor and he'd say, "What do you think you're doing?" and it wouldn't matter what I said because he'd tear the paper into shreds and they'd be outside in some gutter like Joe Pepitone's hat. So I had to work fast.

I started on the left wing, and I figured out that I

could get these thin lines by angling the pencil tip. I tried to remember the rows on the tern, how the feathers on the wings got larger as they moved down, how they slanted a little bit into the body, how they kind of jumbled together above the long tail feathers. How the feathers were different—rounder—before they suddenly speared into the tail. How the wing feathers were long and sharp, but the feathers on the body were like whispers.

You think it's easy trying to remember all that?

You think it's easy trying to draw all that? It isn't.

I messed up the whole left wing. I think I got the rows right, but I got all the feather lines too close or something, and so when I curved them around they looked like a kid in kindergarten practicing his sixes. You couldn't imagine them brushing against the air.

I tried the feathers on the body, and I think I got those okay. You had to use the lightest stroke, the very lightest. But even though it looked good from far away, the closer in you got, the worse it was.

I started on the right wing, and the whole thing looked messed up again. Until I finally figured it out: You can't draw every feather! You can't! I bet you hadn't thought of that either.

So for the bottom rows of the bigger feathers, I drew just a few lines and curved them in, and I think it was right! You could imagine these feathers moving in the air. You really could.

I looked at the feathers, and rolled the paper up to

hide it beneath my bed, and unrolled it to look at the feathers again, and finally rolled it up and hid it beneath the bed. Then I turned out the light and lay down with my hands—with the pencil smudge on my thumb—back behind my head and I looked out the window. There was still a little bit of light left in the summer sky, and the birds were having a riot before turning in. A few stars starting up.

I couldn't keep myself from smiling. I couldn't. Maybe this happens to you every day, but I think it was the first time I could hardly wait to show something that I'd done to someone who would care besides my mother. You know how that feels?

So that's why I went to the Marysville Free Public Library every Saturday for the rest of August and on into September.

Not to read a book or anything.

September.

Washington Irving Junior High School.

The first Monday of September was The Night for All the New Kids Coming to Washington Irving Junior High School to Get Acquainted—which meant a whole bunch of seventh-graders who had probably lived in stupid Marysville their whole lives and one eighth-grader who had moved to town that summer.

Me.

Terrific.

I went with my mother, who got all dressed up like she was heading for Mass and who held my hand until we got close, when people might see. Washington Irving Junior High School looked like the same people who built the Marysville Free Public Library, built it. Six steps—again—and columns on each side of the door and then marble floors once you got inside, which made everything cold and echoey. We all headed into the auditorium and everyone seemed to know everyone else, probably because they had all been in the same elementary school since first grade. Even the mothers, who were all wearing these dresses that looked a whole lot cooler than what my mother was wearing, acted like they had all known one another since forever.

We sat pretty much by ourselves. Didn't talk. My mother took off her hat and held it in her hands. She took off her gloves too.

At seven o'clock, the principal got up and welcomed us all to an exciting new year of growth and opportunity at Washington Irving Junior High School. His name was Principal Peattie—I'm not lying—and Principal Peattie was there to keep us all in line, he said. (We were supposed to laugh politely at that, and all the mothers did. Even mine, after she saw she was supposed to.) Principal Peattie would like to introduce the teachers, he said, so the whole front row of them stood and turned toward us. There were only a couple of teachers who looked happy to be introduced. The rest looked like they knew they still had a few days of summer freedom coming and they sure didn't want to start thinking about school any more than we did. After they sat down, Principal Peattie announced the school theme for the year—Washington Irving JH! Catch the Spirit! and then he called on a bunch of ninth-graders who were all wearing the same orange T-shirt with the school theme on the back—Washington Irving JH! Catch the Spirit!—and they handed out a stack of dittos, and for the next thirty minutes, Principal Peattie stood on the stage and read them to us. The heat trapped inside the auditorium during the whole stupid summer turned up a degree or two with each new ditto.

After that, when even the ninth-graders who had Caught the Stupid Spirit were pretty much drooping, Principal Peattie announced that parents were to stay in the auditorium for an informational session on school expectations as well as a discussion of what supplies they were to provide in a year of austerity budgets. Students, meanwhile, were to go to other classrooms for small group sessions that Principal Peattie and Mr. Ferris would be leading in just a few moments.

I leaned close to my mother. "Let's go," I said.

She smiled. "We should stay for the whole thing," she said. "I'll see you afterward."

So I went out of the auditorium, and one of the Spirit-filled ninth-graders asked me what my last name was, and then she pointed to the room I was supposed to go to, and I went in and sat down with a bunch of seventh-graders whose last names started with M to Z.

They all knew one another.

Terrific.

We waited at our scrubbed-clean desks. Guess who had no one to talk to? We waited, and I looked around for a pen so the desk wouldn't be so scrubbed-clean. But finally Principal Peattie came in. He had this huge smile taped across his face, like seeing us was making him the happiest man in the world.

"This will just take a few minutes," he said. He handed out another ditto. "Principal Peattie wants to go over a few rules with you all so we can get started on the right foot. Principal Peattie thinks that he recognizes most of you from our Looking Forward to Junior High Day last May. But some of you may be new to town, and some of you may come from different school systems." He looked around. "Or at least one of you may."

Guess who.

"We all need to know what to expect of each other so that in a couple of weeks no one says to Principal Peattie, 'Principal Peattie, I didn't know.'"

He found a kid in the second row. "Tell Principal Peattie your name," he said.

"Lee," he said.

"Your entire name."

"Lee Rostrum."

"John's brother?"

Lee Rostrum nodded happily.

"Principal Peattie is sure we'll get along fine, then. Lee, why don't you read the first rule on the sheet?"

Lee Rostrum smoothed his ditto out on the desk. "'School begins with homeroom each morning, starting at eight ten, when each student should be in his seat and ready for the day.'"

"Thank you, Lee," said Principal Peattie. "And eight ten means eight ten, not eight eleven or eight twelve or eight thirteen." His eye roamed around the room. "Your name?" he asked.

"Lester Shannon."

"Lester, would you read the next rule?"

That's how it went. There were rules about the time between classes, and about lockers, and about the combination locks and not giving your combination to anyone except to Principal Peattie if Principal Peattie asks for it, and about lunch, and about making sure your shirt was tucked into your pants for boys and skirts no more than a handbreadth above the knee for girls, and about always wearing socks, and about how long a boy's hair could be — Principal Peattie looked at me when this got read aloud — and about how we were to address teachers, and even about how many times we could go to the bathroom in one day. I'm not lying.

After the bathroom rules, Principal Peattie roamed

his eye around again and then called on me. "What's your name?" he said.

"Doug Swieteck."

"Douglas, would you read the next rule?"

"Doug Swieteck has a question," I said. I know: sounding like Lucas being the biggest jerk he could be.

Principal Peattie frowned. I guess he didn't like questions.

"Suppose Doug Swieteck has to go to the bathroom more than three times?"

Principal Peattie set his ditto down on the desk in front of him. "Then Doug Swieteck would need to see the nurse," said Principal Peattie.

"How's that going to help?" I said.

Every kid in the classroom laughed. Every one.

Principal Peattie did not laugh.

"Read the next rule," he said.

I looked down at the sheet. "I think Doug Swieteck has to go to the bathroom now," I said. "But he'll only need to go once, probably. He's pretty sure, anyway."

Exploding laughter all over the place.

Principal Peattie did not laugh.

"Then Douglas may go to the bathroom."

I stood up.

"And while he's there, he should see that his T-shirt is properly tucked in. He may as well get in the habit now. And he might think about when he's going to get his hair cut, since I don't let boys who look like girls into my school."

More exploding laughter all over the place.

What a jerk.

I left. Principal Peattie closed the door behind me.

On the way to the bathroom, I went by the classroom where the A-to-L kids were in their session. They were all quiet and kind of sitting forward, and I could hear Mr. Ferris's voice. "Within a year, possibly by next fall," he was saying, "something that has never before been done, will be done. NASA will be sending men to the moon. Think of that. Men who were once in classrooms like this one will leave their footprints on the lunar surface." He paused. I leaned in close against the wall so I could hear him. "That is why you are sitting here tonight, and why you will be coming here in the months ahead. You come to dream dreams. You come to build fantastic castles up into the air. And you come to learn how to build the foundations that make those castles real. When the men who will command that mission were boys your age, no one knew that they would walk on another world someday. No one knew. But in a few months, that's what will happen. So, twenty years from now, what will people say of you? 'No one knew then that this kid from Washington Irving Junior High School would grow up to do'...what? What castle will you build?"

I didn't go to the bathroom. I waited outside the auditorium for my mother to come out. And when she did, we went through the lobby doors and I looked up at the moon. Then we headed on home by way of this ice cream place around the corner and down a block from the library. We had black-and-whites, my mother and me. And I paid for them.

You know how that felt?

My brother came upstairs later that night, while I was thinking about Audubon's birds, and buying a black-and-white for my mother, and planting daisies with Lil Spicer, and looking out the window at the spectacular moon.

Remember how I said that when you're feeling good, something always happens to wreck it all? Remember?

"Hey, Douggo," he said. I think you can figure out for yourself how my brother said *Douggo*. "Hey, Douggo, what are you doing with yourself these days?"

"Nothing," I said.

"That's not what I heard," he said. "I heard you were going to the library."

"So?"

He started to laugh the way you'd imagine someone with a twisted criminal mind would laugh.

"So, you don't even know how to read," he said.

"I do too know how to read."

The twisted criminal mind laughed again. "Douggo," he said, "if you had to read directions to pee in a toilet, we'd be spreading newspapers for you all over the house."

Okay, here comes this weird moment. I know I should have jumped off the bed and stomped across the room and flattened him against the wall and punched his lights out. *Now let's see* you *read,* I would have said. If Joe Pepitone had been in the room right then, that's what he would have done.

But I didn't think about that at first. At first, all I could think about was the Arctic Tern, heading down into the water, about to crash, his neck yanked back because he knows he's going to smack into it. The eye.

And then—and this is the even weirder part—I thought of Lucas and wondered where he was and if he was looking out from wherever he was, if he was seeing the spectacular moon like I was seeing it.

Then my stupid brother took off his stupid sweaty socks and lobbed them over at me. "Hold on to these until I need them tomorrow," he said. I threw them on the floor. More twisted criminal laughter. "It's all right, Douggo," he said. "Don't get mad. I'm sure lots of kids in the eighth grade can't read."

I turned over. He was snoring a long time before I finally fell asleep.

* * *

After the deliveries the next Saturday, I decided to see if the Marysville Free Public Library had a back door, in case someone with a twisted criminal mind was waiting for me out front.

It turned out that the library did have a back door—locked, of course. But it didn't matter. My brother wasn't waiting out front. Probably the pack had found some new place to prowl.

So I climbed the six steps and went in by the front door. Mrs. Merriam was at her desk, cataloging like crazy because I guess it's the most important thing in the whole wide world. She had her loopy glasses on, and when she looked up and saw me, she smiled. Sort of. It was the kind of smile that said *I know something you don't*. The kind of smile my brother would get when he knew that my father was looking for me. The smile of a twisted criminal mind.

But who knows? Maybe something lousy had just happened to her. Maybe she was lonely. Maybe she hated stupid Marysville too. Who knows? So maybe I could, once, try being nice to her. Once. What did I have to lose?

"Hey, Mrs. Merriam," I said. Pretty cool.

"Hey, yourself," she said. "You're not always going to get everything you want, you know. That's not what life is like. Maybe after today, you'll understand that."

See what trying to be nice will get you?

I went upstairs to see if Mr. Powell was with the Arctic Tern. I held the rolled paper in my hand. The one with the feathers.

"You don't need to run up the stairs," hollered Mrs. Merriam.

Mr. Powell was by the case, looking down into it. His hands were on the glass like he was trying to press it down.

"Hi, Mr. Powell," I said.

He looked up. "Hello, Mr. Swieteck," he said. He puffed his breath out and ruffled the light hairs all around his face. "How did the problem with the feathers go?"

"I think I solved it, but it took a few tries."

"That's how it should be," he said. "Let's see." He took a couple of steps toward me and reached out his hand.

And that's when I knew that something was wrong. He should have asked me to spread the paper across the glass so we could compare what I did with what Audubon did. But he was reaching out his hand.

So I handed him the paper and then walked over to the glass case and looked inside.

The Arctic Tern was gone.

"Mr. Swieteck," Mr. Powell said.

I looked at him.

"They're Large-Billed Puffins," he said.

I looked down into the case. Whatever they were, these birds were chumps. Fat-bodied and thick-legged and looking about as dumb as any birds could possibly be and still remember to breathe. One looked like he had just fallen into the water and was doing everything he could to keep his face from getting wet. The one on land stood there watching like a jerk, as if he didn't even care that the other one was bobbing up and down, trying not to drown. Probably he was too stupid to care. Or maybe he had a twisted criminal mind and that's why he didn't care.

"I know," said Mr. Powell. "They look a little bit different than the Arctic Tern."

A little bit different? A little bit different? I don't know. You take away the sleek white feathers of the tern and put on stubby dark ones. You take away the pointed wings and stick on dumb oval wings. Then you take away the long neck and throw in a body like an old football, and stick a stupid yellow cup over the stupid bird's face instead of the pointed beak, and I guess a puffin looks a little bit different than a tern.

Mr. Powell walked over to the case and looked down at the puffins. "It was about time to change the page anyway." He shook his head and coughed lightly. "I thought I'd show you some elements of texture since you're already getting into it. Let's take a look at what you did with the feathers first."

"You didn't just change the page," I said.

He looked at me. "No," he said. "I didn't."

He spread my page over the stupid Large-Billed Puffins. He pointed to the left wing. "I see you figured out the problem pretty quickly."

"You can't draw in every feather," I said. "They start to look like nothing but a bunch of lines next to each other."

His hand moved over to the bottom rows on the right wing. "Tell me what you did here."

"I drew just a few lines to show how the feathers curve in."

"And that," Mr. Powell said, nodding, "is what an artist does. "You're right: you can't draw in every feather. But you can draw in the patterning of the feathers so I can see how they are shaped and how they lie on the bird's body. When you draw in the pattern, your viewer's eye will fill in the rest. Now, look at this."

He took an eraser out of his pocket and rubbed out one of the lines for the tern's body. "Draw in these feathers like you've done the others."

"I don't have a line to show where they stop."

"That's right," he said. "So you'll have to suggest it."

So I drew, while the Large-Billed Puffins bobbed in the water below me like the chumps they were. And by the time I was done, Mr. Powell had erased all the lines, and my tern's feathers were plunging against the air like all get-out.

Mr. Powell asked if he could keep my drawing.

You know how that feels?

A few nights before Washington Irving Junior High School was doomed to start, Spicer's Deli on Main Street, Marysville, got broken into. It happened sometime after ten o'clock. And in case you were wondering, my jerk brother was home then, and for the rest of the night.

And if you *were* wondering, you weren't the only one.

Mr. Spicer was wondering too.

And so were the policemen he sent to find my brother.

They came the next day when my mother and I were washing up the dishes after breakfast. They were mostly polite — probably because my father was out somewhere with Ernie Eco and he wasn't there with a whole lot to say and letting himself say it. So my mother did the talking. No, she hadn't heard that Spicer's Deli had been robbed last night. No, she had never shopped there, but her youngest son worked for Mr. Spicer. She did not know Mr. Spicer and she had no idea why he would think that her son had anything to do with the robbery. Yes, she knew exactly where he had been last night: home. No, he had not gone out after nine o'clock. Yes, she was sure of that. Yes, she was very sure of that. Yes, very sure.

The two policemen did not look very sure.

They looked at me. Yes, I knew Spicer's Deli—I worked there. No, I didn't hear my brother go out last night. No, I'd never seen him near Spicer's Deli. Nope, I was sure. Never. Just ask him.

The policemen said they would do that. Did I have any idea where he was right now?

I didn't. My mother didn't either.

They looked at each other. They said they'd ride around some and if it was okay with my mother, they'd ask my brother the same questions—if they happened to see him, that is.

My mother said that would be fine.

When they left, she leaned against the sink. Her breathing was quick and short.

"Douggie," she said, "you don't think..."

"He was here all night," I said.

She looked at me.

"He was," I said.

And in case you think I'm lying because of the lie I told about not seeing him at the deli—which, by the way, isn't that big a lie and one you probably would tell too—I know that he didn't leave last night because I was awake for most of it. I was awake with a flashlight and drawing the tern's feathers again, the way they were supposed to be. On a new page, I drew in the body lines lightly, and then I erased them as I went. The feathers came out pretty good. You could feel them moving through the air. They were moving the way no stupid Large-Billed Puffin's feathers could ever move. And I'm not lying.

So my brother didn't rob Spicer's Deli, no matter who says he did.

This didn't matter a whole lot to my father, who came home really late with Ernie Eco after someone had told him that he'd seen the police talking to his son. I heard the door slam open and his feet on the stairs — taking them two at a time — and him calling for my brother, who probably wished he hadn't come home that night, who sat up in bed and said, "I didn't — " before my father was on him.

I guess I should have been happy about what happened to him. Like he was when it happened to me. But I saw my brother's face when my father flipped on the light switch.

The terrified eye.

"Look at the way Audubon has arranged the two puffins," said Mr. Powell.

"You mean the two stupid puffins," I said.

"All right, the two stupid puffins. Remember the tern? Remember how everything was pointing down? The horizon lined the very bottom of the painting, but your eye hardly saw it. What's different about the setting of this painting?"

"You mean except for the two stupid fat birds?"

"Yes, Mr. Swieteck, except for the two stupid fat birds."

I leaned over the glass case. "The horizon is halfway up the painting," I said.

"That's right. If you drew lines out from these rocks, do you see how they would go across the page, just like the horizon?"

"So everything is going side to side instead of up and down."

"Good. That's thinking like an artist. Now, put one finger at the tail feathers of the bird on the left. Now another on the far foot of the one on the right. I'll put my finger at the top of the head of the left bird, and we've made..."

"A perfect triangle."

"Right. And a triangle whose longest side is at the bottom. So what is different about the feel of this painting?"

"Except for the —"

"Yes, except for the two stupid fat birds."

I shrugged. "Not much is moving."

"Not just that. What else? Think like an artist. Think of everything in the painting, not just the birds."

And then I saw it. The long horizons. The flat lines. The triangle resting on them. So solid. I traced the lines with my fingers.

"Exactly right," said Mr. Powell. "Do you see how if he had used the horizon lines and the triangle for the Arctic Tern, it would have been wrong? It would have warred against the downward motion. But for these birds, it's perfect. The artist gives them a stable horizon that you can't help but see."

I spread the paper across the glass case.

"Draw the horizon line at midpoint — lightly," he said. "Then we'll add in the lines for the two puffins and see where they intersect."

I suppose it was only a matter of time before Lil found me in the library. I didn't hear her come up the stairs. I was trying to trace the triangle and figure out how Audubon made you see a triangle without drawing a triangle and even while sticking things outside it — like the stupid foot of the stupid puffin on the right who was trying not to drown. This isn't easy work, so I was concentrating pretty hard. And that explains what happened.

"Your tongue sticks out of your mouth when you draw," Lil said.

I looked up. "It does not."

"It does too. Your tongue sticks out of your mouth when you draw. That's why you drool." She pointed to the paper. "There," she said.

"It isn't drool," I said.

"Maybe it's because of that funny thing you do with your Adam's apple."

"Is there something you want?"

"Mr. Powell said that you were up here drawing and that you were pretty good. So I came up to see if you were." She looked at my Large-Billed Puffin. "Mrs. Merriam says you're a hoodlum in training."

"What does Mrs. Merriam know?"

"What are these lines here for?"

"Nothing. Just something a hoodlum in training would draw."

She put her hands on her hips. "You don't have to be angry with me. I'm not the one who said it."

"You're the one who told me."

She sniffed. "Maybe she's right and I was wrong. I told my father that whoever robbed the deli, it wasn't you, even when he thought it might be. But maybe you did. Maybe you are a hoodlum in training. Maybe you're just a drooling hoodlum." She turned and went back down the stairs. Her hair waved back and forth with each step down.

When her head was level with the floor, I said, "Lil."

She stopped, looked up at me.

"Sorry about my jerk brother and the daisies."

She looked at me a little more.

"Mr. Powell was right," she said. Then she was gone.

I went back to the drawing. I erased the three triangle lines I had used to guide where I put the birds.

And then I looked up and over at the stairs.

Mr. Powell thought I was pretty good.

And Lil thought I was pretty good too.

I tried to remember the last time anyone told me I was pretty good at anything.

You know how that feels?

I went back to the drawing. I kept my tongue in my mouth. No drooling.

The police came back to The Dump twice more. The first time, they came with Mr. Spicer so that he could identify my brother, which he could. My brother swore up and down that he didn't break into anyone's store. But Mr. Spicer didn't listen — mostly because he was looking at me. He didn't look happy.

The second time the police came back, my father was there, and he swore up and down, until one of them took a step closer so that he was practically standing on top of my father's feet and said that if my father wanted to say one more thing — just one more thing — he could say it in a cell. I could see my father's quick hands twitching.

The whole time the police were there, I sat with my mother on the couch.

The police only came those two other times, and

since they couldn't prove a thing, they stopped coming. Their last line was to my brother: "We'll be keeping an eye out." You could tell they thought he was as guilty as sin, which usually wasn't a bad way to describe my brother. But not for this.

So he wasn't arrested. Still, word got around anyway. That's how it is in a small town like stupid Marysville. All you have to do is spit on the sidewalk, and the whole town figures you're the kind of guy who might commit homicide, and everyone in your family is likely just the same. You could see it in the eyes of the mailman, the eyes of the guy who came to collect our rent, the eyes of Mrs. Merriam—who was sure now that I was no longer in training—even the eyes of the priest at St. Ignatius, who asked my mother her name when we went for our first Mass in stupid Marysville and then right away looked down at me like I was the one with the twisted criminal mind and not my brother.

You could see it in the eyes of Mr. Spicer, who didn't say much when I came in that Saturday for the deliveries but who looked at me in a new way and who told me that I could let Mrs. Windermere put her bill on account. He would ride up some other time to collect the money.

You could see it in the eyes of Mrs. Mason, who didn't invite me in for a chocolate doughnut, even though she had ordered two dozen. And Mr. Loeffler, who didn't have any chores for me, thanks anyway, not today. And Mrs. Daugherty, who kept her kids back from the front door like I was contagious and who didn't even answer the door. Her husband came out instead. Mr. Daugherty. Who happened to be a policeman.

You could probably have seen it in the eyes of Mrs. Windermere, except she never stopped typing while I put her groceries away.

I hate this stupid town.

You could see it in the eyes of the secretary in the Main Office of Washington Irving Junior High School that first day too, and in the eyes of Principal Peattie, who came out of his office so that he could identify me better if he ever had to pick me out of a lineup, and in the eyes of the guidance counselor who worked on my schedule, handed it to me, hesitated, and then decided to walk me to my homeroom because, she said, I didn't know my way around the school yet — but probably because she thought I was going to rob some lockers while I was passing by.

And you could see it in the eyes of my teachers: Mr. Barber in geography, who handed out brand-new textbooks while holding a huge cup of coffee and who made us all swear to keep our new textbooks neat and clean like they were Joe Pepitone's cap or something and who paused a couple of seconds before he handed the book to me because he probably thought I was going to throw it in the gutter like it was a piece of junk.

Mr. McElroy in world history, who announced that we were going to start by studying the barbarian hordes of western Russia, and then looked at me.

Miss Cowper in English, whose first words were "This fall, we will be reading *Jane Eyre* by Miss Charlotte Brontë, and I am not naive enough to believe that you will all like it." Then she looked right at me. "The original novel is over four hundred pages long—no groaning, please, you are not cattle being led to slaughter—but you will be reading an abridgment. Even this is a hundred and sixty pages long, but that should not discourage you. Those of you with character should see this as a challenge. Those of you not so favored..." And she looked at me again and didn't finish the sentence.

One hundred and sixty pages of *Jane Eyre*.

Terrific.

You could see it in the eyes of Mrs. Verne in math, who wouldn't call on me even when I raised my hand—even when I raised my hand and the only other hand up was Lil's and Mrs. Verne had already called on her twice. When Lil got called on again, she looked back at me and then turned to Mrs. Verne and said, "I think *he* knows," and Mrs. Verne's face got all pinchy and she said, "I will choose who is to speak in this classroom, Miss Spicer," and she went on so that no one answered the question.

$x - 17$, by the way.

You could see it in the eyes of Coach Reed in PE,

who lined us up in platoons—he was just back from being a sergeant in Vietnam, and he still had his army crewcut—and told me in his sergeant's voice that I'd better not try to pull any funny business in his class, no sirree, buster, just before he toured us through the locker room, taking us past his office that was Forbidden to All Students, and then told us to shoot baskets the rest of the period.

So that's how it went until I got to Mr. Ferris in physical science. I'm not lying, he was wearing a white lab coat and—I couldn't believe it—dark glasses on a chain looped around his neck. Don't people know how stupid that looks? Worse than a Large-Billed Puffin. His hair was cut like he had just gotten back from Vietnam too, and up on the lab table in front of the class, he had a toy horse that he set rocking back and forth while he talked with us. "His name," Mr. Ferris said, "is Clarence."

I don't know why, so don't ask.

Mr. Ferris told us how we were going to have lab partners and do experiments and create vacuums and aspirin tablets and investigate the concept of mass versus weight and how we'd have to measure with the metric system and we didn't need to fuss about it because it was for our own good and how the first thing we needed to become familiar with was the periodic table starting with H for . . . does anyone know?

"Hydrogen," said Lil, who turned out to be in every one of my classes, except for PE, of course. Did I tell you that she has green eyes?

"Right!" said Mr. Ferris, and he started Clarence rocking happily.

Terrific again.

Physical science was the last period of the day, and when the bell rang, everyone gathered up their books—and I'm not lying, I was really careful with *Geography: The Story of the World*—and was heading to their lockers when Mr. Ferris asked me to wait for a moment. You think there was a single eye that wasn't looking at me when they left? Even Lil's? They probably figured that Mr. Ferris was going to tell me that I'd better not try to pull any funny business in his class, no sirree, buster.

I thought if I had to hear that again, I'd start plummeting into the sea.

"Doug Swieteck," Mr. Ferris said, "do you know the basic principle of physical science?"

A trick?

"No," I said, sort of slow.

He rocked Clarence. "The basic principle of physical science is this: two bodies cannot occupy the same space at the same time. Do you understand that?"

"I think so," I said.

"Do you understand what the principle means?"

I shook my head.

"It means, Doug Swieteck, that in this class, you are not your brother."

Mr. Ferris started Clarence rocking again, and I felt the horizon settle.

The next Saturday, after a week of being my brother in everyone's class except Mr. Ferris's, I found Lil waiting by the Large-Billed Puffins when I came back from the deliveries. "You can't really say that they're beautiful, can you?" she said.

"They're not."

She looked down at the birds. "I didn't mean to embarrass you in math. Everyone knows that Mrs. Verne is mean. But I didn't think the other teachers would—"

"They're jerks. It doesn't matter."

She reached out her hand. "You're right. It doesn't matter. Let's shake on that."

You know, maybe the puffin in the water isn't bobbing around like a chump just because he's trying not to drown. Maybe he's swimming, but he has no idea what to do because there's this other puffin standing beside him, and maybe she's a girl puffin—and no matter how dumb Large-Billed Puffins look to us, they probably look pretty good to each other. And so the puffin in the water is looking at the girl puffin standing next to him, and he doesn't know what to do, because suddenly he's thinking, *I should tell her that she has the most beautiful green eyes in the world,* but he doesn't know how to say it, so he just bobs in the water like the chump he is.

"You're supposed to shake my hand," said Lil.

That is what I did.

After she left, I worked on my drawing of the Large-Billed Puffins. And even though their round eyes are looking away and out of the picture, I decided to change one small thing, so when Mr. Powell came up to see how I was doing, he looked at them, then at me, and then back at them. "It seems that they like each other," he said.

"Maybe," I said.

A week later, while we were taking another try at the puffins—you can't believe how hard it is to make a puffin not look like a chump—I told Mr. Powell about Miss Cowper and Charlotte Brontë and *Jane Eyre.* Mr. Powell wanted me to work on the bills and the feet, since they were at crux points in the composition, he said. (Artists know what this means.) But it was hard to make these look right, mostly because they look so stupid.

"*Jane Eyre,*" he said. "*Jane Eyre,*" he said again.

"The original novel is four hundred pages long," I said.

He nodded.

"We have to read an abridgment, and it's still a hundred and sixty pages long."

Nodding again.

"I'm not reading it," I said.

"Mr. Swieteck, if it's an assignment—"

"I'm not reading it."

I went back to getting the feet right, and the stupid bills.

"I can help," Mr. Powell said after a bit.

"I can't get this one foot that's underwater right."

"With *Jane Eyre*," he said.

I looked up at him. "I don't need any help with *Jane Eyre* because I'm not going to read it."

We didn't talk about *Jane Eyre* anymore. I went back to the puffins.

And I know you think you know why I don't want to read *Jane Eyre,* but it's not really any of your business, is it?

When I got home from the library, my mother was cooking everything in sight. Here are the stats for what was on the kitchen table and counter:

Three loaves of fresh-baked white bread.
One angel food cake with chocolate icing dripping down
its sides—Lucas's favorite.

Probably two hundred carrots she'd sliced.
Probably three hundred green beans she'd cut.
Probably four hundred yellow beans she'd cut.
Three dozen ears of corn shucked.
Thirty-five huge patties of hamburger already cooked
    and wrapped in tinfoil.
One bowl of Italian macaroni salad.
Two bowls of German potato salad.
One bowl of green grapes.
Two platters of tomatoes, sliced.
One platter of onions, sliced.

"Mom," I said.

Everything was piled almost on top of everything else. Bacon was frying on the stove. She was cutting up canned peaches and pears to go in three chilled Jell-O salads.

"Oh, Douggie, Douggie," she said. "I'm so glad you're home. Look at this."

She held up an envelope.

There was a U.S. Army insignia in the left-hand corner.

"It's got to be from Lucas," I said.

"But the address isn't his handwriting," she said.

She was right. She went back to cutting the peaches and pears into smaller and smaller pieces. The liquid Jell-O was cooling on the stove.

"You better open it," I said.

"You open it," she said.

I opened the letter and took it out. It was in script, so it was really hard to read. I held it out to her.

She looked at me, turned to wash her hands, looked out the window, turned back and looked at the letter, and finally took it.

Her terrified eye.

Then she read aloud the most important parts.

That a friend of Lucas was writing the letter for him. That Lucas had been wounded pretty bad, but was mostly okay now. That he would be home in a couple of months, maybe three, maybe a little more, depending on how things went. You know the army. That he hoped we wouldn't mind if he looked a little bit different. Everyone comes home from Vietnam a little bit different.

That Lucas couldn't wait to see us.

She held the letter against her chest. She looked at me. She closed her eyes.

"What is it?"

"He says he can't wait to see us," she said in this squeak of a voice.

She put her hands to her face.

"Mom?"

"And he says that he loves us."

She opened her eyes and looked at the letter again, folded it, put it back in its envelope.

She put it up on the window ledge, over the kitchen sink.

You know, you know, how can you smile like that, and be sobbing and sobbing all over the peaches and pears?

Black Backed Gull
LARUS MARINUS

CHAPTER FOUR

The Black-Backed Gull
Plate CCXLI

"THAT LEFT FOOT has to feel like it's in the water. *In* it, Mr. Swieteck. Not in front of it. You want to give the impression of depth."

"I know the stupid foot is in the stupid water," I said.

"So how does Audubon help you to know it?"

"He changes the color of the foot."

"How else?"

"The lines aren't as sharp."

"Exactly. The whole form of the foot starts to blur. The texture fades away. You can't even see the webbing between these two toes."

"So how do I . . ."

"Take your pencil and we'll lighten the strokes here, and bend them just a bit, since light is bent when it enters the water. Now, follow my hand."

You think this is easy? I'm not lying, it isn't. I'd been working on the Large-Billed Puffins all September, and most of the time I was working on the stupid fading foot, because an artist doesn't draw two-dimensionally, in case you didn't know. An artist draws three-dimensionally on a two-dimensional surface, which Mr. Powell pointed out to me and which I pointed out to Lil Spicer.

"How do you do that?" she asked.

"You have to be an artist to know," I said.

And if you think she said, *Then how do you know?* or something snotty like that, she didn't. Figure out why.

Things at Washington Irving Junior High School were going mostly okay. Mostly. Nothing had happened to *Geography: The Story of the World,* which was good because Mr. Barber checked on my book every time he passed down the aisle drinking his huge cup of coffee. I think he didn't care that I wasn't turning in my answers to the Review Questions at the end of the chapters because that meant I wasn't messing up his new geography book. Mr. McElroy had been showing us filmstrips about the barbarian hordes of Russia with records that gave little pings to let him know when he was supposed to advance the strip. You can't believe how many filmstrips there are about the barbarian hordes of Russia. Miss Cowper still hadn't made us start stupid *Jane Eyre,* so we had all 160 pages to look forward to—not that it mattered, because I wasn't going to read it. Mrs. Verne hadn't called on me yet when I raised my hand, but she *had* called on me when I didn't raise my hand so that she could trip me up and show everyone what a chump I was. But I figured that's what she was up to, and so when she asked if I knew what a quadratic equation was when she thought that no one in the room knew except for her, I knew. I hadn't pulled any funny business in Coach Reed's PE class—no sirree, buster—except that I sneaked over to the Shirts Team from the Skins Team when we finally played basketball after two weeks of dribbling and shooting drills. And in Mr. Ferris's class, Lil and I had done our first lab report together on creating a supersaturated solution, which meant that I did all the smelly chemically stuff and Lil took down the notes and wrote it up.

Oh, and I don't mean to brag or anything, but that lab report that Lil and I turned in for the supersaturated solution? Let's just say that Mr. Ferris started Clarence rocking when he saw it.

But I still couldn't get that left foot of the Large-

Billed Puffin right. It always looked like it was in front of the water.

I worked on it all weekend when my brother wasn't around (which was most of the time) and when my father wasn't around (which was all of the time). I even showed it to my mother, but you can't trust mothers to tell you the truth about stuff like this. They just tell you how good it is and what an artist you are and how they don't know where you got that talent since no one else in the family can draw.

But I still couldn't get the foot right.

On Sunday night, after my mother and I ate four thawed hamburgers and one large bowl of Italian macaroni salad, I decided to try for some inspiration, which is something that every artist needs. So I went downstairs to the basement and got Joe Pepitone's jacket and put it on. Then I went back upstairs to my room and rolled out the paper and tried to fade that foot into the water, because an artist has to know how to give an impression of depth, you might remember.

And I started to get it. I really did.

And then my brother came home — and upstairs — and into our room. And first he said, "How come you're wearing a jacket when . . ." and then he saw the drawing of the Large-Billed Puffins and then he laughed because he wouldn't know a decent drawing if it walked up to him and punched him in the face, so he grabbed it like the jerk he is and looked at it and laughed again and said, "Can't you even draw a foot right? It looks like it's underwater, Douggo," and then he tore it up and said, "I guess you'll just have to try again," and then he scattered all the pieces on my bed because that's what twisted criminal minds do.

Then, still laughing, he left, not even noticing that I had Joe Pepitone's jacket on, the chump—which, of course, I was glad about, since it was a pretty close call. I went back down to the basement and hung it up beneath the stairs again.

And you know what?

I was smiling. I was smiling like all get-out.

If you were paying attention back there, you'd know why.

So on the first Saturday of October, after a week when Mr. McElroy had had enough of the Russian hordes and had probably run out of pinging filmstrips anyway and so we were now headed across the Great Wall into China, and a week when Mrs. Verne finally did call on me when I had my hand up and when I answered right—not to brag—that it was negative x and not negative y, and a week when I had snuck over to the Shirts team again and Coach Reed couldn't figure out why his platoon system wasn't working and how someone was pulling some funny business on him, I went over to the Marysville Free Public Library after my deliveries, ready to tell Mr. Powell that I had figured out how to give the impression of depth. Mrs. Merriam with her loopy glasses looked up when I came in.

"He's in a meeting," she said.

"Is he done soon?" I said.

"He's in a meeting. That's all I know. It's not like I've memorized his schedule. I'm just supposed to do all this cataloging by myself, I suppose."

I went up to see the Large-Billed Puffins. Maybe I ought to give them names, since it felt like we'd gotten to know each other.

But they were gone. Just like the Arctic Tern.

This time, the page was turned to a dying bird. And I mean, really dying. Most of the picture was this one wing, held straight up. All its feathers were spread out, and you could see how Audubon got their pattern down—three rows of long, overlapping dark feathers, tipped white at the ends. You could feel how the wind would cruise over them. It was so beautiful, and it's what you looked at first.

And then you looked down at the second wing, which was crushed.

And then you looked at the belly of the bird, which was spouting thick red blood all over the dark feathers.

And then you looked beneath the bird, where the blood was in a puddle.

And then you looked at the bird's head. After that, that's all you looked at.

I would have given Joe Pepitone's jacket to save this bird.

His beak was wide open and his tongue was stretched out into a point. He was screeching while his blood ran. His head was pulled far back, like he was taking one last look at the sky that he would never fly in again. And his round eye told you he knew that everything was ruined forever.

It was a horrible picture, and I couldn't stop looking at it.

I was still looking at it when Mr. Powell puffed up the stairs after his meeting. He came over to the bird and took off his glasses to rub his eyes. (Just so you know, he didn't have his glasses on a loop because I had finally told him how dumb that looks.)

"Mr. Powell," I said, "he's dying"—as if anyone needed to point that out.

He nodded and put his glasses back on. "That's how Audubon got his specimens," he said. "For some reason, he wanted to show the Black-Backed Gull after he had shot it." He leaned against the case.

"What happened to the puffins?" I said.

"I want you to work on this gull now," he said. "You see how Audubon has combined some of what we've worked on before? When he stretches out this wing, the bird seems so still, like the Large-Billed Puffins. But the bottom half of its body is in movement, like the Arctic Tern."

"Not like the tern," I said.

"No. Not exactly."

"So what happened to the Arctic Tern? And to the puffins?"

"Do you see how he's left the space white and blank behind the gull? He doesn't want anything to distract the eye from the outstretched wing."

"He doesn't even want to give the impression of depth."

"No," said Mr. Powell.

"Which we'd be able to see if we compared the puffins to the gull."

Mr. Powell nodded.

"So can we do that?"

Mr. Powell took off his glasses and rubbed his eyes again. "We can't do that," he said.

"Why not?"

"Because the Large-Billed Puffins are gone."

"The page is . . ."

"Sold."

"Sold?"

"The puffins are gone, Mr. Swieteck. And the Arctic Tern, to an anonymous collector from overseas, I'm told. And the Red-Throated Diver, sold because the buyer thought it would make such a nice picture over the fireplace in her parlor. And the Brown Pelican. And if you were in the meeting with me downstairs, you would have seen Mr. Ballard's secretary hand over a check for twenty-four hundred dollars made out to the Town Council of Marysville. She'll stop by tonight to pick up the Yellow Shank."

"You can't sell the pages of a whole book one by one."

"That's exactly the problem. When it's an Audubon, you can. Most buyers can't afford a whole book, but they can buy one plate at a time — if they find someone low enough to cut them out of a folio."

I looked back at the dying gull. At his ruined wing. In the ruined book.

"Is it Mrs. Merriam who — "

"She doesn't have anything to do with it, and even though she doesn't show it, she's distraught. The three trustees of the library happen to be on the Town Council. Sometimes, the town needs money. Sometimes even for good things. They'd like to sell the whole set of books, but the other three volumes belong to the Marysville Historical Society, and they're preserving them as they should be." Mr. Powell tapped the glass. "This is volume three. And since Marysville's public library is not so scrupulous as its historical society, this is the only volume that is missing any of its pages."

"They're chumps for selling them," I said.

"There are only a few perfect sets in the entire world," Mr. Powell said quietly.

"And this isn't one of them."

Mr. Powell nodded. "Not anymore. So, let's find some paper and begin on this wing."

I looked back at the eye of the dying gull, who knew that everything was ruined forever, because that's how it always is.

On Monday, Coach Reed caught me sneaking over to the Shirts Team and finally figured out the funny business. He told me in his sergeant's voice that I had to go over to the Skins Team and I had better not try to mess up his platoons again, no sirree, buster.

I told him that I wanted to play on the Shirts Team and he should send someone else over to the Skins Team if they wanted to go.

He said he'd send over to the Skins Team who he wanted to send over to the Skins Team, and buster, that was me.

You can probably figure out that everything else in the gym had gone pretty quiet. Not a single dribble anywhere.

I said that it didn't matter who went where as long as the teams were even, and I pointed out that with me on the Shirts Team we had even numbers so it didn't make much sense to send me to the Skins Team.

Coach Reed said that he was the teacher.

I said I thought you had to be able to count to be a teacher.

He said, One, Two, Three, he sure could count the three days of After School Detention I had now and he wanted to know if I'd like to see him count even higher.

I said sure.

He said, Four, Five.

I clapped.

He said, Six, Seven, and before I could clap again he grabbed my arm and dragged me out of the gym and through the halls to Principal Peattie's office. Principal Peattie, who had been waiting for this moment and who decided to stretch things out and make me sweat, told me to sit in this chair by the secretary, which I did in my stupid gym uniform for almost half an hour before he opened his door and told me to come in and sit down and said that Principal Peattie had been expecting something like this all along and Principal Peattie was surprised that it hadn't happened sooner and Principal Peattie was going to throw the book at me so I learned my lesson and learned it good, and dang it, I should take this like a man and look Principal Peattie in the eye.

He really wanted to see me sweat.

"Look Principal Peattie in the eye!" he said.

And I did. For a moment.

"You're not here to look at a pelican," he said. "You're here to look at Principal Peattie!"

I'm not lying. If you had been there, you wouldn't have looked him in the eye either. You would have looked past him, like me. You would have looked at the wall over his desk. And you would have seen what I saw: the Brown Pelican, the beautiful Brown Pelican, the beautiful and noble Brown Pelican.

One of the pages razored out of Audubon's book.

I got seven days of After School Detention and one more for not looking Principal Peattie in the eye. But I couldn't help it.

Could you?

It wasn't the best day I'd had at Washington Irving Junior High School. Tuesday was a little better, even though that morning in English we finally started reading *Jane Eyre,* by Miss Charlotte Brontë, which we were likely to be reading for a whole long time, since it was 160 pages long even in the abridgment, as you might remember.

For the rest of that week, Miss Cowper read it aloud to us. I know. You're probably thinking that we were dying of boredom. But what was kind of surprising was that it wasn't so bad. By Friday, we were at this part when Jane is at the boarding school, and this jerk who runs it — who sort of reminds me of the principal of Washington Irving Junior High School — makes Jane stand on a stool because he wants everyone to think that she's a liar, like she's been going over to the other team in PE or something absolutely horrible like that. So she's standing there and everyone is supposed to stay away from her because the principal says that they should and you think she's going to crumple and just give up. But you know what?

She doesn't.

She sort of reminded me of Lil—which I did not tell her—and which you shouldn't tell her I said either.

So the story wasn't so bad. But what *was* bad was that Miss Cowper decided that beginning next week, she would make us take turns reading it *aloud*. She would read for the first five minutes of class to give us a running start, she said, and then she would call on the next alphabetical victim to read for the next seven minutes.

Terrific.

So on Monday, she started with Otis Bottom, who read like he had written the thing himself. When he finished—and he read the parts after Jane was off the stool and trying not to wish that she could get even with Mr. Brocklehurst, the jerk—I almost wanted to stand up and clap, he was that good.

Except that I really wanted to throw up, he was that good.

Terrific again.

When the period was almost over and Miss Cowper said, "We'll have five more new readers tomorrow," like she was promising a gift or something, I figured I'd better talk to her—because, you remember, I wasn't going to read *Jane Eyre*. So I waited until everyone left, even though I might be late for Mrs. Verne's class and I knew that Principal Peattie would love to see me waiting outside his office for another thirty minutes.

"Miss Cowper," I said.

She was putting pages away in a notebook, but she looked up at me.

"I don't know if I want to read *Jane Eyre* out loud."

"Everyone takes a turn, Douglas, even if you think you don't like the book."

I looked around to be sure that no one was in the room to hear what I was about to say. "I like it well enough."

"So what's the problem?"

What was I supposed to say? I looked at her, like a chump.

"Douglas, I know that Otis Bottom is a wonderful reader. It's a gift that he has. You may have different gifts. But that doesn't mean that you shouldn't try to read aloud."

"I know that," I said.

"Is it reading aloud in front of others that bothers you?"

"No."

"Good. Then I'll look forward to a gallant attempt when your turn comes," she said.

You see how it is? Sometimes things go bad even when other things are going bad.

I headed to Mrs. Verne's class looking at the next few pages of *Jane Eyre*. I think that Charlotte Brontë ought to be shot. I mean, who uses words like these? I didn't know half of them.

Well, most of them.

Okay, I'm a chump. So what?

And what was I supposed to do?

I thought of Jane Eyre standing on her stool, everyone looking at her.

I thought of the dying gull.

I hate this stupid town.

Detention that afternoon was with Mr. Ferris, because the eighth-grade teachers took turns monitoring After School Detention — which probably put them in really good moods. So I stayed in his room after school and waited for the other twisted criminal minds to come join me for ninety minutes of forced study. It didn't help that it was one of those perfect, blue, cloudless days where the trees are starting to golden up and the breezes are cool like they are during a World Series and you could imagine having a catch with Joe Pepitone or Horace Clarke or someone like that but instead you're sitting in the physical science room and it turns out that *you* are the only twisted criminal mind so you're all alone while Mr. Ferris works on his next Lab Preparation.

I flipped through the pages of *Jane Eyre*. Hopeless.

Somewhere, far away, a dog barked. A happy bark.

I flipped through *Jane Eyre* again. Very hopeless.

Mr. Ferris looked up from his Lab Preparation. "So, Doug Swieteck, what are you in for?"

"Mouthing off to Coach Reed."

He thought about this for a minute, his hand on Clarence. "Generally," he finally said, "it is neither wise nor prudent to mouth off to a junior high school teacher. Especially to one who has been a sergeant in the United States Army."

"Not even if the teacher is wrong?"

"Consider: Is it Coach Reed or you who is sitting in this somewhat dreary room that smells of vinegar on a beautiful October afternoon?"

"I see your point," I said.

"However, since it is you and not Coach Reed, perhaps we can put the time to some good use, as you seem to have given up on *Jane Eyre*."

"Have you ever seen the pelican in the principal's office?" I said.

"Are you trying to illustrate a principle of randomness, Doug Swieteck?"

"No. Really. Have you seen it?"

"I have."

"Don't you think it belongs back in the book it came from?"

Mr. Ferris rocked Clarence thoughtfully. "I understand it was a gift to him from the Town Council when he was appointed."

"So you *do* think it belongs back in the book it came from."

Mr. Ferris smiled. "In general, I adhere to the notion that things belong in the class to which they have been assigned—which leads us to the periodic table. No, no more about the pelican." He walked over to the glossy chart hanging beside the chalkboard on the front wall. "The periodic table arranges elements according to their physical properties and to what else?"

"Their atomic number."

"Good. The table gives us the name of the element —here, hydrogen—the atomic number—here, one— and the symbol—here, H. I know that you know the symbol for hydrogen already, so let's see if you can learn six more. Look at the symbols for the inert gases: helium, neon, argon, krypton, xenon, and radon."

I looked at the chart. He might as well have been speaking Ancient Egyptian.

"All right," he said, and he walked to the other side of the board. "Look at me, and tell me that symbol of the first inert gas, helium."

I shook my head.

He looked at me. "Glance back at the chart, find neon, and tell me what the symbol is."

I looked back at the chart. I shook my head again.

Mr. Ferris looked at me for a long time, then he walked back over to the chart and pointed.

"Ne," I said.

"Good. Try xenon," he said. "It has an atomic number of fifty-four."

"Xe," I said.

"Good. Now look over here at the transitional elements." He pointed to element 29. "This is copper," he said. The symbol is . . ."

"Cu."

"Good." He moved his finger down one element. "The symbol for this one is . . ."

"Ag," I said.

"Good." He moved his finger down again. "And this one?"

"Au," I said.

He moved his finger over one. "And this one?"

"Hg."

"Good," he said. "Doug, of Ag, Au, and Hg, which one is the symbol for silver?"

I didn't even have a guess.

"Ag," he said.

And that was how Mr. Ferris figured out what no teacher had figured out before.

Terrific.

* * *

I think Mr. Ferris told Miss Cowper, because in English on Wednesday, we all opened up *Jane Eyre* and Miss Cowper read her five minutes and then she called on Glenn Thomas, who was probably surprised but he didn't say anything and got right to it.

And Miss Cowper—and you may think I'm lying here, but I'm not—Miss Cowper didn't look at me until the end of class, just before the bell was about to ring and Jane Eyre was about to leave Lowood Institution.

"Douglas," she said.

I looked at her. I had been waiting for something to happen, and I figured that this was it.

"Douglas, do you think that Jane Eyre should feel guilty for not being able to save Helen Burns from dying?"

"It wasn't her fault."

"That's right," she said. "It wasn't her fault at all." She looked at the whole class. "There are some things in this world that we cannot fix, and they happen, and it is not our fault, though we still might have to deal with them. There are other things that happen in this world that we can fix. And that is what good teachers like me are for."

A general groaning from everyone in the class. But not from me. Miss Cowper and I, we looked each other in the eye. *Maybe,* I thought, *maybe everything is not ruined forever.*

* * *

That day I was supposed to have my last After School Detention with Mr. Ferris again, but when I came in, he told me to report to Miss Cowper's room.

"How come?" I said.

"Because I am a mean old crank who is likely to beat you if you don't," he said.

"I think I better go to Miss Cowper's room," I said.

"I think you better," he said, and started Clarence rocking.

Miss Cowper was waiting for me when I got there. "Just the person I need," she said. She held up a batch of dittos. Their blue, alcohol smell fluttered around them. "I've been developing a County Literacy Unit, and I need a student to practice on. Would you be willing?"

"What do I have to do?"

"You play the part of the student who is learning how to read."

Are you a little suspicious here?

"The student who is learning how to read?" I said.

She nodded.

"Miss Cowper, if this is because you think—"

"Show me what you've been working on with Mr. Ferris."

I set my books down on my desk. I went up to the chalkboard. I wrote

Ag

"This is the symbol for silver," I said.

She came up to the board and took the chalk from my hand. She wrote

Silver

"So is this," she said. "Let's get started."

I bet Clarence was rocking.

I bet Clarence was rocking every day for the rest of the week, and every day for the next week, when I stayed after school with Miss Cowper—and not for After School Detention, just remember, but so we could work together on her County Literacy Unit and I could play the part of the chump student who didn't even know how to read. So she took me through the letters and the sounds they made by themselves and the sounds they made when they were working with one another. And then we opened up *Jane Eyre* and picked out words that pretty much looked impossible but we figured them out because of what we were learning about letters and their sounds working together.

No one ever told me this stuff! How come no one ever told me this stuff?

How come?

And by the way, in case you want to know, Au is the symbol for gold, which has a hard *g* and one vowel that's a long *o*, and Hg is the symbol for mercury, which has two vowels—*e* and *u*, even though *y* is sometimes a vowel in words like *my, fry, try, cry,* because every word has to have one vowel at least (Did you know that?) and the *c* is hard, not like in *pace* or *cent,* where the *c* is soft, but like in *cure* and *cur* and *care.*

How come no one ever told me this stuff?

On Saturday mornings during deliveries, I'd practice picking out new words in *Jane Eyre,* sounding out the ones that needed sounding out—and I'm not lying, there were plenty. "'A new servitude! There is something in that,' I soliloquized." I mean, who talks like that? Do you know how long it takes to sound out a word like *soliloquized?* And even after you do, you have no idea what the stupid word means except that it probably just means "said," which is what stupid Charlotte Brontë should have *said* in the first place.

When I delivered Mrs. Mason's groceries, she saw that I had *Jane Eyre* stuck under my arm. "Oh," she said, "that was my favorite novel in school."

"It was?" I soliloquized.

"Yes," she said. "Have you gotten to the part where Bertha bites her brother and almost kills him?"

"Mrs. Mason," I said, "I haven't gotten to anything half as good as that."

"Keep with it. You will." That morning she gave me three powdered sugar doughnuts.

When Mr. Loeffler saw *Jane Eyre,* he said, "You poor kid."

"Did you have to read this in school, Mr. Loeffler?"

He nodded. "Fortunately," he said, "I got appendicitis in the middle of it and almost died. Best thing that ever happened to me. I couldn't go back to school for three weeks. How are you feeling?"

"It's a new servitude," I said.

"If I were you, I'd start thinking about pains in my gut."

When Mrs. Daugherty saw *Jane Eyre,* she said, "Do you like to read?"

"It's complicated," I said.

She thought for a minute or so, pushing back her kids like they were a tide about to flow out the door.

"I'm looking for a babysitter for some Saturday nights," she finally said. "But you'd have to like reading since not a single one of these kiddos goes to sleep without a book."

I looked at how many kiddos there were. I figured she must have had trouble finding a babysitter if she was asking me, the brother of the twisted criminal mind. I looked at the five kids. Three of them had something red dripping all over their hands. I was afraid to ask what it was.

Mrs. Daugherty was probably desperate.

"It pays very well," she said.

She was definitely desperate.

Now, this is the part where I should tell you

something. You know how I'm making five dollars plus tips every Saturday? And we both know that's good money, right? You might remember that my father knows that I'm making five dollars every Saturday morning. And he thinks that's good money too. So he takes it, since I'm supposed to be helping out with the household expenses. "It's about time," he says.

So I'm living on the tips that I don't tell my father about—which is what you would do too. Don't lie.

"It's a deal," I said to Mrs. Daugherty.

"Seven o'clock?"

"Yup."

"I'll have the books waiting for you."

Terrific.

Up at Mrs. Windermere's house, everything was quiet. No typing. No dinging. She came into the kitchen when she heard me putting things away. "What kind of ice cream did I order?"

"Mint chocolate chip."

"That's a good kind of ice cream to eat when the god has fled," she said.

I guess that means no one was folding his wings beside her desk.

"What is that book in your back pocket?" she said.

"Jane Eyre."

"Ah," she said, as if she had made a great discovery or something. "Come with me."

I put the mint chocolate chip ice cream into the freezer and followed Mrs. Windermere to her study. She ranged over a bunch of shelves, and then pulled out three smallish, darkish books. She handed them to me. "That," she said, "is a first edition of *Jane Eyre*."

I looked at her. I guess she thought this was pretty all-fired important.

"A first edition," she said again. "All three volumes."

"Wow," I said.

She sighed. "Skinny Delivery Boy, do you have any idea how hard it is to collect a first edition like that?"

I looked over all the books on the shelves in her study. "It looks like you're doing pretty well."

"But this is *Jane Eyre*. One of the world's great stories. Love. Betrayal. Jealousy. The search for the true and complete self. It's worthy of a play!"

She stopped, and stared at me. This smile slowly comes across her face and starts to fill it.

"And there's the god," she whispered, and she rushed to her typewriter. She rolled a page into it and her hands started flying. You already know how.

I put the first edition of *Jane Eyre* back on the shelf, and slid all three books in carefully because I guess it was all-fired important.

I sounded out words from *Jane Eyre* — the paperback edition, not the first edition — all the way back into town. And I stopped at Spicer's Deli for the really cold Coke that Mr. Spicer always gave me. I would have bought a pastrami sandwich if Mrs. Windermere had given me a tip, but I wasn't getting a tip anymore because the bill was going on her tab, which you might remember, and the other tips weren't enough to cover a pastrami sandwich and leave me much for the rest of the week.

And I don't want to complain or anything, but a tip would have been nice, since it was me, after all, who brought the god back to her.

That afternoon when I got to the Marysville Free Public Library, Mr. Powell and Lil Spicer were waiting for me. Mr. Powell was trying to get ahead on his cataloging so that Mrs. Merriam wouldn't fuss at him, and Lil was speeding ahead on *Jane Eyre*. (She was almost done. Terrific.) We went upstairs together to work on the Black-Backed Gull—or Mr. Powell and I did. Lil helped by letting me know what I was doing wrong.

"Isn't there too much blood there?" she said when I spread my drawing out.

"It gives the drawing drama."

"His wing is slanted off to the side."

"Point of view," I said.

"And I think his neck is too far back."

"It's called composition."

And on like that until Mr. Powell told us both to hush because he wanted to talk about Audubon's use of the white space around the wing and the contrast in spatial perception that the two wings gave and artist stuff like that.

Lil hushed for a while, but she started again before too long.

And do you think I minded?

Do you think I minded when she leaned in right next to me to point something out?

Do you think I minded that she smelled like daisies would smell if they were growing in a big field under a sky clearing after a rain?

Do you think I minded when she touched my hand?

You remember how I told you that when things are going pretty good, it usually means that something bad is about to happen? This is true. Just ask the Black-Backed Gull.

About halfway through October, as I was thinking that I'd have to start wearing Joe Pepitone's jacket to school because there wasn't anything else I could wear with sleeves that even pretended to reach my wrists, someone broke into the Tools 'n' More Hardware Store. It happened on a Sunday afternoon. The register got forced open and all the cash taken. There was a bunch of tools gone: a chain saw, a drill set, a wrench set. And a bike too, which made the brilliant policemen of stupid Marysville come to the conclusion that it must have been a kid who broke in.

So guess whose house they came to on Sunday night? And they didn't want any of the thawed hamburgers or German potato salad my mother offered.

Mr. Daugherty was one of the policemen.

"Is your son home?" he asked.

"He's off with his friends," my mother said.

"Is your son ever home?" the other policeman asked. I think he was a little upset.

"What's he doing with his friends?" said Mr. Daugherty.

"Just playing," she said. She said it kind of hopefully.

Mr. Daugherty looked at me. "Do you know where he's playing?" he said. "We have a few questions. We want to be certain he's all right."

Sure. That's what they wanted.

I shrugged.

"Thanks," said the other policeman. "You've been real helpful. We'll go look for him ourselves."

They did—and it probably didn't help my brother that when he saw them, he took off on his Sting-Ray and made them chase him about ten miles and he made them crash one—no, two cop cars, and finally they had to call the state police, who ran him down when one of his tires popped because he had taken a sharp turn on one wheel, which was something only a few people knew how to do and he was one of them. He told us all this after Mr. Daugherty brought him home and sat with us while the other policeman searched through our garage and basement and afterward asked my brother about fifteen different ways if he had ever been inside the Tools 'n' More Hardware Store.

I could tell the other policeman didn't believe him all fifteen times.

It was harder to tell with Mr. Daugherty, except he said that maybe we should hold off on the Saturday-night baby-sitting until things got cleared up.

Terrific.

After they left, my mother asked my brother the same question.

"You already heard me tell them."

"Tell me," she said.

"I didn't steal anything."

"Did you take anything from Mr. Spicer's deli?"

"No. Just because Lucas—"

"What Lucas did is over and done. I'm worrying about what you're doing."

"You don't have to worry about anything," my brother said.

"I am worried."

"You don't believe me?"

My mother went into the kitchen.

My brother watched her leave. He just stood there, watching her back as she worked at dishes in the sink.

He stood there a long time. Then he said something she didn't hear, dared me to say anything — just one little thing — and went upstairs.

I did my homework at the wobbly kitchen table. Mostly Mrs. Verne's stuff. And copying a map of the Mississippi River from *Geography: The Story of the World* — which I want you to know was still as clean and perfect as the day Mr. McGraw-Hill sewed the cover on. I also drew costumes of the samurai tradition of Japan, where we'd gone with Mr. McElroy after we left China. And of course, I did a few pages of *Jane Eyre,* who was settling in at Mr. Rochester's house even though he hadn't shown up yet. At least, I think he hadn't shown up.

I took my time.

When I finally did go upstairs, all the lights were off and my brother was in bed. The covers were drawn up over his head.

You know, when someone has been crying, something gets left in the air. It's not something you can see, or smell, or feel. Or draw. But it's there. It's like the screech of the Black-Backed Gull, crying out into the empty white space around him. You can't hear it when you look at the picture. But that doesn't mean it isn't there.

The trees were reddening and yellowing. You could see the color moving like a slow tide down the hills that rose on both sides of stupid Marysville. One day it was only the trees toward the top ridges, and then the next the color was coming down, first where the trees stood mostly by themselves, and then in bigger patches of red and yellow, until the green was holding out only in the cut-ins on the hills. And then when the tops started to thin out and you could see the bare rock beneath them, the red and yellow reached the bottoms of the hills, and then the trees around town colored quickly, like they didn't want to miss the parade.

Except the trees around The Dump. Their leaves turned brown and dropped.

Terrific.

My mother and I raked them across the front dirt and burned them in the street. Do you know what that smells like?

"It's the smell of fall," said my mother. "Lucas used to love to play in the leaves before we burned them. He'd rake them up, and jump in and scatter them all, and rake them all up again, and jump in again, until he was covered in bits and pieces of leaves. Then he'd come get me, and we'd burn the piles, and he'd stand there all serious and still, like he was watching something far away."

She shifted some of the leaves closer to the low flames.

"He'll be back soon," I said.

"I know he will."

I looked at her face.

She was watching something far away too.

"I hope there isn't any more trouble," she said.

And so you know, that's what I was thinking about in PE these days. I didn't want there to be any more trouble, mostly because my mother already had enough. So I was really trying not to get sent to visit Principal Peattie again, even though it would almost have been worth it to see the Brown Pelican. But I was really trying. No funny business. No sirree, buster.

And things were going okay, even though Coach Reed and I didn't talk much. We were finishing up the Apparatus Unit, which meant messing around on leather horses and parallel bars and ropes and the high bar, which people who are skinny and wiry like yours truly can do without breaking a sweat. Not that Coach Reed would ever say anything to me about that in a million million years. I could have thrown a triple-somersault full-layout dismount, and he wouldn't have said a thing. Pretty much he walked around the gym and hollered at Otis Bottom or someone else and he wouldn't talk with me and I wouldn't talk with him and then he'd tell us to line up in platoons and he wouldn't look at me.

Which was fine. No trouble.

Until the day he announced that he didn't feel like spotting us for another hour, so we should line up and he'd count off two teams and we'd play basketball, and he divided us into Shirts and Skins, and I got on the

Skins team and Coach Reed went into his office and I walked over to the Shirts team and asked James Russell if he'd trade and he said "Sure" and so we did and Coach Reed must have been watching because he came back out of his office, yes sirree, buster, and he was not a happy coach.

He wondered what I thought I was doing. Sergeant's voice.

I pointed out—and I think I pointed this out politely—that I thought I was about to play basketball.

He told me—and I don't think he did this politely at all—that I should shut my mouth and get over to the Skins team.

Is this starting to sound familiar?

Then James Russell said that he had switched with me.

Coach Reed told James Russell that he wasn't talking to him and he should mind his own business and then he looked back at me and wondered if we hadn't already been through all of this before and hadn't I learned anything at all?

I could have said that I'd learned a whole lot. The periodic table and *Jane Eyre* and even the location of the Brown Pelican. But I didn't say anything, which is important for you to know so that you don't blame me for what happened.

Coach Reed guessed that I hadn't learned anything at all, but he was going to give me a chance now. He told James Russell to put his shirt back on and get over to the Shirts team, and when James said he was fine on the Skins team, Coach Reed gave him the kind of look that said he was going to gut him if he spoke one more word.

James put his shirt on and went over to the Shirts team. "Sorry," he whispered when he walked by me.

"Shut your face," Coach Reed said to him.

Then Coach Reed—who is the kind of person that Joe Pepitone would probably want to pound into the dirt with his baseball bat—looked at me again.

"Get over to the Skins team," he said. Growled, really.

I shrugged. What was I supposed to do? I walked over to the Skins team.

You can see I was really trying.

"With your shirt off, Swieteck. You have to have your shirt off if you're on the Skins team."

I looked around at the two teams. "I think we're all smart enough to remember who's on our team," I said. "It's not like we're gym teachers or something."

Okay. So, there I wasn't really trying. I guess that was sounding like Lucas.

Coach Reed said, "Over there now," in a kind of double sergeant's voice. Each word slow. And apart. And long. Carrying a whole lot of atomic weight.

"So are you going to shoot me if I don't?" I said.

I think Coach Reed crossed the floor almost without touching it, and the words "Who do you think you're talking to" filled the gym.

He reached for my shoulder, but when he reached, I pulled back, and all he got was my PE uniform shirt.

Maybe that was what he wanted anyway.

And I don't know if it was him reaching or me pulling back, but whatever it was, the whole stupid gym shirt got torn right down, the whole way.

Everything in the gym stopped—again. But this time, it wasn't because I was mouthing off to Coach Reed. It was because of what they saw.

And what they saw—it's not any of your stupid business.

It got around the whole stupid school in probably a minute and a half. When I walked down the hall after PE, it was like I was in a circle of silence. Ahead of me, people would be talking and laughing their heads off, and then they'd see me and stop talking. They'd hold their mouths shut like the funniest thing in the whole stupid world had just happened and they wanted to bust out talking about it but they couldn't until I walked by. So they'd watch until I got past them, and then wait a couple of seconds, and then I'd hear them start up again, laughing their heads off, and talking, but low enough so I couldn't hear exactly.

You know what this feels like?

When I got to Mr. Ferris's class, I walked in the door to this: Otis Bottom was standing over a group of guys—and he's tall, so he can look pretty threatening—and he was saying, "Shut up, just shut up," and Mr. Ferris was going over to calm things down, I guess, when everyone saw me come in and everything went that eerie quiet.

Mr. Ferris looked at me for a second and then said, "Let's all sit down and get started," except that I turned around and walked out. He came to the door and called after me, and I started running.

So did he.

We reached the front doors of Washington Irving Junior High School at the same time.

He grabbed the bar handle so I couldn't open it.

He grabbed the bar handle of the next door so I couldn't open it.

And the next.

I reared back and hit him in the stomach as hard as I could. I know: After School Detention for Life. Didn't care.

He grabbed my arm. (So I was crying by now. So what? So what?) He walked me across the school lobby. Slammed through the auditorium doors. Shouted to the Washington Irving Junior High School Brass Quintet that they'd have to go practice somewhere else—Now!—which they did, in a hurry. He pushed me down into one of the auditorium chairs. Sat next to me. He said, "Tell me."

I tried to get up and he pushed me back down.

"Tell me," he said again.

So I did.

How my father came home late on the night of my twelfth birthday, and how he'd missed everything because he'd been with Ernie Eco. How he sounded when my mother told him that. How he came up into my room with beer on his breath and told me we were going someplace for my birthday present and I should get dressed right now. How I said he didn't have to and he smacked me and said he'd better not have to tell me again. How he'd taken me past my mother, who wasn't smiling. How we got into the beery car and he gunned it and said hadn't I always said I wished I could have a tattoo like Lucas did? Hadn't I? I nodded because I was afraid not to. How we arrived at the mostly dark place and got out of the car and I said I wanted to go home but he looked at me with beer in his eyes and said I better get in there so I did. How I lay down on this couch and my father talked with this guy and they laughed and my father covered my eyes with his beery hands because this was a present and he was picking out a real surprise and this fat sweaty guy bent over me and I could smell and feel him close when he pulled up my shirt. How it started and I said it hurt and my father pushed me down with his hand over my eyes and said I'd better be still if I knew what was good for me and so I did even though I was crying then too. How when it was done after a long time I looked into the mirror and saw the scroll and the flowers at each end and the words I couldn't read so the fat sweaty guy read them for me: *Mama's Baby*. And I told Mr. Ferris how they both laughed and laughed and laughed and laughed and laughed. The funniest thing in the whole stupid world. *Mama's Baby*.

How I spent days trying to wash it off, and then trying to scratch it off until it bled.

How I hadn't gone swimming since then.

How I changed for PE in the locker room stalls.

How I wished he would ...

Mr. Ferris didn't say anything the whole time. He sat next to me and listened. And when I finished, I looked at him.

He was crying. I'm not lying. He was crying.

I don't think it was because of how hard I hit him.

I know how the Black-Backed Gull feels when he looks up into the sky.

Maybe, somehow, Mr. Ferris does too.

CHAPTER FIVE

The Yellow Shank
Plate CCLXXXVIII

HERE ARE the stats from the last two weeks of October:

> *Three fights in the downstairs hall. No wins. One loss.*
>   *Two ties. Mr. Ferris stopped them.*
> *One fight in Mr. McElroy's class with barbarian hordes.*
>   *A tie. Mr. McElroy stopped it.*
> *Two fights in the upstairs hall. No wins. One loss. One*
>   *tie. Mr. Ferris stopped it.*
> *Two fights in the PE locker room. Two ties. Otis Bottom*
>   *stopped them both, since the So-Called Gym Teacher*
>   *was nowhere around.*

One fight while running the cross-country course in PE.
One loss.

One fight in the boys' bathroom. A tie. James Russell
stopped it.

Two fights between school and The Dump. No wins. Two
losses. But they were close.

Twelve near-fights. Probable record: Eight wins. Four
losses. You don't believe me? So what? So what?

Five days of After School Detention.

Two threats of school suspension, because I was the
instigator of the PE locker room fights, according to
the So-Called Gym Teacher. Liar.

Things were not going so well at Washington Irving Junior High School. Mr. Barber told me I needed to put a new brown-paper book cover on *Geography: The Story of the World,* which I hadn't bothered doing since I was leaving it in my locker instead of bringing it to class and I think Mr. Barber was starting to suspect that I'd taken his new book and destroyed it. I hadn't turned in my Chapter Review Map on the culture of China to Mr. McElroy, and no, I didn't know if I was going to get it done or not. Jane Eyre still hadn't figured out that she was in love with Mr. Rochester, and I mean, how many more clues do you need? I didn't raise my hand anymore in Mrs. Verne's class, and after the first time I didn't bother answering even when she called on me, she stopped calling on me. I spent PE running the cross-country course while the rest of the class started in on the Wrestling Unit. No one said anything when I went out, not even the So-Called Gym Teacher. And I didn't do anything on the next two lab experiments in Mr. Ferris's class. Lil did them both. Even the smelly chemically stuff. And so what that *Apollo* 7 successfully detached from the Saturn rocket to practice the rendezvous they would have to perform perfectly for a moon shot? So what that they landed a mere third of a mile from the landing site? So what? Clarence is a stupid toy horse. Who cares if he's rocking like anything?

Because no matter where I went in stupid Washington Irving Junior High School, there was the look. And the laugh. And the smirk. Jerks.

And no matter where I went in stupid Marysville, there was the look. And the laugh. And the smirk. Jerks.

Do you know what that feels like?

I stopped helping Miss Cowper with her County Literacy Unit. Who were we kidding?

I did do the Saturday deliveries. Guess who wanted the money and wouldn't let me stop?

I didn't meet Mr. Powell at the library afterward either. I don't know if Lil was waiting there or not.

I didn't draw anymore.

I didn't even want to.

It was like the Black-Backed Gull had laid its head down and given up the sky.

So you can see why, on the day of the Annual Ballard Paper Mill Harvest-Time Employee Picnic, I wasn't overcome with happiness and joy.

Neither was my father.

It was pretty clear that Mr. Big Bucks Ballard was an idiot, he said, and that my father or Ernie Eco could run the paper mill blindfolded and do it better, a hundred times better, than he could, he said. All Mr. Big Bucks Ballard did was sit around his big office wearing his nice white shirt and silk tie and telling everyone else what to do, he said. But he never got *his* freaking hands dirty, no he didn't. You never saw *him* at a forklift. You never saw *him* backing a truck into the loading dock. Wood pulp? Big Bucks Ballard wouldn't recognize it if he tripped and fell into it over his freaking head, he said. That's what happens when you get rich. You leave all the real work to the little guy, and you sit back and enjoy all the profits, he said. And it was going to take a whole lot more than a Harvest-Time Employee Picnic to change things to the way they ought to be.

When my father was home—and it wasn't often, since Ernie Eco came over most nights and they drove off together—but when he was home, that's pretty much what he told us.

So no one wanted to go. Not to a picnic thrown by a jerk like Mr. Big Bucks Ballard. But on the last Saturday in October, my father made all of us get in the car and drive to the Annual Ballard Paper Mill Harvest-Time Employee Picnic — even my brother. You can imagine how happy we were. Especially when my father said that Mr. Big Bucks Ballard was the skinflint of skin-flints, and there probably wouldn't be much to eat. And what there was wasn't going to be all that good. You don't expect a jerk and a skinflint to be grateful to his employees, do you?

The only reason we were going, he said, was the Trivia Contest. And this Trivia Contest, according to Ernie Eco, was all about Babe Ruth. And who knew more about Babe Ruth than my father? No one, and I'm not lying. Do you know how many World Series home runs Babe Ruth hit? No, you don't. But my father did. Fifteen. You probably know that in 1927, Babe Ruth hit his famous sixty home runs in a single season. But do you know when he hit fifty-nine home runs? Probably you don't. But my father did: 1921. Do you know how many home runs Babe Ruth hit in the final game of 1928? Three. In one game.

My father could tell you that and a whole lot more, because he had once met Babe Ruth. He shook Babe Ruth's hand and bought him a beer, and Babe Ruth had winked at him and said, "You're a helluva good guy."

My father loved Babe Ruth.

And Ernie Eco said that the prize for the Trivia Contest was going to be a baseball signed by a Yankee. It was probably, Ernie Eco said, a baseball signed by the Babe.

So we all went to the Annual Ballard Paper Mill Harvest-Time Employee Picnic, because my father wanted to win a baseball signed by Babe Ruth.

Terrific.

I had to run through the Saturday-morning deliveries pretty quickly, which wasn't hard, as you might remember, since not everyone knows the basic principle of physical science. Mrs. Mason hadn't ordered any doughnuts. Mr. Loeffler didn't have a single light bulb to change. Mrs. Daugherty's kids were playing upstairs when I came. And Mrs. Windermere never came into the kitchen.

I really wished that at least the Daugherty kids had been . . .

So what? So what? I'm not a chump.

I made it back as quickly as any human being could, which wasn't good enough for guess who.

It was a Saturday that you somehow knew was going to be one of the last beautiful days of fall. The sun was shining hot, like it thought it was still July, and November drizzles were a whole season away. The sky was blue, and a few white clouds were easing themselves along like they didn't care. The grass was warm and sweet, like April, but the trees hadn't forgotten it was October. They were all on fire, and behind their leaves, the birds were singing their last songs. Waves of heat shimmered above the stone walls, and the granite sparkled.

"Such a beautiful day," said my mother.

My father didn't say anything. He was probably thinking about Babe Ruth.

The Annual Ballard Paper Mill Harvest-Time Employee Picnic was always held at Mary's Lake, and since we got there late, we had to park about a mile away—all because, my father said, I hadn't finished the deliveries on time, not that it mattered, since Douggo couldn't hurry up if there were an atomic bomb on his butt. But even from a mile away, you could smell the chicken grilling as soon as you got out of the car. And you could hear hollering and cheering. People called and waved at each other as we walked toward the lake, and then they waved at us, and two women came to meet my mother and took her by the arms and brought her over to introduce her to someone else she had to meet because they didn't live very far from each other at all, and hadn't they seen her this fall at St. Ignatius?

My father and brother and I passed by some long tables and someone called out to us and my father grunted back and then the someone looked through a bunch of wrapped packages and picked two up and called to me and my brother and handed them to us.

Inside was a Timex watch. I'm not lying. A Timex watch with a second hand and a real leather band and numbers for regular time and numbers for military time. A Timex watch. Compliments of the Ballard Paper Mill.

My brother looked at me. I looked at him.

Sometimes—and I know it doesn't last for anything more than a second—sometimes there can be perfect understanding between two people who can't stand each other. He smiled, and I smiled, and we put the Timex watches on, and we watched the seconds flit by.

It was the first watch my brother had ever owned.

It was the first watch I had ever owned.

My father looked at our wrists. "The metal will turn your skin green," he said. "Wait and see."

I did not know that so many people worked at the Ballard Paper Mill. It looked like all of Marysville was there. There was a group playing volleyball, and no one was even pretending to keep score.

There was a baseball game going on, husbands against wives. I guess you can imagine how funny that was. My father went over to stand with Ernie Eco, to laugh and smirk.

There were about ten guys throwing horseshoes,

and the clangs and the cheers that came from them made it seem like it was all-fired important — like it probably was to a bunch of chumps.

I went down to the lake, and it was so hot that there was a whole bunch of kids swimming (which I decided not to do because of you know why) and about eight teams were doing chicken fights and some were diving off each other's shoulders, and James Russell was there and he waved at me to come in but I shook my head and he nodded.

And drifting over everything was the smell of grilling chicken, and the snap of buttery fat when it fell in the fire, and the smoke that drew up over the baseball game and the volleyball and the horseshoes and drifted over to the rows of long tables with bright white cloths over them, where the women — including my mother — were setting out the bowls of salad and plates of rolls and pitchers of pink lemonade and platters of corn on the cob that were steaming and more bowls of salad until people started to crowd away from the baseball game and then one of the cooks by the grills hollered out, "We're all set here!" and everyone came and found a place in line while the cooks carried the long trays heaped with chicken, and the smell in the hot blue air was so wonderful and I looked over at my mother and she was smiling to beat the band, like she had come home after a long time away.

It turned out that my brother was the first one in line. There's a shock.

But it didn't matter, because even if the whole town of Marysville had been there, they couldn't have eaten everything that was loading down those tables. It was like something out of a fairy tale. When a platter was empty, it got lifted away, and another one, even fuller than the first, magically appeared in its place. And there was more chicken cooking, and more vats of hot water with steaming corn, and then onto the line came all the kids from the lake, who were dripping wet, and they were all hollering that it didn't matter if they ate like slobs because they were just going back into the water anyway, and then everyone finishing the salad and chicken and corn and trying to sit back and rub their stomachs and then big aluminum carts being wheeled across the lawn and every kid in the place running to them and reaching in for lime Popsicles and strawberry shortcake and ice cream sandwiches and James Russell grabbing me and yelling "C'mon!" and I was running over too and reaching in for an orange Dreamsicle.

An orange Dreamsicle. You know how good an orange Dreamsicle tastes on a blue fall day when you're full of grilled chicken and your mother is laughing a real laugh like she used to and once you look over and your father is holding her hand like they haven't in a long long long time?

Until Ernie Eco came and she walked away.

Then all the mothers cleared the tables and swept

off the long white tablecloths and, all laughing, folded them together and boxed up the extra food, and there was a lot. The kids ran down to the water again and James Russell yelled, "C'mon!" but I shook my head again. So he ran down to the lake and I tried not to hate him when he took a flying dive and skimmed into the water, came up laughing, and some little kid was climbing on top of him for more chicken fights.

Then most of the adults started to gather around the cleared tables and I went over to the deserted horseshoe pits to see what was so all-fired important about throwing horseshoes. Someone yelled that the Trivia Contest was going to start soon and everyone should choose a partner to work with. I looked back. My father was standing with Ernie Eco. They were whispering together. They'd probably win.

I picked up a horseshoe and threw it. It came up short. By a lot.

I tried another. It came up short again. By a lot.

I heaved another. Long. By a lot.

Terrific.

I threw the last one. It hit short again, but rolled until it flopped in the sand near the post. Not bad.

Which is what an old guy said when I went to gather up the horseshoes. "Not bad. But I think if you hold it on the bend, you might get a little more distance."

I picked up the four horseshoes. "You want to show me?"

He took a shoe and held it with the ends out. "Like this," he said. He walked over to the post. "You stand with your heel here, and swing it back." He did this a couple of times. "Then you release it on the upswing." Which he did. It wasn't a ringer, but it clanged the post. "Everything after that is just practice," he said.

So I tried it. I stood with my heel like that, and swung my arm a couple of times like that. I looked at him. He nodded. So I let one fly like that.

"I think," he said, "you might want a little more arc to the throw. That way they won't run away after they hit the ground."

I let another one fly. Short. Too much arc.

"Not bad," he said.

I handed him the last shoe. I'm not a chump.

He took the shoe into his hand like he had done it a million and a half times. He set his heel. He swung his arm.

The horseshoe left his arm and carried up into the blue air. It turned once, slowly, like it was taking its time. As it fell down toward the post, it threw out its two ends like a diver and dropped onto the sand without even bouncing, without even touching the post, but circling it so perfectly that it was like someone had walked up there and set it down that way on purpose.

I looked at him.

"I told you, it's all practice from here," he said. "But

what I could use some help on is the Trivia Contest. I've been working at it for twenty-five years and never even come close to a ringer."

He held out his hand.

We shook.

"Partners," he said, and we went over to the cleared tables.

Back there, a few kids were eating the last of the ice cream sandwiches, while a bunch of the men had lit cigars, and their long smoke whispered up into the golden trees. Piles of yellow pads and pencils were on the tables, and partners were taking them and writing their names on top. Some of the partners were pretty serious about it all, and they sat there numbering their pads. (This was my father and Ernie Eco.) Most were leaning back and laughing, probably because they didn't know two cents about the Babe, and they figured they weren't going to win anyway.

They were right.

Then some guy wearing a tie—a tie! at a picnic!—this guy stood up on a chair and held a black notebook over his head and everyone cheered. I figured the guy with the tie must be Mr. Big Bucks Ballard, the jerk who didn't know how to run the paper mill as well as my father and Ernie Eco could blindfolded. "The Trivia Contest Questions!" he hollered, and everyone cheered and clapped again. "Ten questions," he said, "and a tiebreaker if we need one. The team with the most correct answers is the winning team. The prize this year: a baseball signed by..."

Okay, you're going to think that I made this next part up, but I didn't. Sometimes, you just have to trust me. This is what the guy with the tie said:

"...a baseball signed by Roger Maris, Mickey Mantle, and Joe Pepitone!"

Cheers from all around, except from my father and Ernie Eco.

"Plus, this year, a fifty-dollar bonus for each partner."

You can bet there were cheers at this.

"Plus, assigned parking spots right by the mill entrance for one whole year."

I guess this sounded good to a whole lot of people, since there were a whole lot of cheers with this too.

"So let's get started."

A baseball signed by Roger Maris, Mickey Mantle, and Joe Pepitone! Who, if you remember, were the three Yankees to hit home runs in Game Six of the 1964 World Series against the St. Louis Cardinals.

Who cares if Mr. Big Bucks Ballard is an idiot!

I looked at my partner.

"Do you think we have a chance?" he asked.

"You bet," I said.

"Question Number One," said Mr. Big Bucks Ballard. He was still standing on the chair. "How long was Joe DiMaggio's hitting streak in 1941?"

My partner looked at me. "Do you know?" he said.

I took the pencil and wrote down *56*. If he didn't even know that one, I thought, he wasn't going to be much help.

"Are you all ready? C'mon, folks, either you know it or you don't. I wouldn't bother guessing if you don't. Next question: How many consecutive scoreless innings in World Series play has Whitey Ford pitched?"

Groans and laughter all around us. "Are you kidding?" someone hollered.

I handed the pencil back to my partner. "Thirty-three and two-thirds," I whispered. He wrote it down.

"Next question. In 1960, the Yankees hit more home runs than any other team in baseball history. How many did they hit?"

More groans. More laughter. I whispered, "One hundred and ninety-three." My partner wrote it down.

"Okay, ready for an easy one?"

Cheers.

"What two years did Roger Maris win back-to-back MVP awards?"

"Even I know that one," said my partner. He wrote down *1960* and *1961*.

"All right, let's see how you are with batting averages. What is Joe DiMaggio's lifetime batting average?"

"Three twenty-five," I whispered.

"What was Mickey Mantle's best batting average for any year of his career?"

"Three sixty-five," I whispered.

"What was the team average for the Yankees in the 1960 World Series?"

Groans.

"Three thirty-eight," I whispered.

"Calm down, calm down," said Mr. Big Bucks Ballard, pulling at his tie. He must have been getting hot. "There have to be some hard ones to separate the men from the boys—apologies to Mrs. Stenson there." Laughter. "Okay, try this one: How many American League pennants did the Yankees win under Casey Stengel?"

My partner looked at me. "Ten?" he said.

I nodded. He wrote it down.

"Question Number Nine: We all know that in 1961, Roger Maris broke the Babe's home-run record with sixty-one home runs. How many did Mickey Mantle have in that same year?"

"Fifty-four," I whispered. My partner wrote it down.

"The last question: Which five years in a row did the Yankees win the world championship?"

"That, I can remember," said my partner, and he wrote down *1949, 1950, 1951, 1952,* and *1953.* "I was at the last game for every one of those," he said.

"Every single one?" I said.

He nodded. "There's no pleasure in getting to be an old coot unless you have some fun along the way."

Do I need to tell you that when Mr. Big Bucks Ballard read out the answers, we had every one right? Do I need to tell you that my father and Ernie Eco did not? Do I need to tell you what my father thought about that? Or what my father thought about a Trivia Contest on the New York Yankees that didn't have a single question about the Babe?

But it wasn't over yet. When Mr. Big Bucks Ballard asked if anyone had gotten all ten right, three teams raised their hands.

Terrific.

"Here you were all grumbling and carrying on," said Mr. Big Bucks Ballard, "but I guess it wasn't as hard as everyone thought." He took a sheet of paper from inside the black notebook. "So now we go to the tiebreaker question, and this time, I admit, it's a doozy! Okay, here we go, for just these three teams, to see who gets the baseball, the bonus, and the parking spots. Ready? You all ready? Okay, and no help, folks. Ready? Okay: What is important in baseball about the number two hundred and sixteen?"

It was like all Creation stopped, it was that quiet.

"Could you repeat the question?" called one of the teams.

"What is important in baseball about the number two hundred and sixteen?"

I watched the other teams. You might as well have

asked them to name the atomic numbers of all the inert gases.

My partner looked at me. "I have no idea," he said.

I whispered to him.

"Are you sure?" he said.

I nodded.

"Really?"

"Really."

"How do you know that?"

"I counted once."

He smiled — not like my mother, but it would do.

"Does anyone know?" hollered Mr. Big Bucks Ballard from his chair.

The other two teams shook their heads. My partner kept smiling. He leaned down to me. "Tell them," he said.

So I did.

But if you think I'm so all-fired smart, you won't think so after I tell you what happened next.

There was some scattered clapping, and Mr. Big Bucks Ballard came down off his chair, walked over, and shook our hands. "How did you know that last one, kid?" he asked.

"He counted once," my partner said.

Mr. Big Bucks Ballard worked at his tie some more. He looked really hot. "How are we going to award these prizes?" he said. He looked at me. "You're not driving yet, so you don't exactly need a parking spot. And it's hard to give you a bonus when you're not even working at the mill."

"We'll figure it out," said my partner.

Then Mr. Big Bucks Ballard looked at my partner. "And how about you? You know you're not supposed to win."

"How come?" I said.

He laughed. "Kid, how do you think it would look if the boss won all the prizes?"

"Pretty bad," I said. "But you weren't even playing."

"Not me," he said. He pointed to my partner. "But he was."

I looked at my partner. "Bob Ballard," he said, and held out his hand.

The ride home was pretty quiet except for my father, who pointed out how unfair it was not to have a single question on the Babe, not one, and how the whole contest was a setup anyway, how Mr. Big Bucks Ballard knew the questions all along, because how else could anyone know that last question about *316*?

"*Two* hundred and sixteen," I said.

He glared at me in the rearview mirror. "Don't you get it?" he said. "He set you up more than anyone. He just strung you right along and made it look like you were answering when he knew the answers from the beginning. What a freaking cheapskate. He didn't want to give away the money. He didn't want to give up the parking spots. He probably doesn't even have the stupid baseball. What a con artist. He probably didn't figure that anyone would see right through him. Did he even give you the baseball?"

"He told me to come to his office tomorrow after school."

"You shouldn't count on anything. That's the way it is in this freaking world. You're nothing but a jerk if you do."

I looked over at my brother. He was polishing the glass face of his Timex watch.

Maybe my father was right.

I didn't go to Mr. Big Bucks Ballard's office on Monday.

I didn't want to find out if that's really the way things were in this freaking world.

Here are the stats for the first week of November:

No fights in the downstairs hall, even though I came close.
One fight in the upstairs hall. A loss.
Two fights in the PE locker room. Two wins, after I showed I would kick just about anywhere.
Two fights in the boys' bathroom. Two losses. There

might have been a whole lot more fights in there,
but I stopped going. You're right. It was pretty
uncomfortable.
Four fights on the way home from After School Deten-
tion. Four losses.

After After School Detention on Friday, I decided I didn't want to make it a week with five consecutive losses on the way home, so I gave the jerks who were waiting the slip by going out through the gym entrance—I had to hope the So-Called Gym Teacher wouldn't see me, which he didn't—and across the track and out the back field and around toward The Dump.

It took me right past the Ballard Paper Mill. So I figured, Why not?

When I got to the mill—and I'm not lying, you know when you're getting close to a paper mill, and it's not because of the pretty scenery—when I got to the mill, I walked around to the mill entrance, facing the river. Right by the front door, right next to the stupid front door, in the best parking spot in the whole paper mill, my father's car was parked. Next to it was Ernie Eco's pickup.

He never said a thing. Not one thing.

I went inside, where a woman on the phone smiled and raised her hand to tell me she'd just be a second. It was a swell place, a really swell place. Thick green carpet. Paneled walls. Pictures of the board of directors. Lamps with green shades. Red leather furniture. And by the windows looking out to the water, plants with long stems and these flowers that—well, it's hard to describe. They didn't even look real.

The woman hung up the phone. "They're orchids," she said. "Mr. Ballard grows them. Most of these will be gone in a week or two."

"Gone?"

"When they start to blossom like this, he sends them to his old employees who still live in town. You're Douglas Swieteck, aren't you?"

I nodded.

"I'm Mrs. Stenson. I'm sure he'll see you. Just let me call in."

But she didn't need to, because a door in the paneled walls opened and there was Mr. Ballard himself, silk tie and all. "My partner!" he said. "Mrs. Stenson, have you met my partner?"

She smiled, laughed.

"Come in, come in," he said. And I did. I guess I don't need to tell you about what his office was like, except that it was mostly like the room outside, but one wall had pictures of Mr. Ballard throwing horseshoes with a whole lot of people I didn't know and a couple I did: Mayor John Lindsay and—I'm not lying—President Lyndon B. Johnson, which he saw me looking at. "Never throw horseshoes with a Texan," he said. "They don't like to lose. So, partner, what are you going to do with the hundred dollars?"

He went and sat down at his desk, put his feet up on it, next to a long, long tube.

I looked at the tube.

"If you ask me—and you don't have to, since it's your money—I'd put it in a savings account for college. It would be a good start."

"A hundred dollars?"

"The hundred dollars I sent home with your father. When you didn't come by on Monday, I gave it to him for—" He stopped. He took his feet off the desk and leaned forward. "You didn't get it."

"No, no," I said. "No, I got it. Thanks. A savings account for college is a good idea."

He stared at me for a long time.

"What?" I said.

"You didn't get the baseball either."

"I got it. It's great. It's in my room right now. Thanks."

"You sure?"

"I'm sure."

It was just like my father said. You shouldn't count on anything.

Mr. Ballard sat back, nodded, smiled a little. "So what can I do for you?"

I looked out his windows, past the orchids on the windowsill, and down toward the river. It was wide, and the trees on the far side were starting to shake their leaves down. It was getting colder.

"You practice horseshoes here?"

Mr. Ballard had horseshoe pits down by the river, and we played in the cool with the sound of water in our ears, and the clanging of the shoes against the posts when he threw them, and the thud of the shoes against the ground when I threw them.

Here are the stats:

Mr. Ballard threw four ringers in a row, and five in a row another time.
He had fourteen ringers all together.
And six leaners —which still count, by the way.
I had one leaner —which, you remember, counts.
And I had one ringer where the shoe wrapped itself around the top of the post, spun around a couple of times, and then dropped onto the sand.

I think Mr. Ballard was happier about my ringer than I was.

"Doug," he said, "you got the arc just right on that one. And it doesn't matter how many times it spins around, as long as it comes down flat like that."

And just so you don't think I really stink at horse-shoes, you should know that even though that was the only ringer I threw, I did come close four more times, and I rang the post twice, and even though it doesn't count, it still isn't bad.

"A little more practice," Mr. Ballard said, "and you'll be a better thrower than President LBJ ever hoped to be. You come by anytime, okay? The shoes will always be waiting for you." He set them down against a stake. "Right here."

We walked back up from the river, and Mr. Ballard told me to stop by his office and he'd have Mrs. Stenson see if she could find us some lemonade to celebrate my first ringer, and when we got up there, Mrs. Stenson was standing by his desk, and there was someone else there holding a stack of frame pieces, and a picture of a bird from you know where was spread out on Mr. Ballard's desk, and Mrs. Stenson said, "You're just in time. We're down to three choices for the Yellow Shank," and Mr. Ballard went over to see.

I did too.

It was about as far from the Black-Backed Gull as you could get. The Yellow Shank wasn't the first thing you saw at all. You saw his world first. It was fall, and the grass was getting duller, and the trees were gold and that reddish brown that looks like the color of old bricks. The Yellow Shank was walking in a sunny spot, looking like he owned the place. The water in front of him was dark, and the woods beyond were darker still. Really dark. But Audubon knew something about composition: he kept the top of the bird's back as straight as the horizon, right smack in the middle of the scene, with a beak held up just as flat and just as straight, and an eye that said *I know where I belong*. You couldn't help but be a little jealous of this bird.

I leaned in close. The lines in the water matched the line of the bird's beak. That would be easy to get. What would be hard to get were the legs. The back leg was poised as if it was about to leave its toehold and push ahead, and the way of it, the whole way of it, said that the head and back wouldn't be moving at all — just those legs. How did he give you the way the bird was going to move, even though he didn't show him moving?

"Any closer and we'll have to frame you too," said Mrs. Stenson.

"I think," said the guy holding the stack of frames, "that if you're going to put it over the bookcase there, you'll want this mahogany frame to go with that wood."

"But we're not sure it's going there," said Mrs. Stenson. "It could go by the window, as if the bird were looking outside. Then the mahogany wouldn't do at all."

"What do you think?" Mr. Ballard said. I looked up. He was asking me.

"I think it belongs back in the book," I said.

I know. That made me sound like a jerk. A real jerk. I didn't even mean to say it. Mr. Ballard had supposedly already given me this signed baseball and a hundred dollars and stuff. I was wearing his Timex watch! I should just shut up.

But he asked.

The guy holding the stack of frames looked at me like I was trying to take bread from his mouth.

Mrs. Stenson looked at me like I was going a little too far.

And Mr. Ballard said, "Why?"

"Because," I said, "things belong in the class to which they have been assigned."

The guy with the stack of frames put another one on the corner of the print. "Perhaps the mixture of the darker and lighter tone in this one would allow you to hang the print in either spot," he said.

Mrs. Stenson looked down at the new frame, then back at me.

Mr. Ballard drummed his fingers along the edge of his desk. He looked at me, then at the Yellow Shank, and he let his fingers light on the sunny spot beneath it. "Let's roll the thing up and put it back in its tube," he said. "I think I heard a ringer."

There aren't too many things around that are whole, you know. You look hard at most anything, and it's probably beat up somewhere or other. Beat up, or dinged up, or missing a piece, or tattooed. Or maybe something starts out whole and then it turns into junk, like Joe Pepitone's cap getting rained on in a gutter somewhere. Probably you can't even tell it's a cap anymore. Probably you wouldn't even want to pick it up if you saw it. But it didn't start that way. It started as Joe Pepitone's cap, and when he was out in the field, the sun was beating down on it from above the stands of Yankee Stadium and he could smell the grass and the dirt of the infield beneath its brim.

When you find something that's whole, you do what you can to keep it that way.

And when you find something that isn't, then maybe it's not a bad idea to try to make it whole again. Maybe.

I mean, what would you do if you found a baseball with only 215 stitches? Wouldn't you want to put in one more to make it right?

I know, that all sounds cosmic. But that's what you would have thought too if you had been in the Marysville Free Public Library the next day when I brought the tube back in, and when Mr. Powell took one look at it and knew what it was. You would have thought it too when we went back upstairs and Mr. Powell slid the Yellow Shank out of the tube and opened the glass case and turned the pages until he found the place between plate CCLXXXVII and plate CCLXXXIX and laid the print back in.

And if you looked at Mr. Powell's eyes, you would have thought what I thought: *I am going to get the birds back*. The Arctic Tern, the stupid Large-Billed Puffins, the Brown Pelican, and all the rest of them.

I am going to get the birds back.

And I'm going to start drawing again.

Ernie Eco came by for supper that night before he and my father were going off somewhere to look at a new pickup that some idiot was selling for some price a whole lot less than he should be selling it for and all he wanted was a hundred-dollar down payment. It would be a steal, Ernie Eco said, eating another ham slice, and would I pass the mashed potatoes?

My mother didn't say anything. She wasn't smiling.

"I went down to the mill yesterday," I said.

My father and Ernie Eco looked at me. My mother did too, with worried eyes. She held her fork in midair.

"Yeah?" said my father.

"I guess you two got the parking spots I won," I said.

"So?" said Ernie Eco. "It doesn't cost Mr. Big Bucks Ballard a thing."

"It just makes him look good to all the little guys who work for him," said my father.

"He said that he gave you the—"

"He didn't give me a thing," said my father. "Did you see me bring anything home? Did you? That's because he didn't give me a thing."

"He said that he gave you the signed baseball and a hundred dollars."

My father put his two hands down flat on the table. He looked at me a long time. "What are you trying to say?"

"I'm telling you what Mr. Ballard said."

My father's hands twitched. "If Mr. Big Bucks Ballard said he gave me the signed baseball and a hundred dollars, then he's a liar. You got that?"

You know what I should have said. Even my brother knew what I should have said, because after what felt like a whole long time, my brother whispered, "Doug's got it."

My father looked at my brother. "Shut up." He turned back to me. "I said, Mr. Big Bucks Ballard is a freaking liar. You got that?"

Then I figured it out, how Audubon got the Yellow Shank to move. He's staring into this dark place, and he's just about to cross the river that divides him from it, and his back foot is halfway up because he's about to push off, and he knows what he's getting into, but he does it anyway, calm and smooth and straight. He's going to step into the middle of the picture, where he should be, with the light in back of him and the dark ahead. His whole world is waiting for him to do that.

I was waiting for him to do it.

I looked at my brother.

Even though whatever is in the dark is waiting for the Yellow Shank, he's going to do it anyway.

"Someone's a liar," I said.

Here are the stats for that night:

He missed me the first time because I leaned away.

He missed me the second time because I pushed the chair back and got up.

He just clipped me when I had to push through Ernie Eco's arm, the jerk.

And he missed me again when I spun around and got to the back door first.

I count that a win.

I went back to the Marysville Free Public Library and stayed until it closed at nine o'clock. Mr. Powell had left the book open to the Yellow Shank. That bird, he knew where he was going, even if he was going on stupid yellow legs.

He knew.

But that doesn't mean anything is going to be easier.

When I got home late that night, my father was gone, my mother was in her bedroom, and my brother was flipping baseball cards all by himself, which tells you something about how much he has going on between his ears.

I started up the stairs.

"Do you know what a jerk you are?" he said.

"Shut up," I said.

"All you had to do was say 'I got it.' That's all you had to do."

I leaned over the banister. "Don't you ever want to say 'I don't got it,' just once? Don't you ever want—"

"Every day, Douggo," he said.

"Then why don't you?"

"Because after you left, Douggo, who do you think he hollered at? Who do you think? That's why she's upstairs, so you don't see her face, because she's been crying since supper. Do you get it now?"

I sat down on the stairs.

"Do you get it, Douggo? Do you get it?"

"Shut up. It's not like you—"

"Like I what? Like I what, Douggo? Do you ever wonder what it's like to be so angry that you... And then something happens, and after that, everyone figures that's what you're like, and that's what you're always going to be, and so you just decide to be it? But the whole time you're thinking, *Am I going to be like him? Or am I already like him?* And then you get angrier, because maybe you are, and you want to..."

He stopped. He wiped at his eyes. I'm not lying. My brother wiped at his eyes.

"Go upstairs," he said. "There's something on the dresser. Put it somewhere he can't find it."

I started up the stairs.

"And Douggo," he said. "Even if you're a jerk, you still got guts."

Yup. My brother said that. I'm not lying.

And you know what was on the dresser, right?

I carried the baseball downstairs.

"How did you—"

"Drunks keep everything they want to hide in their cars."

Flipping baseball cards. Wiping at his eyes. Flipping baseball cards.

I went down to the basement and put the signed baseball in the pocket of Joe Pepitone's jacket. When I went back into our room, my brother was deep under the covers, his face turned away.

"Thanks," I said.

He didn't answer. But I got it.

On Monday, it was like I was walking into the center of the picture.

I got a new brown-paper book cover for *Geography: The Story of the World* and decorated it with an Arctic Tern on one side, and a Yellow Shank on the other—right in the middle of the paper. When Mr. Barber walked by my desk holding his coffee, he opened my book and flipped through the pages, which were perfect. "Thanks for taking care of it so well," he said. And when I nodded, he smiled, then hit me lightly on the shoulder. Like Joe Pepitone would do.

I turned in my Chapter Review Map on the culture of China to Mr. McElroy and added a list of Chinese characters and their meanings that I wrote myself to make up for being late. Not bad for someone who at the beginning of the year could hardly ... well ...

In English, when we got to Chapter 38 of *Jane Eyre*— which I had read twice already because of Miss Cowper's County Literacy Unit—Miss Cowper turned to me and said, "Let's have Douglas finish the novel for us," and I looked at her, and I started to sweat, and I looked down at the page. You know how many words in *Jane Eyre* have more syllables than any word has a right to?

But you know what? I got it. I really got it. Most of it.

Lil Spicer said I was the best reader of all. Which was a lie. But so what? So what?

I raised my hand in Mrs. Verne's class, and even though it took a few tries, she finally called on me, and I'm not lying when I'm telling you that no one else in the class had even imagined a *z* axis. Mrs. Verne was pretty impressed and said that I must have a fabulous visual imagination.

Did you get that? *Fabulous.*

In PE the Wrestling Unit was still going on, but the So-Called Gym Teacher didn't say anything when

I ignored the lined-up platoons and went outside to run. It was November now, and most of the trees had dropped their leaves off and were all bare and dark. But as long as the So-Called Gym Teacher was going to let me run, I'd run. And it didn't hurt any that James Russell and Otis Bottom started to run with me. I didn't ask them to. They just saw me going outside and decided to come along, I guess. We mostly ran without saying anything.

And in Mr. Ferris's class? Imagine yourself handing in lab reports that get Clarence rocking his little wooden hooves off, and you have it.

So after school on Monday, I asked Lil if she wanted to walk over to the Ballard Paper Mill, and she said, "Why?" and I said I'd show her how to throw horseshoes, and she said, "How hard can it be?" and I said, "Harder than you think," and she said she guessed she'd try and so we went down behind the mill to the horseshoe pits. The shoes were there, just like Mr. Ballard promised.

I showed Lil how to hold the shoe at the top, how to stand with her heel at the post, and how to swing her arm a couple of times, and she threw the first one about ten feet, which isn't, in case you don't know, even in the neighborhood of how far it has to go. Then she threw the second one ten feet again and got so disgusted that she threw the third one as hard as she could and it hit on its side and rolled almost all the way to the post. Then she figured that she had the technique down and she threw the last one as hard as the third, except that she didn't let go until the end of her swing, and the horseshoe went straight up into the air and she screamed and ducked and I bent over her and held her so it wouldn't hit her when it came down except it came down next to us instead of on top of us and when we stood up, she looked at me like—like I'd done something noble and heroic.

You know how that feels?

Fabulous.

Then we collected all the horseshoes and walked over to the other post and she said, "Why don't you throw one?" and so I did.

It was perfect. I swung my arm twice, let the horseshoe go just right, and it flew up, slowly, gracefully, and then it turned once and let its two ends come down and it landed flat and skidded on the sand just enough to ting the post.

It was a beautiful sound that . . .

Well, I'm lying.

I missed the stupid post by a mile.

But it doesn't matter, because something else happened when we finished throwing horseshoes that was even better.

Reader, I kissed her. A quiet walk back we had, she and I.

CHAPTER SIX

The Snowy Heron
Plate CCXLII

BUT THE THING about being a Yellow Shank is this: once you move into the middle of the picture, you're that much closer to the dark woods.

By the middle of November, it was pretty obvious that November in stupid Marysville, New York, is about the crummiest month there is for running. You never know; things could always get worse. But in November the valley traps thick clouds and holds them low, so the air is always wet and cold, and every day, right around the time I went outside to run with James Russell and Otis Bottom, every day, and I'm not lying, it rained. And it rained the kind of gray rain that's only a few degrees short of being snow and goes down your back and pretty soon—like, right away—your sweat-shirt and T-shirt and all the rest are wet through and they're so cold that you don't want them touching your skin but what can you do?

The one thing the cold made me do was pick up the pace, so even James Russell was panting by the time we got back, and Otis Bottom kept looking at me like he was wondering why we had to go so all-fired fast. But I couldn't exactly go to Mr. Ferris's class in a sopping wet T-shirt, and I had to change it before everyone else came back to the locker room because of you know why. James Russell and Otis Bottom figured it out, I guess. They never said anything when I took my dry clothes over to the bathroom stalls.

But the week before Thanksgiving, things got darker in PE. The So-Called Gym Teacher announced that we were going to start a new unit—Volleyball—and Every-one, and he meant Everyone, was going to Cheerfully Participate because this was a Team Sport that required Every Single One of Us to be a Part of the Team.

Terrific.

So we strung up nets while he sat in his office and we used masking tape to mark off the boundar-ies and we knocked the balls around some and then served overhand as if we knew what we were doing, and the So-Called Gym Teacher came out of his office and said we were supposed to practice passing back and forth, which he'd never told us, and he went back into his office and we passed back and forth until we all got sick of it and then we started dodge ball with the volleyballs until the So-Called Gym Teacher came out of his office again and hollered and that was pretty much the end of the period.

One more blah day of PE at Washington Irving Junior High School.

Except that in English the next day, a runner from the Principal's Office came in and handed Miss Cowper a note. She read it, and looked at me. "Douglas, Principal Peattie would like you to stop by after school."

Every eye in the classroom turned toward me. They probably figured that my twisted criminal mind had made me do something awful again.

"How come?" I said.

"If you mean to say 'Why has Principal Peattie requested to see me?' my answer is 'I do not know.' But I'm sure he will tell you."

"I'm sure he will," said about twenty-two voices around me.

"That'll do," said Miss Cowper, and with one last look at me—a little worried, maybe?—she turned back to the chalkboard.

Lil leaned over. "What did you do?"

I shrugged. "Do I have to do anything?"

"Pretty much you don't have to go see the principal unless you've done something."

"All right. I'll tell you. Principal Peattie has a mad wife and he's hidden her in the school attic, except that every so often she escapes."

"The school," said Lil, "doesn't have an attic."

"In the basement. I went down by accident and there she was. And she came at me, Mrs. Peattie, like she was going to bite me to death or something. But I got away, and now Principal Peattie wants to keep me quiet. He'll probably lock me up too. And then, Lil, you alone will know the terrible secret."

I should tell you that I was revealing this terrible secret to Lil while Miss Cowper was trying to teach us the Wonders of the Adverb and that when she asked if Lil and I had anything we'd like to share with the whole class, we stopped, quickly understanding that Miss Cowper was watching us angrily and would beat us mercilessly if we did not cease immediately. And I'm giving you that last sentence just to show that you can too talk and learn at the same time.

Principal Peattie made me wait for half an hour—again. I guess it was his technique. Then he opened the door and told me to come in, and to sit, and then he sat down behind his desk and underneath the Brown Pelican and looked at me like I was personally responsible for causing all the problems of Washington Irving

Junior High. He shook his head a couple of times before he began.

I'm not lying—this Brown Pelican, he was beautiful. He could have been as funny-looking as the Large-Billed Puffins, because he was mostly bill. Put him next to the Arctic Tern, and you could hardly imagine him flying. The feet, the curve of the neck, the colors—he could have been a hoot. But he wasn't.

When you looked at him, it didn't matter how he was put together. He was noble. If you were a bird, you could imagine bowing down to him.

"Principal Peattie has been speaking with Coach Reed," Principal Peattie said.

You had to wonder what the Brown Pelican's voice would be like if he could speak. Something deep, but still able to laugh. Warm. Easy.

"Coach Reed says— Douglas, would you mind terribly giving Principal Peattie your full attention?"

You could imagine the Brown Pelican standing over the Black-Backed Gull at the moment when the gull most needed him and saying that maybe the sky won't be lost after all.

"Listen, kiddo, you look Principal Peattie in the eye!"

I did. It wasn't easy.

"I said, Principal Peattie has been speaking with Coach Reed."

You remember that feeling of cold, freezing rain down your back I was telling you about?

Principal Peattie held up a piece of paper. "Coach Reed has had the secretary type up this report for your Permanent School Record."

Just so you know, I should tell you this: I did not say, *I didn't know the So-Called Gym Teacher could write a report.* I did not say that. Even though I was tempted. Sometimes I really do get it.

"He tells Principal Peattie that you have been cutting his class for weeks."

"I've been running," I said. "He sees me go out every day at the beginning of the period."

"Has your class been doing a Running Unit?"

"*I* have."

"The rest of your class hasn't, and guess what? You're not the teacher." He looked down at the piece of paper. It was a blue piece of paper, which I guess made it all-fired important. "It says here that you've missed the entire Wrestling Unit."

I didn't say anything.

"How are you going to make that up?"

I still didn't say anything. I figured that keeping my mouth shut was my best option. I got it.

"Principal Peattie will tell you how you're going to make that up. Coach Reed staggers his units, so he's starting another one on Wrestling for his fifth-period class. You be there for that one—and don't even think of missing a day."

"Fifth period is my lunch period," I said.

"Fifth period *was* your lunch period," he said.

"Do I still have to do his—"

"Yes, you still have your other period with him too." Principal Peattie looked at the blue piece of paper. "Volleyball."

"He must really love me to want to see me twice a day," I said.

"He doesn't," said Principal Peattie. And then he said something that I don't think I want to tell you.

It only gets me closer to the dark woods.

Saturday deliveries in November are, of course, cold and gray and wet. The sky is as dark and lousy as it is in the background for the Snowy Heron, which is the Audubon picture that Mr. Powell had turned to because he wanted me to think about Composition on Several Planes at once.

But things weren't like they had been in October.

On Saturdays now, Mrs. Mason was taking out a couple of doughnuts again from the two dozen I was bringing, and she was putting them on a white plate, and setting that beside a mug of hot chocolate that was waiting for me. And Mr. Loeffler, who was reading *Jane Eyre* because he said I inspired him, liked to tell me that I should see the movie with Orson Welles sometime, and then he'd act out a scene or two and we'd start to laugh because Mr. Loeffler is no actor, and I'm not lying. Afterward we'd change whatever light bulbs needed changing. Then when I got to the Daughertys' house, Phronsie and Davie and Joel and Polly and Ben would all be waiting to tackle me, and I let them. I never came away from them without two or three new bruises somewhere. It was great.

And Mrs. Windermere. You know how cold it gets when you're walking out to Mrs. Windermere's, and Mrs. Mason's hot chocolate is a long time ago, and it's misting and freezing and Joe Pepitone's jacket isn't as warm as it could be, and you have to walk fast so that you don't start to shiver but you can't walk too fast because you don't want to tip the stupid wagon over? It's that cold.

So when you walk into Mrs. Windermere's kitchen and it's all warm and cozy like my mother would keep it if this were her kitchen and you hear Mrs. Windermere typing in the distance with the god probably sitting beside her with his wings folded, you take your time because you don't want to go out into the cold again. And besides, there's the Red-Throated Divers to look at and wonder what spectacular thing the mother diver is thinking about showing her kid next. And then Mrs. Windermere comes in and says, "Skinny Delivery Boy, do you want a cup of coffee?" I'm not lying. Coffee. And I say, "Sure," and she says, "How do you take it?" and I say, "Black," and she says, "Fine," and I'm warm all the way back home.

And then, on November Saturday nights, I'd be over to the Daughertys', who had decided to give me a chance after all. Maybe they were desperate.

Mrs. Daugherty wasn't kidding: five kids, and every single one of them needed to get read to before going to sleep. And it wasn't like you could read to all of them at once, or even three of them, or two. It was five kids, five books.

This takes a long time. I'm not lying.

But I didn't care, because I figured it all out, thanks to Miss Cowper's County Literacy Unit.

I figured out Sam-I-Am for Phronsie.

I figured out Circus McGurkus for Davie.

I figured out Jack, Kack, Lack, Mack, Nack, Ouack, Pack, and Quack for Joel.

I figured out Andy and the thorn in the lion's paw for Polly.

And I even figured out why Wilbur is one terrific pig for Ben.

You know what this feels like, to figure all this out?

Do you really know what it feels like?

And after the Daughertys came in at night, Mr.

Daugherty would drive me back to The Dump in his police car.

So you might think that things were going pretty well. And I guess they were. But even while eating cinnamon doughnuts, and changing light bulbs, and walking back from Mrs. Windermere's, and driving to The Dump in a police car, and working on the Snowy Heron, I'd be thinking about what Principal Peattie told me, and you really don't care about Composition on Several Planes at Once when you're thinking about what he told me.

"Look at the diagonals that Audubon sets up first," Mr. Powell said. "Go from the tip of the heron's feet to the tip of his beak, and you have the first diagonal. But look at the second diagonal. It's a lot subtler. He starts at the end of *this* broad leaf in the upper left, right here, and then brings it down across the top edge of *this* broad leaf, and the bottom edge of *this* rise in the shore. And the two diagonals form . . ." He waited.

"An *x*," I said.

"Exactly right. And the center of that *x* is . . ."

"The lake."

"Which is drawn linearly, long and narrow. Do you see?"

I got it.

"So," Mr. Powell said, "you have one plane of action in the forefront, marked by the diagonals. In that one, the heron is stepping out from the higher brush and is trampling this plant. In the other plane, the one on the horizontal, the hunter is in the background, holding his gun and advancing."

I nodded.

Principal Peattie is a jerk.

"What's interesting is that the two planes are going to come together sometime soon after the moment we are seeing, because both the bird and the hunter are approaching the center of the diagonals, which in a composition such as this always intersects at the middle of the page, just like the action will intersect at the middle of the page."

"It doesn't look like the heron is going to come off too well," I said.

Mr. Powell looked at the approaching hunter. "Probably not."

"So this is one dead heron we're looking at."

Lil got up from her table where she was doing our English class exercise that was supposed to show us More Wonders of the Adverb. She looked at the Snowy Heron. "He doesn't look dead to me," she said.

"Shows how much you know," I said.

Okay, that was sounding like Lucas — and dumb. I know. But nobody else in the room had Principal Peattie tell him that . . . nobody else in the room knew what it was like to have someone blast away at him, like this heron was going to find out.

Lil went back to the adverbs. Mr. Powell was quiet;

then he got out a sheet of paper. "Try drawing the contour of the heron without a line—suggest the feathers," he said. "At least until you get to the base of the neck."

I tried, but I couldn't get it. And after Lil closed her book and got up and left without saying a thing, I didn't even want to try to get it.

"Mr. Swieteck," said Mr. Powell, "take the paper home and try it."

I shook my head. I left the pencils and the paper there. And I left the Snowy Heron too, forever in the moment before he was going to be blasted, which he had no idea was coming.

He didn't know how lucky he was.

On the day before Thanksgiving, we got a postcard from Lucas—still not in his handwriting—that said he was coming home, finally. He'd be back by the middle of December. "Remember, I don't look exactly the same," someone wrote for him. My mother cried, and she said that we had a lot to be thankful for this Thanksgiving, and I guess that was true, especially since Mr. Ballard sent home a twenty-two-pound turkey—which, I'm not lying, is a big turkey—for every one of his employees. On Thanksgiving Day, my mother put it into the oven right after she got up, and it cooked all morning and half the afternoon so that the whole house was filled with the scent of it.

My mother went around smiling — until Ernie Eco came.

On the Monday after Thanksgiving, I went to fifth-period PE class instead of lunch.

I sat down at the end of one of the squad lines. The So-Called Gym Teacher made us count off by twos — no, I didn't say anything about how this was probably as high as he could count — and then he divided us into two platoons and told each platoon to line up by height (which took a lot longer than you might think) and then he told us to sit on opposite sides of the mat spread across the floor to see who our opponent would be. It was supposed to generate aggression, he said.

Terrific.

And you know, you have to wonder if the world is fair when it was one of those late-fall days in stupid Marysville when a tropical front or something had come up from who knows where — South America? — and everything was warm and the yellow sun was shining and what a sweet day it would be to run, or to eat lunch outside. Instead, I was messing around on a gray mat that smelled of the sweat of a thousand wrestling matches. It was, I had to admit, hard to give the Wrestling Unit my full attention.

Here are the stats from my first match of the period:

One takedown . . . of me.

One pin . . . of me.

One loss . . . for me.

Match time: Eight seconds.

I guess you can tell I wasn't paying much attention.

The So-Called Gym Teacher came up behind me before my second match while my opponent was staring at me across the mat generating aggression. "I'm not going to pass you for the unit if you don't try," he said.

Here are the stats for the second match of the period:

One takedown . . . of me.

One pin . . . of me.

A second loss . . . for me.

Match time: Thirty-six seconds, which is four and a
half times longer than the first match.

The So-Called Gym Teacher eyed me from the other side of the mat. I eyed him back. Then he leaned down and said something to my next opponent, who turned to look at me. The So-Called Gym Teacher said something to him again, and then he walked away. It was sort of creepy. Like you were the Snowy Heron and you could feel that something was wrong but you weren't sure, because you hadn't seen the hunter with the gun coming across the horizontal yet.

But I'm not lying, the stats for the third match were different.

When the So-Called Gym Teacher blew his stupid whistle, this other guy and I got into the circle, and I crouched down as if I cared at all, and as we started to circle each other he said, "Reed wants me to call you a Mama's Baby."

I almost lunged at his throat.

"But I'm not," he said quickly. "I'm not." We circled some more. "He's a jerk," the guy said.

"Let's get something going," hollered the So-Called Gym Teacher.

We circled some more. And when my back was to the So-Called Gym Teacher, I said, "Keep circling."

So we did. And someone on the edge of the mat started to laugh, and then someone else, and then we started to circle faster, and pretty soon the whole place was laughing except for the So-Called Gym Teacher, and this kid and I were laughing so hard we could hardly keep circling but we kept going until we were dizzy and finally the So-Called Gym Teacher hollered at us to sit down and we did except we both kept swaying, we were so dizzy.

The So-Called Gym Teacher was about as angry as you can see a teacher get, and when he called the next two guys up for their match, he could hardly keep the roar out of his sergeant voice.

But you know what the two guys did?

That's right.

They circled. And circled. And circled.

I think you can imagine what the So-Called Gym Teacher did. If it had been legal, I think he would have called in firing squads. But since it wasn't legal, he told us that he was going to give every boy in class a big fat zero for the day, and we could see how we all liked that, yes sirree, buster.

We all went in to get changed. We were still laughing.

No one in the locker room looked when I took my shirt off.

Maybe the Snowy Heron is going to come off pretty badly when the planes come together. Maybe. But he's still proud and beautiful. His head is high, and he's got this sharp beak that's facing out to the world.

He's okay for now.

On the first Saturday of December — the month that Lucas was coming home — I waited for Lil outside the library after the deliveries. It was cold, and I'm not lying. The sky was iron, and Mrs. Windermere's coffee had worn off way before I got back into town, even before I passed the open meadow. A few snowflakes blew past in a hurry, which is how most people went by too, all huddled together and their heads down and their arms close in. So you can see it was kind of noble for me to wait outside for her. But I hadn't really talked to her since Thanksgiving, and I guess I wanted to make sure that she wasn't still thinking of my stupid "Shows how much you know" like I was still thinking of Principal Peattie's stupid . . . what he said.

She came up the street with a load of books and stomped up the six steps to where I was waiting and I said, "Hey," and she said, "Hey," but she said it in a way that meant she wasn't really saying "Hey," she was really saying, *You are such a jerk and I wish you would drop into some crack,* so I knew she hadn't forgotten.

"Are you coming into the library?" I said, and she looked at me like she was generating aggression and she said, "Not now."

"I wish you would," I said. "It's not much fun just drawing with Mr. Powell."

"Oh," she said. "I didn't realize. Well, I don't know very much about it, do I?"

"If we stop in at your dad's deli, we could get two Cokes," I said.

"Do you have any money?" she said.

"No."

"Then what you're really saying is that if we stopped in my dad's deli, I could get you a Coke, right?"

I shrugged and smiled.

Lil Spicer shook her head, and then she laughed, and I'm not lying, she smiled too. "You know," she said, "you should smile more often." She handed me her books and took my arm. "Let's go," she said.

That afternoon, after our Cokes, I drew that Snowy Heron like I was John James Audubon himself. Except my heron, he was strutting out into the world like that hunter would never, never come.

Finally, finally, finally, in the middle of December, we drove down to New York City in my father's new pickup, my father, my mother, and me. We left my brother home, first because we wouldn't have room for him in the pickup once Lucas got there, and second because my father wanted him to move the furniture around in our bedroom upstairs so that we could fit another bed in. This wasn't going to be easy, which my brother had pointed out and which my father had answered with . . . you know.

I sat between them. My father was glaring at the cars on the expressway as if he were daring them to try, even try dinging up his new pickup. I wasn't sure why he was so all-fired worried about it—it was already pretty dinged up. You don't get a whole lot for a hundred-dollar down payment, I guess. But whenever someone closed in on him, he rolled his window down and let them know, even though they had their windows rolled up because it was about zero degrees outside. Of course, when my father opened his window, it made it about zero degrees inside too. And it didn't get warm again, because the heater didn't work in his new pickup. I guess he forgot when he bought it that we weren't living in, say, Miami.

My mother was wearing her best blue coat. She looked out the window too, most of the time. It was like she was trying to peer across the miles, right into the city, to find Lucas. Every time a bus passed us, she looked into all the windows. Who knew? He might be there.

Me? I was watching for Joe Pepitone whenever a Ford Mustang drove by, because Joe Pepitone is the kind of guy who would drive a Ford Mustang.

We got lost three times in New York City because, my father said, no one knew what they were doing when they laid out all the streets. Nothing made sense. And if you were there, you wouldn't either have pointed out that it made perfect sense since the whole city is on a grid. You know you wouldn't.

When we finally found the Port Authority bus station, we drove around it eight times because he wasn't going to park in one of those garages where they take your money and then go joy-riding in your truck. Not him! He was going to find a spot on the street — which we finally did about a half mile away, which took a whole lot longer to drive than you might think because we had to creak through a Stop the War protest that was spilling into all the side streets. By the time my father edged the pickup into a spot, my mother was near frantic. When he finally switched off the ignition, she got out and I got out and my mother started to walk toward the Port Authority. "Just hold on," my father called.

"If we don't hurry," she said, "we won't be there when his bus pulls in."

"So what?" he said. "He's been gone a—"

My mother didn't wait for him to finish. She turned away and began walking.

I could have cheered.

We were there on the bottom level of the Port Authority when Lucas's bus pulled in. My father, a couple of minutes after.

I wish I could tell you what it was like, watching my mother smile while the bus parked. I wish I could tell you.

But maybe you know, and I don't have to.

There was the smell of diesel, and the screech of air brakes, and the big engine of the bus echoing off the cement walls and ceiling. There was the crowd of people all looking for someone they cared about who was on the bus and coming home for Christmas. There was the driver switching off the engine, taking off his hat and stretching, pushing back his hair. He reached forward and pulled a lever and the doors opened and he got out and stretched again, then walked over to the lug-

gage bins and bent to open them. And there were the
passengers starting to get out, and they weren't Lucas,
and they walked slow and unsteady, like they'd been
crinkled up for a while in a seat too small. And one by
one they turned to the crowd and waved at someone,
and that someone would run up and they'd hug and kiss
and then go find their luggage.

That's how it was, one by one everyone coming
off the bus, holding the rail as they stepped out, until
everyone was off the bus and the bus driver was standing by the empty luggage bins and closing them up and
then he looked over at us.

"You folks waiting for a kid in a wheelchair?" he
said.

"No," said my father.

But my mother gasped, and then she was running.
She flew past the bus driver and up the stairs of the bus.
We could hear her steps as she ran to the back.

I came up behind her, and this is what I saw: My
mother was kneeling down in front of my brother Lucas.
One of the overhead lights was shining brightly on her
hair, turning it all gold. She held Lucas's face in both
her hands. Her blue coat was spread out, and it covered them both like wide wings, covered even the chair
my brother was sitting in. She was kissing him, but I
couldn't see his face until she reached to hold him close
to her, and she put her head beside his. Then I could

see him. I could see the wide gauze bandage across his eyes.

And oh God, it wasn't until she stood and turned to me that I could see why Lucas was in the chair: Both his legs were missing. Above the knees.

My mother looked at me. That smile.

Next to them stood a smart soldier, his uniform perfect, his hat off and under his arm, looking away like he wasn't supposed to be seeing this.

I walked down the aisle, touching each of the seats as I passed them. My mother watched each step I took. When I was in front of the wheelchair, she put her hand on the back of my brother's head, and he leaned into her.

"Lucas," I said.

He tilted his face up to me. "Hi, Doug," he said. He reached out and I took his hand. It was trembling a little. "I got dinged up," he said.

"A little bit," I said.

He smiled.

I never saw it before, but he smiles like my mother.

The soldier and I got Lucas down from the bus. It wasn't easy, and I think we hurt Lucas twice trying to get him down the bus steps, and again when we crowded him into the elevator. And again when we crowded him out of the elevator. But he never said a thing, and when we finally got him on the ground floor, he reached out and the soldier shook his hand and Lucas said, "Thank you, sir," and the soldier said, "It was an honor," and he saluted Lucas — who couldn't see him, but Lucas saluted back as if he somehow knew. Then my mother took his hand and I got behind the chair and pushed him through the Port Authority and out onto the street.

"Where are we?" he said.

"New York City," I said.

He lifted his face up to the air. The bright cold sunshine shone down on him, but he couldn't see it. He was smelling instead.

And then he turned his head, because he was hearing what suddenly we were all hearing.

The Stop the War protest was marching toward us, people holding up signs with letters that dripped like blood, screaming into bullhorns, chanting, and sort of looking like the hunter coming across on the horizontal to the meeting of the diagonals, which is where we were standing. When the marchers in the front saw us, they tried to hold back, but the power of the marchers behind heaved them forward, and so instead they turned sideways and skirted around us until we were in a pocket with the crowd touching us everywhere. And you know what they said when they saw my brother in his uniform sitting in a wheelchair with bandages around his eyes, his legs gone? You know what they said?

They said he got what he deserved.

They said they were glad his eyes were gone.

They said they were glad his legs were gone.

They said he got done to him what he did to Vietnamese babies and how did he like it?

They said that's what happens when you let yourself get used by fascist pigs.

My mother tried to get in front of Lucas, but the crowd was so thick and so close that she couldn't work herself around the wheelchair. She looked back at my father, and he pushed himself past her and stood in front of Lucas, who sat there the whole time, facing straight out, even when someone spit on him. He didn't say anything. He just took it, like there was nothing else he could do.

You know what that feels like?

It feels like having Principal Peattie tell you that not a single teacher in the whole school gives a rip about you — not a rip — because they all gave up on you a long time ago, like on the day you started.

That's what it feels like.

It probably went on like that for only a few minutes, but it felt a lot longer. And when the crowd finally thinned out and the last protester had hated him, we got back to the pickup and my father started it up while my mother and I helped Lucas out of the wheelchair and into the cab and my father swore when he had to get out after my mother came around the front to get in through the driver's side. I got in the back and pulled the wheelchair into the pickup. It was heavier than I thought it would be, and I had to be careful because my father sure hoped I wasn't dinging up his pickup while I was getting that thing in.

I put the wheelchair down on its side and leaned against it so it wouldn't roll around as we headed out of Manhattan and back up toward Marysville to a house my brother had never seen. And maybe wouldn't see now.

Not that he was missing much.

It was a long drive, and I think you can imagine how cold it was for one of us especially. But I kept wondering every time we hit a bump and the stupid shocks in the pickup didn't do a thing how much it was hurting Lucas.

Probably a lot.

When we pulled into the driveway, my father got out and went into The Dump. I lowered the wheelchair over the side and jumped out and opened the door. Lucas's face was pretty grim. I'm not lying. My mother had been crying, so her face was pretty grim too. I wasn't sure how we were going to get Lucas out of the pickup, especially without hurting him more. I guess he wondered about that too, because he said, "Doug, if you wheel the thing below me, maybe I could sort of fall into it." It took me a couple of seconds to see that he was kidding, even though there's nothing funny about missing your legs, you know.

Then the front door of The Dump opened, and I thought it was probably my father coming back to help out. It wasn't. It was my brother. He looked at me; then he looked inside the truck at my mother and Lucas. "Lucas," he said.

"Hey," said Lucas.

My brother looked at me again, and then he reached into the pickup. "Tell me if this hurts," he said, and he reached around Lucas and Lucas reached an arm around my brother's neck and he lifted him out, just like that, and set him down in the wheelchair.

"Thanks, little brother," said Lucas.

And my brother, my brother Christopher, he said, "Anytime, Lucas. Whenever you want."

So we wheeled Lucas into The Dump and my father said how did we think we were going to get him up to our room in a wheelchair and Christopher said, "We got it figured out."

And Lucas gave that smile.

I really did try to care during the Volleyball Unit in PE that week. But you have to admit, volleyball is not that great a sport. You don't hear Jim McKay announcing the thrill of victory that comes from winning a volleyball game. I mean, slapping a ball around and getting it over a net? What's the point to that?

There's a reason that no one carries stats about volleyball around in his head.

But I really did try to care. And I even tried to care about the Wrestling Unit — not enough to try to win, but enough to keep things going for a minute or two without a whole lot of circling, which the So-Called Gym Teacher announced would get the two circlers two more big fat zeroes.

And no, I didn't say a thing about my surprise at him being able to understand the mathematical concept of zero. Remember, I got it.

And I didn't even complain about having to be in the Wrestling Unit at all, which I had reason to, since you may have noticed that James Russell and Otis Bottom weren't there with me even though they had missed most of the Wrestling Unit too. But so what? So what? If the So-Called Gym Teacher wants to be the jerk of the world, so what? If he wants to boom around in his sergeant voice, so what?

But maybe you can understand a little when I tell you that when the So-Called Gym Teacher hollered at me during Volleyball that I should go after those balls and not act like a Mama's Baby, you can understand why I got the volleyball and was about to throw it as hard as I could into his sneering face, but I held back — and I'm not lying, it wasn't easy — and I told him to shut up, just shut up, and he sneered some more and said I would never throw the volleyball because I knew what would happen to me, and my mother would be all upset, wouldn't she?

I almost threw it.

I almost did.

But I didn't.

I smiled—the way Lil Spicer likes. Then I took off my shirt and threw it onto the bleachers. I went back and served the stupid ball over the stupid net. Overhand.

Stats for that game:

I don't remember. My platoon lost. It's volleyball. Who cares? It wasn't exactly the agony of defeat. It was something a whole lot better.

But I'm not lying, all that week, the So-Called Gym Teacher did not let up. On Tuesday, he made three guys in the Wrestling Unit run the bleachers all period because they weren't trying hard enough. Guess who was one of the three guys. Then later, during Volleyball, he made two guys clean off the scuff marks from the gym floors with old tennis balls. Guess who was one of the two guys.

On Wednesday, during the Wrestling Unit, he made two guys run the bleachers all period because they weren't trying hard enough. Guess who was one of the two. And in Volleyball, I had to finish all the scuff marks I'd missed on my side of the floor.

On Thursday, he had four guys finally wash the

sweaty wrestling mats down. Guess who was one of the four. In Volleyball, he told four guys that they were going to stand in the middle of the court and try to retrieve balls that were spiked down to them. We were supposed to dive. You know what that feels like, diving onto a gym floor for forty-three minutes?

Then he told us that the next day would be the stunning climax of the Wrestling and Volleyball Units.

Terrific.

So on Friday, the last day before Christmas vacation, the So-Called Gym Teacher said he had picked random wrestling partners by choosing our names from slips of paper he'd cut up and put into a hat. He held up his clipboard. He said he'd call out the names two by two, starting with the first pair to wrestle.

Guess who was in the first pair.

My partner turned out to be Alfred Hartnett. I'll let you guess again: Do you think Alfred Hartnett weighed about the same as me, or about sixteen times more?

The So-Called Gym Teacher smiled when he called my name and then Alfred Hartnett's. He put the clipboard down on the bleacher and leaned back. "Let's get it going," he said.

I'm not lying, even if I had been trying, it wouldn't have made any difference. Alfred Hartnett laid an arm across me, and I went down. It was, for the record, his left arm, not his strong side. He was a good guy.

The So-Called Gym Teacher thought it was hilarious.

After the period, he went back to his office and left two guys — me and Alfred Hartnett, hilarious — to roll up the mats for Christmas vacation. They weren't so bad because, as you might remember, they'd gotten cleaned off earlier that week. When we finished, we walked back toward the locker room, and I saw that the So-Called Gym Teacher had left his clipboard and the slips of paper on the bleacher.

I looked at the clipboard.

Wouldn't you have wanted to know?

Not a single name on it.

The So-Called Gym Teacher had set it all up. There wasn't anything random at all, the jerk.

I flipped over the page.

Blank.

"Hey, Alfred," I said.

I flipped over another page.

It wasn't blank.

It was a drawing. A drawing of James Russell going for a lay-up. Behind him, you could make out every kid in our platoon.

I'm not lying, the So-Called Gym Teacher knew something about Composition on Several Planes at once.

I flipped over another page.

Otis Bottom, hanging about halfway up the climbing rope, looking like there was no way in creation he was going to get up any higher.

Another page.

Me. Running.

Another page.

Our whole platoon, smacking volleyballs around.

Another page.

Our whole platoon really playing volleyball this time. Me serving. No shirt. And no tattoo.

I looked at that awhile.

Then I skipped some pages and turned to the back of the pad.

And stopped.

A drawing of a low road between high grasses.

Bodies. Lots of bodies. All jumbled and thrown on top of one another.

Another page.

A Vietnamese man, old and worn. Dead. His eyes open, and his body lying crooked on the ground. Behind him, a young girl, naked, reaching for his hand. But she never made it.

Another page.

A boy, younger than me. A straw hat broken underneath him. His face — what was left of it — with a terrified eye. Burning huts behind him. Bodies all along the road to the huts. The words *My Lai* at the bottom. And, *I was there.*

"Swieteck, what do you think you're doing?"

It was the So-Called Gym Teacher.

He came across the gym like a thunderhead bearing down across the valley and grabbed the clipboard out of my hands. "What are you doing, looking at my personal things?"

"Coach," I said.

"You get out of here!" Screaming, shrieking sergeant voice. "Get out of here! Never touch my things again. Did you hear me? You get out!"

I went into the locker room to change.

Later that day, Miss Cowper — and I didn't ask for this, it just seemed to happen — Miss Cowper wrote me an excuse from PE so that I could help her refresh her County Literacy Unit. I never did find out what the stunning climax of the Volleyball Unit was.

Lucas didn't talk much, and when he did talk, it was never around my father. It was mostly around my mother. You could hear them late at night, when everything was quiet and dark. There would be these low voices, then quiet, then the low voices again. Sometimes crying. Every night, when they were alone, my mother would change the gauze bandage around Lucas's eyes. Then her voice would call quietly up the stairs, and Christopher would go down to bring Lucas up to our bedroom.

He wouldn't talk about what happened, how he lost his legs and maybe his eyes. Sometimes you'd come into the kitchen and he would be sitting by the kitchen table where the sunlight was coming in, and he'd have his face raised to it like he could see its warmth. Sometimes you saw him try to lift his body up and down in the chair, like he was lifting a weight — which he pretty much was. Sometimes he would get letters from people in his unit or from the doctors and nurses who had worked on him after he was wounded. I told him I would read them for him. He never wanted me to. He told me to throw them all away, which I didn't.

His stumps hurt him, and sometimes he would reach down to where his legs used to be — he wanted to scratch them, but there was no place to scratch. He'd still try, and then he'd give up and put his hands over his face, and you could tell he was doing everything he could not to let himself think that everything was ruined forever.

We were supposed to go down with Lucas to a doctor in New York City every two weeks for who knows how long, but when my father said he couldn't be traipsing all over the state every two weeks, we found a doctor in Kingston who would see him, and when my father put up an all-fired fuss at the first visit about how much it cost, the doctor said he had a son in Vietnam too, right now. A medic. So he'd take Lucas on for as long as his son was over there, and my father said he wasn't asking for any freaking charity, and the doctor stopped talking to him and told Lucas he'd see him in two weeks and he gave him some exercises to work on.

Lucas didn't do them.

Two weeks later, just before school was about to start after Christmas vacation, we went up to Kingston again and the doctor had an eye doctor waiting too. My father said he wasn't going to be gypped and he hadn't brought any money so if he thought that . . . The eye doctor turned his back on him and unwrapped the gauze from Lucas's face.

Then he turned to my father. "Anything else?" he said.

It was the first time my father had seen Lucas without the bandage. It was the first time I had too.

Burns all across his face. Whatever skin was left was shiny and stretched. His eyebrows and eyelashes were gone, it looked like for good. And everything was seeping. Everything looked wet and raw.

He'd lost the sky.

Christmas, as you can guess, wasn't exactly *Ho Ho Ho* around our house. On Christmas Eve, my father went out somewhere with Ernie Eco, and Lucas didn't want to go to midnight Mass, and so Christopher stayed with him, and my mother and I went. We didn't have a tree, and if it hadn't been for the ham that Mr. Ballard sent home to all his employees, I think we would have been celebrating with thawed hamburgers. Presents? Forget it.

So I went to St. Ignatius, and it was cold and damp like it usually was, outside and inside, except inside there were more candles lit than you'd think could fit inside a single church. Up front there were two balsam trees, and their scent mixed with the waxy smell of the candles. And there was a cradle beside the altar, a blue cloth draped over it. And there was a choir of perfect boys in perfect white robes with perfect combed hair singing their perfect notes like everything was perfect. And I thought of Lucas back home in his wheelchair, and so I couldn't understand it when my mother turned to me during "Hark, the Herald Angels Sing" and said loud enough to hear over the organ and the perfect choir, "What a wonderful Christmas this is."

I shivered.

Even with all those candles, it was still cold.

That wasn't the only time I shivered. I shivered late at night after Christopher carried Lucas up to bed and we had gotten him in and covered. Then we would lie awake and listen to his dreams.

And I would see the young boy with the broken straw hat. The burning huts. The girl's hand. *My Lai. I was there.*

Then Lucas would try to turn over, and there would be a low moan, and Christopher would get up, and I knew that Lucas was awake in the dark that he carried around with him all the time.

"What can I do?" Christopher would say.

"You weren't there. You can't do anything."

None of us knew how to make it light.

At the beginning of the first physical science class of the new year, Mr. Ferris set Clarence on the front lab table and started him rocking. "Do you know, Otis Bottom," he asked, "what historic event in the sciences will occur during this new year of 1969?"

Otis Bottom looked like he didn't really want to be back from Christmas break yet. He could have guessed all day and not gotten close.

"Doug Swieteck?" Mr. Ferris asked.

"The moon shot," whispered Lil.

"The moon shot," I said.

"Thank you, Lil Spicer. Yes, the moon shot. *Apollo Eight* has circumnavigated the moon and descended to sixty-nine-point-eight miles over the lunar surface. Think of that. From the very beginning of human consciousness, we have looked at the moon and wondered what it would be like to walk on it. In 1969, what man has wondered about for thousands and thousands of years, you may be able to see on your television screens. It is our first step out into the solar system. It is our first step out into the galaxy."

Clarence was really rocking. I'm not lying.

"So what are they going to find there?" Otis Bottom was trying to recover.

"Ah, Otis Bottom. That is the question. What are they going to find there? Who knows? Maybe everything will be exactly as they expect. Maybe everything will be a surprise. But one day soon, man will walk across the soil of the lunar landscape, and that will be a sign of our progress. In a time when it doesn't seem as if we're making much progress anywhere else, this, ladies and gentlemen, is a sign of tremendous possibility. And that, Otis Bottom, is perhaps the best answer to your question. They will find possibility there."

I thought of Lucas in his darkness. Wouldn't he like to see it?

I went through the rest of that day in a kind of daze. I mean, *the moon!*

Possibility!

Geez, *the moon.*

In January, all of Coach Reed's classes were starting a new unit in PE: Physical Fitness and Endurance. We were going to have a whole lot of tests to see how many sit-ups we could do in four minutes, and how many pushups, and squat thrusts, and leg lifts, and chin-ups, along with timed hundred-yard dashes and mile runs. We were supposed to compare ourselves to the President's Council on Physical Fitness goals that all American boys should be trying to reach so we wouldn't die of heart attacks someday.

So that period we spent practicing the correct way to do pushups and sit-ups, and after that we took turns holding each other's ankles and counting sit-ups, or holding fists beneath each other so that you could tell how far down your chest had to go for a good pushup, and we got timed for a trial run. It was about as exciting as it sounds.

You know how the Snowy Heron has its beak pointed out to the world? How it doesn't care that the hunter is coming up the path? How he looks at the hunter and says, *So what?*

How he sees Possibility?

After class, when everyone was headed into the locker room, I stopped at Coach Reed's office. He was sitting behind his desk, which was covered with Presidential Fitness Charts with lots of little spaces that needed filling in.

"Hello," I said.

He looked up from his clipboard, then turned it over.

"What do you want?" he said.

"I saw some of your drawings. You're good," I said.

He looked at the face-down clipboard. Then he looked at me with suspicious eyes. "So?"

"You drew the war," I said.

Coach Reed not saying anything. His hand pressing down on the clipboard, pressing it into the desk.

"My brother was there too," I said. "He's back."

A long minute passing.

"No, he's not," said Coach Reed finally. Not his sergeant voice. "No one ever comes back from Vietnam. Not really." He picked up the clipboard and held it against his chest.

"He's not reading the letters he gets."

Coach Reed nodded.

"He needs someone who knows what it was like."

Coach Reed looked at me.

I looked at the clipboard.

"Maybe you do too," I said.

"Get out, Swieteck," he said. "I'm busy." Sergeant voice back.

"I could help," I said.

He laughed. Not a happy laugh. "Help," he said.

"I could take care of those charts. I could write down everyone's names and keep track of where they start, what kind of progress they make, where they finish. Stats like that."

Coach Reed got up and sat on the edge of his desk. "Why so helpful?" he said.

"Do you want me to do it or not?"

"Not," he said.

I shrugged. "Okay." I turned to go.

"Wait a minute," he said. He fingered the clipboard. "I'll think about it. Go get changed. I'll let you know when you come back."

I nodded. "Okay."

When I came back, his office door was closed. But on the door, there was a note. *Swieteck,* it said. *Start with the second-period stats.*

I stayed after school to start.

"You know, Mr. Powell," I said the next Saturday. "I don't think Audubon had this right. I mean, about the hunter."

"Do you think he's in the wrong place in the picture?"

"No. He shouldn't be in the picture at all."

"What would you have put there instead?"

"Another heron. He's just seen her, and he's going to fly over to say hi."

"It would be a different story," said Mr. Powell. "What do you think, Lil?"

She came over and looked at the picture. Then she took my hand.

You know what that feels like?

Like what the astronauts will feel when they step onto the moon for the very first time.

Like what might happen if Coach Reed rang the doorbell at The Dump some afternoon and sat down next to Lucas.

Like knowing that Principal Peattie is wrong about what he said.

Like laying a missing bird picture back where it's supposed to be.

Like someone seeing what a chump you are and getting you a cold Coke anyway.

Like Possibility.

CHAPTER SEVEN

The Forked-Tailed Petrel
Plate CCLX

DO YOU KNOW how often it snows in stupid Marysville during a winter? Once a week. Maybe twice. And do you know on what day of the week it always snows? Saturday. Every Saturday for most of January and on into February. Every Saturday.

You remember what I do on Saturday mornings?

And do you think deliveries stop just because it's snowing, and blowing, and blizzarding, and the snow isn't turning to slush like it would on Long Island and it's getting deeper and deeper, and the cold is so bad that Joe Pepitone's jacket doesn't help much at all and my fingers are starting to stick to the handle of the wagon so

I have to pull Joe Pepitone's sleeves down over my hands but I don't have anything for my ears, which were about to snap off until Mr. Loeffler gave me this gray wool cap that Lil says looks great on me but I think makes me look like a chump but I wear it anyway because I really don't want my ears to snap off and besides did I tell you that Lil says it looks great on me?

Every Saturday it was the same. I'd wake up, and it would still be dark because the clouds were thick and it was already snowing hard, and it had been snowing hard for most of the night so the ground was covered, and the sidewalks and the streets too. While Lucas and Christopher slept, I'd put on about everything I had beneath Joe Pepitone's jacket and then I'd put on the gray wool cap that Lil says looks great on me, and I'd lace up my sneakers and head out into the snow, and my feet would be cold and wet in three steps. Mr. Spicer always had a cup of hot chocolate for me to start off each of the runs, and I'd drink it and go out with the first load. In the beginning of January I did this with the wagons, but pretty soon Mr. Spicer figured that I'd do a whole lot better with this old toboggan he had. So that's what I'd use. And it went a whole lot quicker. I'm not lying.

But you can't believe how cold the wind can blow in stupid Marysville.

Mrs. Mason always had a cup of warm milk waiting for me, because I'd told her like a chump that Mr. Spicer always started me off with hot chocolate and she wanted to be sure to give me something different, she said. So it was hot milk. I got used to it.

Mr. Loeffler always had a cup of hot tea waiting for me. I got used to that too.

Mrs. Daugherty always had a bowl of cream of wheat waiting for me. I did not get used to that. Phronsie whispered that it was good if you put a whole lot of brown sugar on it. It wasn't.

Mrs. Windermere always had a cup of hot coffee waiting for me. Black, which, she said, was the only way to drink it if you wanted to be awake to serve the god of Creativity, which she needed to do a whole lot since she was working on a stage adaptation of — guess.

Yup. *Jane Eyre.* I'm not lying.

When I told her that the only people who read *Jane Eyre* were people who had to because their English teachers made them read it and no one in their right mind was going to pay good money to sit in front of a stage and have all this acted out, she sipped her coffee and said, "Skinny Delivery Boy, I'm not even finished with it and people are already lining up to buy tickets."

Can you imagine anyone buying tickets to *Jane Eyre?*

Can you imagine Joe Pepitone buying tickets to *Jane Eyre?*

Me neither.

* * *

I spent that winter with my head down against the wind, pulling the stupid toboggan, my hands up Joe Pepitone's sleeves, and always having to go to the bathroom because of the cold and the warm hot chocolate, milk, tea, coffee.

But afterward, when I got back from Mrs. Windermere's, Lil would be waiting at the deli, and Mr. Spicer would heat up some chicken noodle soup for us — his own recipe, with lots of chicken and onion — and I'd take off my sopping sneakers and lay them beside the radiator, and take off my sopping socks and lay them on the radiator, and I'd stretch my sopping feet as close as I could get them to the radiator, and I'd eat the chicken noodle soup until I was warm again. And then we'd go to the library, where Mr. Powell was waiting for us and where we had started to work on gesture.

Which, by the way, the Snowy Heron would have been good for, but it was gone now too, because of the snow.

I'm not lying.

Stupid Marysville had so much snow that winter that the town ran out of money to pay for the plowing and the salting and the sanding. So the Town Council went over to the library, like it was a bank or something, and took a razorblade with them, and the next time Mr. Powell came in, the Snowy Heron was cut out, just like that, and sold off somewhere to pay for more plowing and salting and sanding.

If you're trying to get Audubon's pages back, and stupid Marysville is selling them off faster than you can find them, it gets sort of discouraging.

So here are the stats for volume three of John James Audubon's *Birds of America* owned by the Marysville Free Public Library of stupid Marysville, New York:

Total number of plates: One hundred.

The Arctic Tern: Missing. Sold to an anonymous collector from overseas.

The Red-Throated Diver: In Mrs. Windermere's house.

The Large-Billed Puffin: Missing. Mr. Powell won't tell me where.

The Brown Pelican: In Principal Peattie's office.

The Yellow Shank: Returned by Mr. Ballard, who is a good guy.

The Snowy Heron: Missing. Mr. Powell won't tell me where.

Total removed from Birds of America: *Six.*

Total returned to Birds of America: *One.*

Total to be returned to Birds of America: *Five.*

Terrific.

"When you're considering gesture," said Mr. Powell, "you're not imagining the birds as if they're posing for you. You're imagining them moving across the page instead of staying put. Your pencil is going to show them not only at the moment of the picture, but the moment before and the moment that is going to come after."

I looked at Mr. Powell.

He started to laugh. "Try this: You're not going to draw a picture of the bird. You're going to draw a picture of the bird's flight line."

"How do I do that?"

"Don't think of the bird as a flat image. Think of it the whole way around, even the parts that you don't see. Then think of how all the different pieces of the bird are working with or against each other. Think how the body of the bird wants to fall . . ."

"And the wings want to keep it up."

"Exactly. All movement relies on that kind of tension. You show the movement by suggesting the tension."

"And how do I do that?"

That was when we looked at the Forked-Tailed Petrels.

Things at Washington Irving Junior High School were going mostly okay.

My *Geography: The Story of the World* was as clean as you could expect after half a year. Mr. Barber still checked it out, leaning down over me when I was working on the Chapter Review Map about India. I could smell his coffee, and even though it didn't smell as good as Mrs. Windermere's — which she percolated before I came — it still smelled pretty good. In world history, Mr. McElroy had found eight filmstrips about the history of the Philippines. The record pinged away at us just about every class.

Terrific.

In English, Miss Cowper was throwing us into the Introduction to Poetry Unit like it was as all-fired important as the moon shot. You know, there are good reasons to learn how to read. Poetry isn't one of them. I mean, so what if two roads go two ways in a wood? So what? Who cares if it made all that big a difference? What difference? And why should *I* have to guess what the difference is? Isn't that what *he's* supposed to say?

Why can't poets just say what they want to say and then shut up?

In math, Mrs. Verne selected a group of students who had shown Excellence and Promise to work together on Advanced Algebra. Guess who was in it? Lil too.

You know how that feels?

In Mr. Ferris's physical science class we were distilling aspirins, very large aspirins, which by the time the last bell rang Mr. Ferris said he needed. Clarence was rocking his little hooves off these days because the moon shot was still on go-ahead, and it looked like it wouldn't be long before there were human footprints on the lunar surface, as Mr. Ferris kept reminding us. When we asked him if making aspirin was as important as men going to the moon, he rubbed his head and looked kind of painfully at us and said, "Believe me, aspirin is pretty darn important."

And in case you're wondering how things have been going with Coach Reed, January and February were mostly okay, too. I filled in all the Presidential Physical Fitness charts for him, in both periods. He'd call out the numbers, and I'd write them down where they were supposed to be. When he had to do the Written Comments at the end of the charts, he told me what to write, and I did it. I told him maybe my spelling wasn't going to be all that terrific, but he said he didn't care.

A few days into this, he brought me a new gym shirt so that I didn't have to wear my undershirt anymore. He handed it to me one morning after we finished a period's chart.

"Thanks," I said. "My brother isn't talking much these days. And he dreams a lot."

"Go shower," he said. "You'll be late for your next class."

There are two Forked-Tailed Petrels. They're in the middle of a green, stormy sea, and the waves are about as high as they're flying. They're heading closer, and their sharp beaks are open, because they're calling to each other kind of desperately.

"Look at the way the wind is blowing the waves," said Mr. Powell. "Anything odd about it?"

I shook my head.

"Look again," he said. "Pay attention to the composition."

He was right. Two winds were blowing the waves in two directions, completely apart.

"So how are the birds' bodies responding to those winds?"

The two winds were pushing them in different directions, but the petrels were using them to meet in the center of the picture. That's what the picture was about: meeting, even though you might be headed in different directions.

All movement relies on that kind of tension, you know.

Because of the snow, we missed most of Lucas's appointments in Kingston. My father said he didn't want to chance driving off the highway in this stuff, and he wasn't about to take a day off just for a doctor's appointment, not with Big Bucks Ballard breathing down his neck. So Lucas would have to do the best he could.

My mother did the best she could by calling up the doctor's office and asking what to do and filling the prescription for the ointment for Lucas's eyes and checking the stumps every day to be sure there was no redness or smell of infection.

You can imagine what that was like.

Lucas mostly sat around the kitchen with a blanket over his lap. Not because he was cold. He didn't talk hardly at all. None of us could know what it was like, he said. We weren't there. So what's the point of talking?

When he did talk, he was his old jerk self again.

When I told him about the moon shot and how one day there would be human footprints on the lunar surface, he said, "I guess they won't be mine."

And when my mother asked me to run down to Spicer's Deli for more milk, Lucas said, "I'd run down for you, but..."

And when Christopher said he was thinking about going out for track in the spring — which is something like a miracle since Christopher has never gone out for anything in his whole life — Lucas said, "I bet I could run my legs off if I tried — oh, wait a minute."

Every time he said something, that was the last thing anyone said for a long time.

Which is what had probably happened the second Saturday of February, when I had been working on the gestures of the Forked-Tailed Petrels and I was starting to get them just right so that they looked like they were about to dance with each other and I came back home and said to my mother and Christopher, "I think I got them dancing," and Lucas said, "I bet you couldn't do that for me," and the Silence Came Down and I thought of the Yellow Shank and I said, "Shut up, Lucas."

I'm not lying. I said, "Shut up, Lucas."

He turned his face toward me. "What did you say?"

"Are you deaf too?" I said.

He threw the blanket off his lap. He tried to raise himself up in his wheelchair. "Listen, little brother—"

"I can hear," I said.

"I got my legs blown off, in case you forgot."

"How could I forget? You tell us about it every day."

I think if Lucas could have gotten out of the chair, he would have pulled my face off.

My mother had her hand up to her mouth. But she didn't stop us.

The thing about the Forked-Tailed Petrels is that they only have a moment. The winds are blowing opposite ways, and each one is riding a different wind, and there's only this one moment when they can meet. It's all-fired important.

They can't miss it when it comes.

"Doug," said Lucas. He said this in a kind of snarl.

"You don't even try," I said.

"Try what?" More snarling. "I can't grow new legs."

"You have two arms," I said. "They used to be strong."

"You used to be able to take me," Christopher said.

"And the doctor said that you should try leaving the bandage off your eyes," said my mother. "Maybe..."

"I'm blind."

I walked over to my brother. I reached for the bandage across his eyes, and when he felt me near him he tried to stop me. Snarling. But I was a lot stronger than him now. I hadn't thought about it, but I was. So I grabbed his arms, pushed them away, and pulled the bandage off.

My mother started to cry.

Most of Lucas's face was still the shiny pink of half-healed skin. His eyes glistened with the ointment smeared over them. No eyebrows. No lashes. His eyes blinked, and blinked, and blinked.

"You want to stop me?" I said, or maybe I snarled. "Try. Hitch yourself up in that wheelchair. Try."

He didn't move. He kept blinking.

"Try," said Christopher.

Lucas blinked again. He turned his face toward my mother. "I think I see you," he said.

The next Saturday it snowed, but it didn't matter; Christopher and I carried Lucas into the pickup, and Lucas, my mother, and my father drove to Kingston early. Lucas didn't have the bandage over his eyes. He kept turning his face from side to side, blinking, trying to make things out.

And he was smiling.

I already told you about his smile, right?

After the deliveries, I drew the Forked-Tailed Petrels with smiles.

"Birds," said Mr. Powell, "tend not to have expressions on their faces."

"This is their one chance," I said. "In a second they're going to be blown past each other, and who knows what will happen next?"

Mr. Powell leaned down to my drawing. "In that case, smiles are appropriate."

But none of the petrel smiles could touch Lucas's smile or my mother's smile when I got home that afternoon, or mine, probably, when I heard that the Kingston doctor thought, *really* thought, that Lucas's eyes might heal, and he was going to send him to a specialist down to Middletown—

"He was going to send him to some guy in New York City, but I set him straight on that," said my father.

—and meanwhile, the doctor had some exercises he wanted Lucas to *really* work at for his arms and upper chest and Lucas said, "I may need your help, little brother," and I said, "Sure." He reached out his hand and I took it and we shook, and his hand felt . . . strong.

* * *

You know, I don't think the Forked-Tailed Petrels are blowing past each other. The more I think about it, it seems to me that they're probably circling, like two wrestlers. And when the waves and the winds smack at them, they spread their wings and skitter around and then they try to come back together again. That's what I think they're doing.

On Monday, James Russell was counting my squat thrusts for the Presidential Physical Fitness chart when he said, "I hear you've been drawing birds at the library."

"Yup," I said, kind of breathless. It's hard to talk when you're doing as many squat thrusts as you can in four minutes.

"Audubon's stuff," he said.

Nodded.

"You know, some of the plates are missing from that book," he said.

Nodded again. I was at sixty-three and still had about a minute to go, which, if you ask me, isn't bad.

"I know where one of them is," he said.

Nodded again. Principal Peattie's office, I figured. I'd seen the Brown Pelican too.

"Puffins," he said.

I stopped the squat thrusts.

"My father bought it from the town."

I'm not lying: I added another forty-two squat thrusts before Coach Reed called time.

If I had James Russell's father's job, I wouldn't talk about it. Probably James felt the same way, because he never talked about it. And when he told me what it was, he said that he was only telling me because I'd probably figure it out the minute I walked into his house. But I couldn't talk about it to anyone, he said. Promise?

I said I'd keep his secret, and probably you shouldn't tell anyone either.

James Russell's father is the First Flutist of the New York Philharmonic.

Do you know what my father would say if he knew that?

And James was right: you could tell as soon as you walked into the house. I mean, how many houses have flute music playing on the stereo in the middle of the afternoon, and loud? And how many houses have books about flutes right out on the coffee table that anyone could see right off, and sheet music everywhere, and this huge piano and next to it a music stand with a silver flute across it?

I'm not lying, you could tell pretty quick.

What you might not be able to tell pretty quick when you meet Mr. Russell is that he is the First Flutist of the New York Philharmonic, because Mr. Russell is bigger than Joe Pepitone and Mickey Mantle put together. And I don't mean he's fat, because he isn't. He's just huge. He stands over you like this little mountain, and he's got this dark beardy shrubbery all around the peak, and arms like pines, and legs like oaks, and feet the size of small lakes. His hands look too big to hold anything but a boulder—one in each.

And I said, "You play the flute?"

And he said, "Sweetly and beautifully."

Then he showed me.

He was right. Sweetly and beautifully.

He started with Mozart, who isn't as bad as you might think. Then some Brahms, who is as bad as you might think. Then some Joplin, who's good, and then some Aaron Copland, who Mr. Russell said was his favorite composer even though he didn't write anything for a flutist. And then he did some Beatles stuff. It didn't sound exactly like the Beatles, but it wasn't bad. And when he finished, I asked him to play the Copland again, and he smiled and did.

Copland knew how to say what he wanted to say. Unlike certain poets I could mention.

Then James took me upstairs. He had a house big enough to fit fourteen of The Dumps into. Maybe more. His own room was the size of our downstairs, and he had his own bathroom and tile with the grout still around it. And on the third floor, they had this room that ran the whole length of the house, about as big as left field in Yankee Stadium, which I have walked on, by the way. And right where the stairs came up to this room, the Large-Billed Puffins were hanging.

Okay, this is going to sound dumb. You know how sometimes when you haven't seen someone in a long time, and suddenly there he is, and you look at him, and for a second it's almost like he's a stranger and then that second is gone and it's all the same? Sort of like when Holling Hoodhood came by and dropped Joe Pepitone's jacket off last summer? That's what happened, except that at the same moment, Mr. Russell was downstairs playing that Copland piece again. And there were those fat puffins, looking like chumps, bumbling around like they had no idea how to get on in the world, looking dumb and stupid, and so beautiful that I wanted to...nothing.

"They're kind of dumb-looking," said James Russell.

"Yeah," I said.

I couldn't take my eyes off them.

And still, the music played sweetly.

"They don't even look like they can swim," he said.

The music played beautifully.

Tuesday after school, I went home to do all the homework that I wouldn't be able to do that night because Mrs. Daugherty had called and wondered if I could come over on such short notice, and so now I had the

Daugherty kids to read to and we were up to this place where this spider is going to die and a pig has to get her egg sac. I know — it sounds dumb. But it wasn't bad. So I had to get all my homework done before I went, especially for Mrs. Verne, who had already dropped two people from Advanced Algebra because they didn't get all their assignments in on time, and I wasn't going to be Number Three.

But on Wednesday, I went home again with James Russell. It was raining, and we got pretty wet, walking home with Otis Bottom too, since his house is only a couple of blocks away from James Russell's. And for the record, Otis Bottom's father has a job you could talk about: he's a doctor, which explains why his house is not on the same side of town as The Dump. I guess that being a doctor and being a flutist with the New York Philharmonic pay pretty good.

At James Russell's house, we visited the Large-Billed Puffins like they were old friends. Then we played speed chess up on the third floor, which I was no good at but he didn't wipe me out too fast. And he had a great dartboard up there, and I only threw a few into the wall instead of into the target. And then we played regular chess and I was better at that but he still won. And all the while Mr. Russell was playing Copland downstairs, and the stupid puffins were bobbling about in the water, sweetly and beautifully.

On Thursday I stayed late with Coach Reed to finish the Presidential Physical Fitness charts. "Thanks," he said when he signed his name on the last one.

"Sure," I said.

I stood up to go.

"Swieteck," he said.

"Yeah."

"How's your brother?"

Surprised?

"His eyes are getting better," I said.

"That's not what I mean."

"I know. He still dreams."

Coach Reed looked at me a little while, his mouth working. "Go on home," he said. "And thanks for writing up the charts."

Then the Forked-Tailed Petrels flew a little closer.

"Do you dream too?" I said.

Coach Reed looked down. He started to fuss with a bag of softballs.

A long time with the fussing.

Then: "There was a kid, younger than you."

More fussing with softballs.

"And an old man, and a young girl. Probably the kid's sister. I don't know."

Fussing with softballs.

"They come every night."

"That's what it's like for Lucas," I said.

He shook his head. "I don't think so. Not like these three."

"Maybe they want you to do something," I said.

He stopped fussing with softballs.

"Maybe they want you to help someone."

He looked at me. "Maybe they do," he said.

That's what I mean about the Forked-Tailed Petrels circling around and around each other, until they finally meet.

On Saturday, we had another snowstorm.

Terrific.

Before I even left the house, there was eight inches on the ground, and I'm not talking light and fluffy here. I looked out the bedroom window and I said to Lucas—who was already doing his exercises at the side of his bed—"I'm going to be soaked up to my knees in three steps," and he said, "Wouldn't happen to me!"

I know. Sounds like the same old Lucas. But if you had been there, you would have seen that he said it smiling.

I was, by the way, soaked up to my knees in two steps. And if it hadn't stopped snowing and the sun hadn't come out and the sky hadn't started to blue over the tops of the mountains, I might have said, "Forget it," and headed back home. But I didn't. I drank my hot chocolate at Spicer's Deli and then set out, and Mrs. Mason was waiting with her hot milk and I got through it. Mr. Loeffler had a cupboard door that was loose, a light bulb that needed changing over the basement stairs, and a cracked windowpane in the bookcase that he needed me to take the glass out of very, very, very carefully and which he couldn't do because of his shaky hands.

Mrs. Daugherty was keeping my bowl of cream of wheat hot, and she had a special treat with it, she said. It was bananas.

In the whole story of the world, bananas have never once been a special treat.

Then I headed off to Mrs. Windermere's, where I knew the coffee was percolating.

No matter how wet and cold you are, black coffee percolating will get you through it.

But I was pretty wet and cold by the time I got there. Wet and cold all the way through. And even with Mr. Loeffler's gray wool cap — which I only wore because Lil Spicer said I looked good in it, which you might remember — my ears were still about to fall off.

I guess you can imagine what Lucas would have said if he heard that, but now, he would have said it while he was smiling.

The coffee really was percolating at Mrs. Windermere's, and the kitchen was that kind of warm that goes right into you, like a blanket. I could hear Mrs. Windermere typing — probably Jane Eyre was falling in love with Mr. Rochester right there in her typewriter—and so I put away the groceries and took two cups down from the cupboard and poured the coffee and brought the cups into her study. I opened the door and set one down next to her—you could see the vibrations of her typewriter in her coffee—and I sat down and sipped at mine and was almost half done before she looked up at me.

"Jane Eyre is falling in love with Mr. Rochester," she said.

See?

"But I'm not quite sure how to show it on stage."

"Maybe," I said, "he should be over at a desk, drawing something."

"Drawing something?"

"And she comes up behind him and sees what he's drawing, and she thinks he's pretty cool."

"What happens next?"

"I don't know." I shrugged. "He doesn't have any idea what to say to her."

"Maybe he should let her draw something with him," Mrs. Windermere said.

"Maybe," I said.

Mrs. Windermere nodded then turned quickly to her typewriter and began smacking at the keys. Her hands flew high. Petrels in the winds.

I sipped at my coffee until I was finished with it. I got up and walked around the table in her study. It was still piled high with books. It will probably always be piled high with books. But the difference was, I could read them now. Not that I'd want to read these particular books, but I could have if I wanted to, and that makes all the difference. I'm not lying.

But I don't know who would want to read these. *Librettos of the Great Operas.* Snore. *Life of Verdi.* Snore snore. *Aku-Aku,* which sounds like someone sneezing. *History of the Old South Church, Boston.* Snore snore snore. Even percolated black coffee wouldn't keep you awake, if you were reading these.

I picked up *Aku-Aku* and looked at the book beneath it.

Aaron Copland's Autobiography: Manuscript Edition.

I read it again.

Aaron Copland's Autobiography: Manuscript Edition.

I picked it up. Mrs. Windermere was still typing.

I opened the book. Inside the front cover a sheet of music was pasted, handwritten. I couldn't read any of it. Maybe I should try that next.

Mrs. Windermere stopped typing. "What book is that?" she said.

"Aaron Copland's," I said. "The guy who writes music."

"You mean the guy who tries to write music," she said.

I looked at her.

"Skinny Delivery Boy, you are talking to a very old woman who doesn't think much good music has been written since Ludwig van Beethoven finished his Ninth Symphony." She turned back to her typing. Her hands rose high.

"So why have the book?" I said.

Mrs. Windermere's hands were still high. "My husband liked to collect quirky books. That one has a page of Copland's music written in his own hand. But neither he nor I ever read the thing, me because I never wanted to, him because . . . because he didn't have enough time." Her hands came down.

"Mrs. Windermere," I said.

"Don't make an old lady cry. What kind of ice cream did I order?"

"Cherry vanilla," I said.

She stood up. "Let's go try some."

"Mrs. Windermere," I said, "if you don't want the book much, I think I could use it."

She looked at me. "Do you like Copland?"

"I do, but it's not for me."

She peered sort of slanted at me. "You have something up your sleeve," she said.

I told her.

Mrs. Windermere smiled. Almost like my mother, which kind of surprised me. "The god of Creativity has folded his wings by your desk too," she said. She took the book, held it lightly to her lips, and kissed it. It wasn't weird. It was beautiful. Then she handed it back to me. "Nothing should ever sit and gather dust," she said, and we went into the kitchen and tried the cherry vanilla ice cream.

On the way home, I carried *Aaron Copland's Autobiography: Manuscript Edition* underneath Joe Pepitone's jacket so that nothing would happen to it. When I got to the library, I showed it to Lil and told her. But I didn't show it to Mr. Powell.

"Mr. Swieteck," said Mr. Powell, "I think I can accept having the petrels smile a little bit. But that is an out-and-out grin."

"I suppose so," I said.

He looked at me. "Rather like what you are doing right now," he said.

"I guess," I said.

Mr. Powell looked at Lil. "And you too, young lady," he said.

Lil started to laugh. She looked over at me and laughed harder. Me too.

Then Lil came up behind me to see what I was drawing. She put her hand on my arm and squeezed.

You know what that feels like?

"I think you two know something I don't know," said Mr. Powell.

Lil squeezed again.

* * *

On Monday, I went with James Russell to his house.

Mr. Russell was playing Aaron Copland's music on his stereo. I call that Fabulous.

Mrs. Russell made us both sit down with a glass of milk. "And I have a special treat for you," she said. I'm not lying. She really said that. I held my breath because of the last special treat at the Daughertys', but it didn't help, because when Mrs. Russell came back, she came back with a loaf of banana bread. Banana bread! And James said, "How about we have some jam with that?" and Mrs. Russell said, "Jam? Then you wouldn't be able to taste the bananas," and James said, "Ma, I hate bananas," and she said, "But I'm sure that Doug enjoys them," and I said, "I think I'm still full from lunch, so the milk's fine," and then Mrs. Russell picked up the plate with the banana bread on it, and you might not believe this, but she started to laugh and laugh and laugh, until Mr. Russell came out to the kitchen to see what was so funny and she showed him the banana bread and he said, "I hate bananas," and we all started to laugh until Mrs. Russell said, "I hate bananas too," and you can imagine us all laughing until we were crying and finally Mrs. Russell took the banana bread outside to break it up for the birds — "Let's hope *they* like bananas" — and then I showed Mr. Russell *Aaron Copland's Autobiography: Manuscript Edition,* and he stopped laughing.

Remember how I told you how big his hands are? How they could carry boulders?

He held *Aaron Copland's Autobiography: Manuscript Edition* like it was a half-cracked egg. "I've heard of this book," he whispered, "but I never thought..." He was talking like you would talk just before Mass. He opened the front page, looked at the sheet of music pasted in.

"It's in Aaron Copland's own handwriting," I said.

Mr. Russell stared at it, then he looked at me, smiling, and we went into the front room and he put the book on his music stand and he played the music from the page with his silver flute, sweetly and beautifully.

Fabulous.

When he finished, he looked at me and said, "Where did you find this?"

I told him. He shook his head. "I can hardly believe it," he said.

"Mr. Russell," I said, "I have an idea."

Here are the stats for the rest of that week:

> *Number of times I wanted to tell someone: A hundred
>   and fifty thousand.*
> *Number of people I told: Four. Lil Spicer, my mother, my
>   brothers.*
> *Number of times I walked by the library, hoping that
>   Mr. Powell might be in: Twelve.*

Number of minutes off the record for finishing the
    Saturday deliveries for Spicer's Deli: Seventeen.
    (Mr. Loeffler didn't have any chores to do, so that
    helped.)
Number of minutes it took me to get to The Dump from
    Spicer's Deli and then back to the library: Twelve.
    Probably a record.
Number of seconds it took between coming to the library
    and Mrs. Merriam telling me not to run up the
    stairs: Less than one.
Amount of time it took Mr. Powell to understand what I
    had: I think he's still working on it.

We laid the Large-Billed Puffins back in their place in Audubon's *Birds of America*. It became a little more whole than it had been before.

Do you know how that feels?

Do you think the Forked-Tailed Petrels were dancing now?

Not much more than Mr. Powell, who first danced around the room with me and then with Lil, and then we all went downstairs to tell Mrs. Merriam, and he took her hands and tried to dance with her but she wouldn't have any of it, even though I think she was smiling just a little the whole time she was shushing him away.

* * *

That night at supper, Lucas said he wanted to go to the library before it closed to see the puffins.

"Don't expect *me* to carry you up those stairs," said Ernie Eco, who was eating with us — again.

"We don't," said Christopher.

Ernie Eco looked up at him from his plate.

Christopher stared back.

Ernie Eco looked down.

"Once we get inside, there's an elevator," I said.

Ernie Eco worked on his string beans.

After supper, Christopher and I went with Lucas to the library. The days were finally starting to get longer, but it was still dark, and the first stars had been out for a while. Lucas looked up toward them as we went, squinting, blinking, trying to see.

We carried the wheelchair up the six steps between the two of us, and it wasn't light. Then we lifted it over the door frame and onto the marble floor of the library, where the wheels ran quiet and smooth. Mrs. Merriam looked up to see who had come in so late, and when she saw Lucas, she walked out from behind the desk and took off her looped glasses — this didn't happen very often — and she said to Lucas, "Welcome home." I'm not lying. She said, "Welcome home." Like she was bringing him into her own kitchen or something.

Lucas turned his face toward her and blinked. "Thanks," he said.

"When did you get back?" she said. He told her. "Where were you stationed?" Told her. "Were you near Saigon at all?" Nodded. "When?" Lucas tried to remember.

Then she asked him, "While you were there, did you ever hear of a Lieutenant Merriam? Lieutenant Leonard Merriam?"

Lucas thought, then shook his head. "I never did."

She leaned down toward him and put her hand on his chair. "He was stationed near Saigon. You might have heard of him."

Lucas shook his head again. "I'm sorry."

Mrs. Merriam stood up again. She twisted her hands together. "I didn't think you would have," she said. "I never really did."

"There's thousands of guys there," Lucas said.

"I know. But your mother must be glad you're home."

"Thanks," said Lucas.

I told Mrs. Merriam that we were going up to see the book, and she went to the bottom of the stairs to turn the lights on, and she watched as we went to the elevator. Lucas didn't exactly like the steel gate that we had to draw across. And he really didn't like the way the elevator rattled around on its way up. And he really, really didn't like the sound of the pulleys straining themselves. And of course, at the top, the elevator stopped a couple of inches below the floor, and we had to pull Lucas's chair over the lip.

So he was sweating — and even shaky — when we got into the room with the petrels and the puffins and everyone else. But he wheeled himself over to the display case and looked in. Mr. Powell had left the book open to the Large-Billed Puffins, and Lucas stared down at them for a long time, trying to make them out.

"There's two of them," he said. "Right?"

He looked down again. And after a while he said, "Lieutenant Leonard Merriam is MIA."

"How do you know he's missing?" said Christopher.

"I know," he said. Lucas looked at the puffins. He leaned so close that his face was almost touching the glass. "Not everyone gets to see who they want to see again. I guess I'm lucky."

Mrs. Merriam was waiting for us at the bottom of the stairs. She turned the lights out when we got down. She held the door open for us. And then — I watched through the window — she went back to her desk, sat, put on her glasses, and looked at something a long way out from the library.

CHAPTER EIGHT

The Brown Pelican
Plate CCLI

YOU REMEMBER how I said that when things start to go pretty good, something usually happens to turn everything bad?

I was starting to think maybe I was wrong.

Maybe things don't always turn bad.

What a chump I am.

One Saturday in the middle of March, I figured out that my baseball—and you know which one I mean, my baseball that I had been keeping in the bottom drawer of the dresser underneath my socks and sweatshirt since I'd started wearing Joe Pepitone's jacket—my baseball was gone.

Then on Monday morning, I found out that Joe Pepitone's jacket was gone too.

When I asked my mother if she knew where my jacket was, she put her hands on the back of a kitchen chair and held on hard.

"Could you have left it at school?" she said.

"I wore it for the Saturday deliveries."

"At the library?"

I shook my head.

"On the stairs?"

"No."

She held on tighter to the chair.

I didn't ask any more questions.

Remember how I said something usually happens to turn everything bad? Remember how I said that?

My jacket from Joe Pepitone.

Then one day in late March, one of those days when the sun is sort of teasing you with the idea that maybe spring isn't so far away after all, the Tools 'n' More Hardware Store was robbed again.

Guess who the police came to question?

Christopher said he hadn't been anywhere near the Tools 'n' More Hardware Store.

Lucas and I both said he hadn't been anywhere near the Tools 'n' More Hardware Store.

One of the policemen said, "Can we see your bike, son?"

"Sure," said Christopher.

We all went outside, my mother and me and Lucas and Christopher and the policemen. Christopher wheeled his Sting-Ray up.

"You're missing a pedal," said the policeman.

"I lost it a few days ago," said Christopher.

"Where did you lose it?"

"If I knew that," said Christopher, "then it wouldn't be lost anymore."

"Chris," said Lucas, low and steady.

"You wouldn't have lost it anywhere near the hardware store?"

"No, I wouldn't have lost it anywhere near the hardware store because I haven't been anywhere near the hardware store since I don't even know when."

The policeman took a bicycle pedal out of his pocket. He slid it onto the rod on Christopher's bike. It slid on easily. "I found this over at Tools 'n' More," said the policeman, looking up at my mother. "Around the back." Then he turned to Christopher. "Looks like a match to me."

It did. We could all see it was the right pedal.

Christopher went with the policemen.

I went to the Ballard Paper Mill to find my father.

I didn't want to run into Mr. Ballard. Not right now. So I went out onto the floor, looking for my father, but no one seemed to know where he was. He wasn't at his station, where he was supposed to be, and he wasn't packing, and he wasn't loading trucks. Finally, one of the loaders said I should try outside past the loading dock. Maybe he was there. And he was. Taking a break, I guess. Smoking a cigarette with Ernie Eco.

I told him about Christopher.

And the funny thing was, my father looked straight at Ernie Eco. It was the first thing he did. Look straight at him.

Ernie Eco shrugged.

My father threw his cigarette away and we went in and across the floor. "Swieteck," someone called, but my father never even let on that he heard. We went across the floor and out the front door and into his pickup and on into Marysville.

It took two hours to get Christopher out on bail. And in that time, he was fingerprinted, and his picture taken for police records, and a policeman tried to get him to confess, but he kept saying he didn't have anything to confess and he didn't know anything about the hardware store and no, he didn't have any idea who did. And when he wouldn't confess they put him into a cell for the rest of the two hours and when he came out he smelled like throw-up.

A sergeant said there would be a hearing—they'd let us know when. And in the meantime—he looked hard at Christopher—in the meantime, if Christopher happened to remember what went on that night and where all the stuff was, maybe things would go a whole lot easier for him.

Christopher didn't say anything. We went out into the pickup. My father got in the front, and I got in the front, and Christopher got in the back.

Maybe because he smelled like throw-up.

We drove home slowly. But word got around Marysville fast.

Things at Washington Irving Junior High School did not go well the next day. Every time someone looked at me, the look said *I know.*

In geography, I didn't draw the Chapter Review Map of Northern Africa, because I didn't read the chapter on Northern Africa. In world history, I told Mr. McElroy, "Who really cares about the creation stories of the aboriginal tribes of eastern Australia?" In English, we were still on the Introduction to Poetry Unit, and I'm not lying, if I ever meet Percy Bysshe Shelley walking down the streets of Marysville, I'm going to punch him right in the face. I cut Advanced Algebra. Coach Reed can chart his own Presidential Physical Fitness charts. And in Mr. Ferris's class, I wasn't so all-fired excited that the command ship and the lunar module of Apollo 9 had separated and flown a hundred miles apart and then come back together, just like they would for the real moon shot, which was now really going to happen, said Mr. Ferris. He put his hand on Clarence's head. It was the first time astronauts had transferred from one space vehicle to another while in space, he said.

Terrific.

The next morning, Principal Peattie was waiting for me when I got to school. He told me to come by his office after Mr. Barber's class—Mr. McElroy already knew I'd be late for world history. And I'd better not try to get out of this, he said.

Terrific.

Do you know what it feels like, reviewing North Africa's geography, which you still haven't read about, while waiting to go to the principal's office, which you'd better not try getting out of?

You wish there was room on the moon shot.

I waited for my half hour and when I finally got into Principal Peattie's office, he looked like he wished there was room on the moon shot too. For me.

"So," he said, "you're up to your old tricks."

Lucas—the old Lucas—might have pointed out that cutting Mrs. Verne's class was a new trick, but I still get it. I didn't say anything.

"First PE, then Algebra."

"Advanced Algebra," I said.

"Not anymore," he said. "Principal Peattie does not give a student who lacks the discipline to go to assigned classes the privilege of attending advanced classes."

Did you know that the Brown Pelican's beak is about as long as its whole body? It's huge. It looks like it could open wide and fit in a whole lot. Like a principal.

"Do you understand that all actions have consequences? That's what Principal Peattie is trying to teach you here," said Principal Peattie.

The pelican is standing mostly on one leg. The other is lying like it doesn't care on the branch, like the pelican doesn't believe that actions have consequences — which he doesn't.

"You are assigned three days of After School Detention," said Principal Peattie. "Starting this afternoon. Principal Peattie will be calling your home to explain why you'll be late."

The Brown Pelican, the way he looks out at you, that eye, he knows he's...

"Are you listening to Principal Peattie?"

...noble.

Principal Peattie stood up.

"Yes," I said. "I'm listening."

"Do you want to explain to Principal Peattie why you cut Mrs. Verne's class?"

I didn't say anything.

"Douglas, is it because of your brother?"

If you wanted to draw the Brown Pelican, I'm not lying, it wouldn't be easy. There's something like nine or ten rows of feathers. Maybe eleven. Maybe twelve.

And they're all shaped differently, and they all layer over each other. And the composition is fabulous. He's standing on this big old branch that's starting to decay, but it's still putting out leaves. The Brown Pelican is right in the middle of the picture, balancing on this one leg, and it doesn't seem like a body with so much beak in the front could be balanced, but it is. It looks like it should tip forward. All movement, you might remember, relies on that kind of tension. But he wasn't moving. He was balanced just right. It would take a while to figure out how Audubon did that.

Principal Peattie sat back down. "If you're not even going to look at Principal Peattie, he can't help you," he said.

I looked at him.

"My brother didn't do anything," I said.

He sighed, like it was him that was in some sort of pain. "Principal Peattie has spoken with the police about this," he said. "Your brother stole merchandise from the Tools 'n' More Hardware store. He almost certainly was the one who robbed the store last fall as well. He probably is also the one who robbed Spicer's Deli last fall."

"You don't know anything," I said.

"The sooner you face the facts —"

"Here's a fact," I said. I might have been yelling, but I'm not sure. "That bird belongs back in the book it was stolen from."

Principal Peattie looked sort of startled. He turned around to the Brown Pelican, and then he looked back at me. "That plate was a gift from the Education Committee when Principal Peattie assumed the responsibilities of being the principal of this school," he said. "It was not stolen. And Douglas, it has nothing at all to do with the problem you and Principal Peattie are talking about."

"I have an idea," I said.

Principal Peattie sighed again.

"When the police figure out who the thief really is, and it isn't my brother, then you have to give the bird back to the library."

Principal Peattie considered this for a long time. A long time. Then he nodded, like he'd decided something, and stood. "All right," he said. "All right. Principal Peattie will take a chance. He will do that. Meanwhile, you, Douglas, have to promise to attend all of your classes without missing a single one."

"And I get to stay in Advanced Algebra."

He considered this, then nodded again. "But you still have three days of After School Detention," he said.

I held my hand out.

He held his hand out.

We shook.

Over us both, the noble Brown Pelican watched, keeping his balance like it was no trouble at all.

* * *

I served After School Detention with Miss Cowper. She gave me three more poems by stupid Percy Bysshe Shelley that she was sure I would enjoy. "'Two vast and trunkless legs of stone stand in the desert,'" she said. "'Near them, on the sand...'"

I really will punch him right in the face.

It was late in the afternoon when I finally got out of school on the third day of detention, and even though it was a pretty nice spring day still, I was a whole lot colder than I wanted to be because, if you remember, I didn't have Joe Pepitone's jacket anymore. Which is why, I think, Mr. Ballard stopped when he saw me while driving past. He leaned across the seat and rolled down his window. "Hey! My partner!" he called.

I waved.

"Get in," he said. "I'll drive you home—unless you have time for a few horseshoes."

I got in. I looked out the window. We drove a few blocks.

"Horseshoes always help me think things out," Mr. Ballard said.

Another block. The Dump came in sight.

"I guess I have time," I said.

Mr. Ballard turned toward the paper mill.

* * *

Mr. Ballard was keeping the horseshoes in his office until it got warmer. So we went in together and he got them from behind the door — you should have seen the orchids blooming with all that sunlight coming in — and we went down to the horseshoe pits. The ground was still pretty soggy from the winter, and the sand around the stakes was all wet through. "It'll be a practice round," said Mr. Ballard.

I threw the first shoe. Way over.

He threw the next one. It clanged the post and bounced off.

I threw the next shoe. Way over.

He threw the next one. A leaner.

And that's pretty much how it went, until it got too cold and we went back to the mill.

Here are the stats for that practice round:

Shoes way over: About fifty for me. Two for Mr. Ballard.
Shoes thrown short: None for me. Four for Mr. Ballard.
One-pointers: Three for me. About fifty for Mr. Ballard.
Leaners: None for me. Four for Mr. Ballard, which he
   said was unusual.
Ringers: None for me, which he said was unusual.
   Twenty-three for him, which wasn't unusual.

"Did you have a good game?" said Mrs. Stenson when we brought the horseshoes back up.

"It was a practice round," Mr. Ballard said.

He went into his office and set the horseshoes behind his door. Then he came back out. I was standing by the window. All that sunshine.

Mr. Ballard stood next to me. He picked up an orchid, put it back, and chose another that was in fuller bloom. It was all purple and white and yellow, like some artist had designed an impossible bloom without worrying about composition, like he went wild and let it all go. "This is for your mother," he said, and handed it to me.

And suddenly, I felt like I was going to cry. Right there in the middle of the office of the president of Ballard Paper Mill. Just start bawling like I was four years old or something. Holding this orchid for my mother.

"It's all right," said Mr. Ballard. "Things will work out." I looked up at him. "Things always do."

I didn't want to tell him that he was wrong. I had seen the Black-Backed Gull. I didn't want him to start crying too.

"I'll drive you home," he said. "Give me a minute." He went back into his office. Mrs. Stenson smiled at me, which was probably her trying not to laugh, me standing there about to cry, holding a flower. Then Mr. Ballard came back out of his office. He handed me a jacket. "This doesn't fit me anymore," he said. "I'd be glad to have someone use it."

I took it. You won't believe what kind of jacket it was.

And no, it wasn't a Yankee jacket.

Even though a Yankee jacket would have been terrific.

It was a flight jacket. I'm not lying. A flight jacket. Dark leather. Lined on the inside with this soft flannel stuff. Deep pockets. Turned-up collar. A flight jacket. Like you'd wear if you were an astronaut on vacation walking around Marysville before you were going to blast off to the moon.

"Try it on," he said.

I did.

"It's a little big," said Mrs. Stenson.

"It's perfect," said Mr. Ballard, and he looked at me with eyes like the Brown Pelican's.

I drove home with him, wearing the flight jacket, carrying the orchid.

I don't think I need to tell you what my mother did when she saw that orchid.

But I do need to tell you what Lucas said when I told him I had a new flight jacket: "Would it fit me?"

"Not in a million years," I said.

He started to laugh. "I guess you're right," he said, and laughed some more.

You know how good it was to hear Lucas laugh?

It was even better than wearing this flight jacket, which—unless Joe Pepitone's jacket turns up—is the only thing I own that hasn't belonged to some other Swieteck before me.

On Saturday morning, Mrs. Mason said that my flight jacket looked "snazzy" and she wondered if someone who wore such a snazzy jacket would still like a chocolate doughnut or if he was too grown up for that. I said I would love a chocolate doughnut, and she gave me a glass of cold milk so I could dunk it.

Mr. Loeffler said my new flight jacket reminded him of something, and he went up into his attic so he could find it while I brought the groceries in. I waited, and when he came back, he was wearing—I'm not lying—a flight jacket! Its brown leather was all creased and soft, and it had a yellow woolly collar and yellow woolly stuff at the ends of the sleeves. "Mr. Loeffler," I said, "that's terrific!"

"Lieutenant Loeffler," he said, and pulled the jacket trim around him. "Not bad. Not bad at all after thirty-five years."

He was right. It wasn't bad at all. So I brought my feet together and my hand up, and I saluted him. Just kidding around. But you know what? He got this serious look on his face, like we weren't just kidding around in his kitchen. And he snapped his legs together and got straighter than I had ever seen him, and he whipped his arm up, and saluted back. His hands weren't shaking. Not at all. And it sort of startled me — not the salute, but because of his eyes.

I think you can probably guess what they looked like.

Ben, Polly, Joel, Davie, and Phronsie loved the flight jacket. They all wanted to try it on, and I let them, even though Joel almost disappeared in it, and Davie and Phronsie could both have worn it together and still had plenty of room.

Mrs. Windermere said my flight jacket made me look like Errol Flynn.

"Who?" I said.

"Errol Flynn. The actor. At least, he thinks it's acting."

I shook my head.

"Never mind," she said. "I've been trying to write Mr. Rochester's dialogue all day, and every time he speaks, he sounds like Errol Flynn. It's driving me crazy." She looked at the packages of groceries I was putting away. "What kind of ice cream did I order?" she said.

"Pistachio," I said.

"Pistachio?"

I took it out of the grocery bag and showed her.

"I hate pistachio," she said. "I would never have ordered pistachio. It's . . . green."

"That's what Mr. Spicer packed."

Mrs. Windermere raised an eyebrow. "Skinny Delivery Boy, Mr. Spicer is not infallible."

I shrugged.

She looked at the pistachio ice cream. "Go get two spoons," she said. "And take off that jacket. I don't want to write with Errol Flynn and I don't want to eat ice cream with him either. Even if it is only pistachio."

When I got to the library that afternoon, Mr. Powell and Lil were already upstairs, and Lil had a stack of books that, she said, she got out for both of us because we were supposed to be working on a project about New Zealand for Mr. Barber and did I remember that we were partners and the project was due in two weeks?

I'm not a chump. I said I remembered.

Then Mr. Powell said I looked great in my flight jacket.

Lil said I looked great too, only the way she said it made it sound a whole lot better than the way Mr. Powell said it.

She smiled and opened up one of the books on New Zealand. You know how pretty someone can be when she opens up a book? Especially if she has brown hair the color of the pelican's feathers?

"Mr. Swieteck," said Mr. Powell, and we got to work.

* * *

"Balance can be achieved in two different kinds of conditions," said Mr. Powell. "Stable and unstable."

"Stable and unstable," I said.

"Let's say that you were going to draw Lil sitting by that table, working on the project that you better get going on as soon as we're done here. Let's say that we draw the table with its legs on the floor, and Lil with her feet on the floor, and maybe the drawing will be wider than it is high so we can show the whole table. That painting would be stable. Why?"

"Because nothing would look like it could fall over," I said.

"Exactly. A stable composition is fixed firmly to the ground."

"So in an unstable composition, I could have Lil floating away to New Zealand."

Lil smirked at me.

"Yes," said Mr. Powell. "What else?"

"Maybe the table could be slanted and the right legs up in the air."

"In such a painting, do you see how much more tension there would be?" said Mr. Powell. "You don't know where anything is headed."

"The Brown Pelican is stable," I said.

And after a moment, Mr. Powell said, "Yes, he is."

He is, you know. It might look like he isn't, standing mostly on this one leg on a curved branch that looks pretty rotten. But he is. He wouldn't move if a hurricane blew in. That's what makes him so noble.

I drew the Forked-Tailed Petrels again, from scratch, because that's what Mr. Powell said I needed to do. They weren't smiling. The water was going every which way beneath them, and the wind was a storm blowing so bad, they could hardly control their wings.

"You sure can't tell where they're headed," said Mr. Powell.

And he was right.

Afterward I got to work on the New Zealand project — alone, since Lil left because she had a stomachache. But she made sure to leave all the books with bookmarks at the right places. She could hardly wait to see what I came up with, she said from the stairs.

Terrific.

The first of April was a gray and half-rainy day that still thought it was early March. After school, Lil and I walked over to the Ballard Paper Mill to bring Mr. Ballard a note from my mother about the orchid and to maybe throw a few horseshoes. You know how good a flight jacket feels on a cold day like this? You know how good it felt walking with Lil to throw horseshoes, even though it was half rainy? Even though everyone in stupid Marysville thought Christopher was...

I went into Mr. Ballard's office and he was talking

with Mrs. Stenson and when he saw us he called, "My partner!" and I introduced him to Lil and they shook hands. I gave him my mother's note and he said thanks and he hoped that my mother liked the orchid. I told him that she turned it every morning in the sun so that it would grow evenly, and when she watered it, it was like she was feeding a baby. He laughed and asked if we wanted to throw some horseshoes, and Lil said we did, and I got the shoes from behind the door, and by the time I turned around Lil was picking out an orchid for herself and the sun had come out suddenly and was throwing everything it could through that window and it was all landing on Lil, and she was smiling and brushing her hair back the way she does and being kind of embarrassed because Mr. Ballard was giving her this orchid that was almost as beautiful as she was, a pale purple one with white just barely on its edges.

She looked at me and smiled, holding the orchid. "What do you think?" she said.

"Beautiful," I said.

We left the orchid and went out of the office and across the mill floor. The sun was still shining when we opened the door, and some of the people on the floor gasped when they saw the light pouring through. "Leave it open," someone said, and we did.

We went outside, and there, standing against the wall, I guess on another break, were my father and Ernie Eco.

They were smoking and laughing like something was really, really funny. The funniest thing in the whole world.

And Ernie Eco? Ernie Eco was wearing...

My father said, "What are you doing here?" I didn't even look at him.

Ernie Eco was wearing my Yankee jacket from Joe Pepitone.

Lil and I went back inside. We walked across the floor. I left the horseshoes outside Mr. Ballard's office door. Lil took my hand.

"You better go in and get your orchid," I said.

"I don't..."

"Go ahead," I said.

She waited for a bit, then she bent down to pick up the horseshoes and went on inside.

I was gone before she came out.

I didn't want her to see me.

I ran. Hard. Really hard. Until I hurt so bad that it didn't matter that the world was so unstable. And it didn't even matter that maybe I was wrong: when the hurricane blew in, it would throw the Brown Pelican as far as it wanted to.

Ernie Eco didn't come to supper that night.

My mother asked if I'd seen Mr. Ballard and given him the note. I said yes. The orchid was in the middle of the table, and every so often she would reach across and turn it so that she could look at it from a different angle, like she was studying its balance.

I didn't say much the whole meal. Neither did my father.

At dessert, Lucas said he thought it was about time he should be looking for work. Christopher said he could help him get around if he could cut school, and my mother slapped at him, and Christopher said he should get credit for trying and Lucas told him he'd get by and Christopher wasn't allowed to miss a day, not a single day, and Christopher said, "How come?" and Lucas got real quiet and said, almost whispered, "Because you're not going to Vietnam, you're going to college," and my father said there wasn't any way in the whole world he was going to pay for that and Lucas said that was why he was getting a job and my father said he wasn't going to get a job because what could he do?

Which pretty much ended dessert.

There's a kind of angry quiet that can lie down over a house. Maybe there are some houses, like the Daughertys', that have never known it — that house probably hasn't ever had a quiet day. But in The Dump, Angry Quiet was an old friend, and he moved in again. No one talked because we all wanted to scream.

Lucas started going out every morning to look for work. You know how many people in stupid Marysville want to hire someone who doesn't have legs?

Zero.

He went out in that stupid wheelchair every day the first week of April. Every day. He wheeled himself up and down every street in Marysville that had some-place where someone might get work. You know how hard it is to go down a stupid curb in a wheelchair? You know how hard it is to get back up on the other side before a light turns red again? You know how many stores even have doors that Lucas could figure out how to open while sitting in a wheelchair?

Here's what they told Lucas:

I don't think you could do this job from a wheelchair.
Sorry, but I couldn't put up with a contraption like
*   that rattling around here all day.*
It'd be too hard on you, son.
The aisles are too small for your wheelchair. You'd
*   never manage.*
Frankly, we don't want our customers feeling sorry
*   about something when they walk in. People who*
*   know they're going to feel sorry don't come back*
*   to the store.*

And more like that.

But Lucas went out every day. I guess being in a wheelchair can be pretty unstable. But Lucas isn't.

* * *

Do you know what it feels like to walk into a house where everything is going along just fine when back at your own house Lucas is going out every day for nothing and Ernie Eco is wearing your jacket?

That's what it was like the next Wednesday night when I went to the Daughertys' on short notice again and Mrs. Daugherty said, "Thanks for coming, Doug," and told me there were marshmallow brownies for me after the kids were in bed but they had already had theirs and they didn't need any more sugar — which I could tell because Phronsie and Davie had me by the legs and Joel was trying to push me over and Polly and Ben were waiting to see if I was going to fall over so they could pounce.

"Don't hurt him," Mrs. Daugherty said, and Mr. Daugherty said I was big enough to take it and he laughed and that was the cue I guess for Ben and Polly because I was down on the floor before Mr. and Mrs. Daugherty were out the door, and they were tickling me until I agreed to play Bloody, Bloody Murderer and they all went screaming to hide. When I found Davie, I tagged him and he became a Bloody, Bloody Murderer too, and then we went into the kitchen and found Polly and she became a Bloody, Bloody Murderer too, and then we went . . . well, I guess you can figure out the rules. And after that we all had some cold milk and I let them have just a tiny piece of marshmallow brownie and then we started in on the reading, which as you might remember takes a while.

Phronsie had a new book, and I don't care what anyone says: elephants don't wear clothes.

Davie made me read about this kid who had a name like Tick Tock Tiddley Wink Tembe something that I could never read right and Joel just about died laughing when I tried and you couldn't do it either.

Joel had a book about Ben that he thought was great because he had a brother Ben and this Ben could figure out how to jump to the top of the castle and could I guess how he did it? "You can't jump to the top of a castle," I said, and Joel started to laugh and laugh and laugh because you can too, you can too, so go ahead and read it!

Polly had this book about a house in a forest where Laura lives with Pa and Ma and her sisters. You'd be surprised how good this was, especially considering that nothing happens.

And Ben had this book about a pig that went to Florida and it turned out to be funnier than it sounds, which was good because there are a whole lot of books with this pig — could I believe it? — and Ben wanted to read every single one.

Terrific.

So by the time the pig got on his way and all the kids got to bed, it was probably later than the Daughertys would have wanted it to be but it usually was, and I was sitting in the upstairs hall listening to everything settle into that kind of sweet and beautiful breathing. Mrs. Verne had given us more quadratic equations than she should have for Advanced Algebra, and then four problems about two men who were driving in different directions at different speeds for different amounts of time and who cares how far apart they could get before one of them ran out of gas, and then the breathing wasn't sweet and beautiful anymore.

It was wheezing. From Joel's room. Breathing like the breather couldn't get enough air. I stood up. Wheezing hard and kind of desperate. I went in. Turned on the light. Joel was looking at me, and his eyes...

Oh God, I had seen the Black-Backed Gull.

I run to his bed and he tries to breathe. He can hardly get anything in. His eyes get bigger. He tries drawing more air in. Hardly anything.

I run into the hall. I call home. Christopher answers. I tell him to get over here now and hang up. I run in to Joel. Hardly anything. Run to Ben's room and tell him I have to take Joel to Dr. Bottom's house and he should stay awake with the others until Christopher comes. "Is it his asthma?" he says. "I don't know," I say. I run in to Joel. He is standing by the bed with his back arched, dragging in air, rubbing at his chest, starting to cry. Sweaty. Ben runs in. "Where's your inhaler? Joel, where's your inhaler?" Joel looks at me like he thinks I can do something. Ben starts tearing the bed apart, and then he runs to the nightstand and pulls out the drawer and empties it on the bed. "I can't find it," he yells. "Joel, where is your inhaler?" Polly comes and stands by the door. She looks at Joel. "Is he going to die?" she says.

I wrap him in a blanket. I carry him downstairs and out the door. Joel puts his arms around me, tight, like he is fighting a bloody, bloody murderer. Start to run.

Do you know what it feels like running in the night, holding this kid who's crying but he can't cry because he can't breathe, and you're running and running and you don't know if it's your sweat or his and he's staring at you afraid and believing in you but you're not believing in you and if the Bottoms aren't home what are you going to do then?

Running in the night running in the night running in the night running.

Their lights are on. I kick at the door as hard as I can. Again. Again. Again. Joel drags another breath, weaker now. Again.

The door opens. Dr. Bottom, I hope. One look at us, and he reaches out and he takes Joel. "Otis, Otis, get the shower running. Hot as you can get it. Now!" Carries Joel into the living room and looks at me and points to another room where he wants me to get something and then sees that I probably can't figure out what he wants and he tells me to hold Joel and he runs and then he comes back with this thing and he hollers, "Here!" and he holds it out and Joel grabs it and holds it to his mouth and pumps.

And pumps.

And pumps.

And pumps.

And I can hear the air dragging in but it's less draggy.

And Joel — who was starting to turn a color that no human being should turn but I didn't want to tell you about that until you knew it was going to be all right — Joel looks at me and he smiles.

Keeps pumping.

Breathing.

Breathing.

Sweet, beautiful breathing.

Beautifully.

Dr. Bottom carries him to the stairs. Then he looks back at me. "I'm going to bring him up into the steam for a bit," he says. He looks down at Joel, breathing, watching me. "Do you know what he's telling you?"

I shook my head.

Dr. Bottom smiled. "I think you do."

I did.

It's the same thing that Mr. and Mrs. Daugherty told me when they got to Dr. Bottom's house and saw Joel asleep on the couch, covered with two afghans and being watched over by Dr. Bottom and Otis and me.

And by the way, Otis made the coffee for us that night, and for the record, it was a whole lot stronger than Mrs. Windermere's. I guess he was used to making coffee that helps people stay awake.

Maybe he's a good guy too.

Mrs. Daugherty stayed the night at Dr. Bottom's house so she would be there when Joel woke up. Mr. Daugherty drove me home, then he went back for Christopher and drove him home. When Christopher came up into our bedroom, I was still awake and sitting on his bed. "So how did it go?" I said.

This is what he told me:

"Piece of cake."

"Really?

"Really."

"They didn't..."

"Hey, I'm not some chump babysitter. I told them all to go to bed, and they did. That's it. Get off my bed and go to sleep."

"Shut up or I'm coming over there and kick you both to death."

You can guess who said that.

I went by the Daughertys' house the next morning. Joel was great. And here's what Mrs. Daugherty told me: When they got home, they saw Ben and Polly holding

Christopher down on the floor, and Davie and Phronsie were beating him around the head with one hand and holding a marshmallow brownie with the other, and Christopher was begging for mercy, and when he saw the Daughertys he picked up Davie and Phronsie — who were still beating at him but not letting go of their marshmallow brownies — and he told Mr. and Mrs. Daugherty where Joel was, and they got into the car right away and hadn't even thought about telling the children to go to bed.

Piece of cake.

After school, Mr. Daugherty was waiting with his patrol car. When he saw me, he waved, told me to come over. He opened the side door and I got in, and he said he was going to drive me home to thank me, and he put the siren on, and off we went.

And here's what Mr. Daugherty told me: The night before, when he got back to the house to pick up Christopher after he'd brought me home, my brother was in a heap of little Daughertys, all asleep on top of him, and he was asleep too, and still holding the book about elephants who wear clothes.

I'm not lying. That's what Mr. Daugherty told me.

Don't tell my brother I know this.

Don't tell him that I know he's not a chump babysitter.

And don't tell him that I think he may be what the Brown Pelican is.

CHAPTER NINE

The Great Esquimaux Curlew
Plate CCXXXVII

IT TOOK A WHILE, but by the first Saturday of May, spring finally decided to stick around. Mr. Loeffler said it was the latest spring he'd ever seen, but that probably meant it would be the warmest, and he was right. I didn't even need my flight jacket anymore, which didn't mean that I stopped wearing it.

By that first Saturday, everything had jumped from brown to green, and if you stood in front of the Marysville Free Public Library and looked at the maples up and down the street, you could watch their gold leaves unfurl like little flags, waving for all they were worth — which, after a long winter, was a lot. I pulled the Saturday deliveries past people dragging last year's leaves from under their bushes, cutting back hedges, digging up gardens by the curbs, and raking, raking, raking like the Marysville Garden Inspector was going to stop by in the afternoon. It was that kind of a day.

Back at Spicer's Deli, I told Lil that everything looked as green as New Zealand, and she said, "How would you know?" which I think meant that I hadn't exactly done half of the work for Mr. Barber's New Zealand project that we handed in together.

But I'm no chump.

"I'll buy you a Coke and show you how green it is," I said.

"Does that mean I'm supposed to go get Cokes for the two of us?"

I shook my head. I took two quarters out of my pocket and laid them on the deli counter. Lil chinged open the register and slid them into the drawer, and I went over to the refrigerator in back and got two bottles of Coke, took their caps off, and brought them up front. There was froth at the tops of the bottles, and Lil could hardly keep from giggling when she took her first sip.

"It always goes up my nose," she said.

She was beautiful.

She walked with me to Mrs. Windermere's, and I'm not lying, everything was even greener than it had been in town when I was making deliveries earlier that morning. By a lot. The maples, the oaks, the grass, the ferns coming up beside the road, the fields. Especially the fields, which even smelled green.

"You were right," said Lil.

She took my hand, and we walked up to Mrs. Windermere's. Slowly.

It was still too short.

At the house, there was a car I hadn't seen before, about a block and a half long. It was so long that it didn't fit in the turnaround. Half of it was on the grass, gleaming everywhere.

We went to the back and I unlocked the door with the so-secret key and Lil and I brought the groceries in and put them all away and we started out because we had the whole slow walk back to look forward to and then Mrs. Windermere came in with Mr. I-Own-the-Gleaming-Car next to her.

"Skinny Delivery Boy," she said.

"Mrs. Windermere," I said, "do you think that maybe you could call me something else?"

"No. Is everything put away already?"

"Yup. We were just going." I reached for Lil's hand.

"And this is . . ."

"Lillian Spicer," said Lil.

"It's nice to meet you, Lillian."

"Thank you," said Lil. "It's very nice to meet you."

She was always so polite. Did I tell you that she has green eyes? Did I tell you that she's beautiful?

"So is Lillian your girlfriend?" said Mrs. Windermere.

Everything stopped.

Everything.

"Skinny Delivery Boy, you know I never beat around the bush. Yes or no?"

I looked at Lil. She looked at me. She wasn't planning to be helpful with this. I looked back at Mrs. Windermere.

"Yes," I said.

I looked back at Lil. Smiling.

"Mrs. Windermere," said Mr. I-Own-the-Gleaming-Car.

"And this," said Mrs. Windermere, "is Mr. Gregory, who is supposed to be producing my play at the end of the month but who is not making much headway."

"Who is making the best headway any producer could possibly make with a writer who is—" started Mr. Gregory.

"Mr. Gregory likes strawberry ice cream," said Mrs. Windermere.

"I do not like strawberry ice cream," said Mr. Gregory.

"Nonsense," said Mrs. Windermere. "Everybody likes strawberry ice cream. What kind did I order?"

"Raspberry sherbet," said Lil.

"Oh dear," said Mrs. Windermere. She shook her head. "That's too bad."

"Raspberry sherbet?" said Mr. Gregory.

We all sat down to small bowls of raspberry sherbet, except for Mr. Gregory, who sat down to a bowl of raspberry sherbet about as big as New Zealand because he hadn't had raspberry sherbet since he was a boy and he thought he should make up for lost time. I think he might be a good guy. At least, he looked like he might be a good guy. You can't look like Mr. I-Own-the-Gleaming-Car when you're eating a huge bowl of raspberry sherbet in someone's kitchen.

"So are all the actors ready for the play?" said Lil.

"That's the problem," said Mrs. Windermere. "Mr. Gregory hasn't cast them all yet."

"You have no idea how difficult it is to find actors for as many parts as we need played for this script," said Mr. Gregory. "If only a certain writer had been willing to—"

"A certain writer won't," said Mrs. Windermere. "Who do you still need?"

"Helen Burns, to start with," said Mr. Gregory.

"Helen Burns," said Mrs. Windermere slowly.

"To start with," said Mr. Gregory.

Mrs. Windermere looked at Lil. "There she is right there. Skinny Delivery Boy's girlfriend."

Mr. Gregory looked at Lil.

"I'm not an actor," said Lil.

"No, you would be an actress," said Mrs. Windermere. "And Lillian, every young girl, once she steps upon a Broadway stage, enjoys the thrill of being an actress."

"Not me," said Lil.

"The right voice. The right manner. Even the right hair. I think she'd be perfect," said Mr. Gregory. "How old are you?"

"I'm twenty-five," said Lil.

"Have you ever acted before?" said Mr. Gregory.

Lil stood up. "No, and I won't be acting now."

"She's really, really good," I said.

Lil looked at me like she was going to throw the rest of her raspberry sherbet in my face.

"Really," I said.

Lil looked back at Mr. Gregory. She smiled sweetly —sort of. Then she pointed at me.

"Do you have a part for him?" she said.

Mr. Gregory shook his head. "No," he said. "Not for a young boy."

I smiled at Lil sweetly —sort of.

"Perhaps the voice of Bertha Mason," said Mrs. Windermere.

"The voice of Bertha Mason?" I said.

"Can you shriek like an insane woman who has been locked in an attic for a great many years?" said Mrs. Windermere.

"I've heard Doug shriek like that lots of times," said Lil. I looked at her. She smiled even more sweetly.

"No," I said.

Lil looked at Mr. Gregory and shrugged. "If he won't shriek like an insane woman who has been locked in an attic for a great many years, then I won't be Helen Burns."

"Then you're not Helen Burns," I said.

"Fine," she said.

"Fine," I said.

I sure did wish we had gotten out of that kitchen as soon as we put the deliveries away.

"Then that's that," said Mrs. Windermere.

"That's that," I said.

"I'll see you next week, Skinny Delivery Boy," said Mrs. Windermere.

"I'll see you next week," I said.

"Fine," she said.

"Fine," I said.

Lil and I dropped our bowls and spoons into the sink, and we went to the door.

"Goodbye, Mr. Gregory," Lil said.

And that was the mistake. She shouldn't have stopped to say goodbye. It's like those horror movies where the person about to be mauled to death could have saved herself if she'd taken only one more step but she stops to be polite or something.

I took Lil's hand. We were almost through the door.

"Gregory," said Mrs. Windermere loudly, "what have you done with the Snowy Heron I gave you?"

I stopped.

"I've already told you: I haven't done a thing with it. I hate birds. And I hate pictures of birds."

"I wonder if we might find a better place for it than rolled up and put away in your closet?"

I turned around.

"Such as . . ." said Mr. Gregory.

"The Snowy Heron?" I said.

Mrs. Windermere turned to me. "Yes," she said. She turned back to Mr. Gregory. "I wonder if we might make a present of it to someone."

"The Snowy Heron?" I said again. "Audubon's Snowy Heron?"

"Excuse me, Skinny Delivery Boy. Yes, we could make a present of it to someone who, say, helped out in the performance."

Mrs. Windermere cupped her chin in her hand.

"Just a thought," she said.

I looked at Lil. "Helen Burns is a great part," I said.

"Wait a minute," said Lil.

"Why don't we all sit down and have another bowl of raspberry sherbet?" said Mrs. Windermere.

You remember the Snowy Heron, right?

If you saw the Snowy Heron, if you saw how beautiful the Snowy Heron was, if you saw how perfect he looks in Audubon's book, then you would be willing to shriek like an insane woman who has been locked in an attic for a great many years too.

You would.

It took more than a little bit of convincing to get Lil to be Helen Burns, which really is a great part, even though she dies. You might wonder how I finally convinced her. It happened on Monday. In geography. When Mr. Barber announced that we were going to be doing one more Team Project for the year. It was going to be on the Role of Transportation in a Country's Development. And when Mr. Barber asked, "Who would like to do the Transcontinental Railroad in the United States?" Lil raised her hand and said that she would do it with me. "Is that okay with you, Douglas?" said Mr. Barber.

Lil looked at me and mouthed the words *Helen Burns*.

"Terrific," I said.

You might wonder who is going to have to do almost everything on this project because one of us has a *real* part in a Broadway play with *real* lines while the other one just has to stand offstage and scream like an insane woman who has been locked in an attic for a great many years and that same one of us did diddly on the New Zealand project and so the one with the *real* part in the Broadway play figures that the one without a *real* part in the Broadway play has a lot to make up for.

I'm starting to feel like a chump.

But whenever I feel like a chump, I remember the Snowy Heron.

If you saw the Snowy Heron...

When Mr. Barber found out about the Broadway play, he said that since Lil and I were going to be working so hard to put on this play we only had to turn in a five-hundred-word report on the Transcontinental Railroad. (I didn't look at Lil when Mr. Barber said this. She couldn't have been smiling, but I was.) When Mr. McElroy found out about the Broadway play, he wanted to take a whole period talking about the role of actors in world history but the only actor that any of us could think of was John Wilkes Booth. "I guess actors aren't so important after all," said Mr. McElroy. "You can't imagine an actor ever becoming president of the United States, for example," which was true. We couldn't. When Mrs. Verne found out about the Broadway play, she took a whole period off from solving equations with at least two unknowns to talk about her own college acting career — which had a whole lot of lines in Greek that she could still recite and which I'm not going to write here because I don't even know how.

When Miss Cowper found out about the Broadway play, I thought she was going to walk on air right there in front of us. She said that she hadn't heard such good news in a long time. We would have to stop the Introduction to Poetry Unit prematurely, she said, and move directly into the Modern Drama Unit so that the class could support Lillian and Douglas. Would we please pass forward our poetry anthologies?

I'm not lying, the whole class loved us. You can only take so much poetry, especially when it's poetry by Percy Bysshe Shelley, who is still going to get it right in the face someday.

When Coach Reed found out about the Broadway play, he smiled and said he wasn't surprised.

Maybe he's turning into a good guy too.

When Mr. Ferris found out about the Broadway play, Clarence didn't stop rocking during the whole lab (which involved sulfur, which is something you really don't want to smell like but which we all did by the time we were finished but Mr. Ferris promised we wouldn't smell like that by the time the curtain came up).

And when Mr. Powell heard about the Broadway play, he went over to *Birds of America* and turned pages until he came to the one he wanted. "Look at this one," he said. We did. "The Great Esquimaux Curlew. An actor if ever there was one."

He was right. The Great Esquimaux Curlew looked like he was just coming onstage, his body leaning forward, his neck stretched out, his bill stuck up in the air like he was about to sing or something. The composition was stable, with his body right in the center against a mound of grasses—also in the center. And the only thing that upset all this was his bill, which you looked at first because it seemed to stick out above the scenery—and it was upside down.

"Am I supposed to look like that when I come on stage?" said Lil.

I'm no chump. I didn't say a thing.

On Tuesday and Friday evenings and Saturday afternoons for the rest of May, Mr. Spicer drove Lil and me down into New York City and dropped us off at the Rose Theater, where Mr. Gregory was always standing outside waiting for us and making it look like we were late. On the drive down, Lil went over her Helen Burns lines again and again. And again and again.

"'Miss Scatcherd is hasty—you must take care not to offend her.' Do you think it's *Scatch*erd, or Scat*cherd*?" she said.

"*Scatch*erd," I said.

She tried it out.

She tried it out again.

"Scat*cherd,*" she said.

That's how it was pretty much the whole way down to New York City. And just so everyone knows the stats:

Number of times I repeated Lil's lines with her:
Something over six thousand.

Number of times I had to correct her: Something over
sixty thousand.
Number of times we drove down to New York City before
I had all her lines down myself: Six.
Number of times she asked me to say my lines: Zero.
(Which is probably because she didn't want me
shrieking like an insane woman who has been
locked in an attic for a great many years while we
were locked inside a car.)

And I'm not lying, I was a great shrieker. I'd been
practicing too. If you're going to get this right, you can't
just shriek. Anyone can do that. To shriek like an insane
woman who has been locked in an attic for a great many
years, you have to practice.

The first time I practiced was in our bathroom,
and when Lucas heard it, he tried to roll his wheelchair
right up the stairs because he figured there was a bloody,
bloody murderer at my throat. He got three steps up
before I heard him.

After that, he said I had to practice outside.

So I went to the green field on the way to Mrs. Windermere's house and hoped that no one was around.

Here's how you practice shrieking like an insane
woman who has been locked in an attic for a great
many years:

You stand in the middle of the field.

You look around to be sure that no one is going to hear you.

You breathe in a couple of times to get as much air into your chest as you can.

You stretch your neck up like the Great Esquimaux Curlew.

You imagine that it's Game Seven of the World Series and it's the bottom of the ninth and Joe Pepitone is rounding third base and the throw is coming in and the catcher has his glove up waiting for the ball and Joe Pepitone is probably going to be out and the game will be over and the Yankees will lose.

Then you let out your shriek, because that's how everyone in Yankee Stadium would be shrieking right then.

That's how you practice shrieking like an insane woman who has been locked in an attic for a great many years. And you keep doing it over and over again until all the birds in Marysville have flown away.

I'm not lying, I got good at this. If you had heard me shrieking, you would have thought someone was being murdered too. It was so eerie, you might have thought that someone who had been murdered was shrieking. You might even have thought that someone who had been murdered had come back and was murdering the murderer, who was shrieking. That's how good I was.

When the cast of *Jane Eyre* heard me shriek from offstage for the very first time, they all looked around to see who had done it, and then they started clapping.

That's pretty good.

Lil said I was a natural. It hardly sounded like I was acting at all. And how was I doing on the Transcontinental Railroad in the United States?

Mr. Gregory said I might have to tone it down a bit since we didn't want people in the first two rows fainting away.

Mrs. Windermere said I might have to tone it down a bit since we didn't want people in the first two rows wetting their pants.

It got so that I liked the rehearsals, even though it meant that I couldn't be drawing the Great Esquimaux Curlew with Mr. Powell on Saturday afternoons. But I loved watching Lil on stage. I loved listening to her lines, which, as you might remember, I already knew by heart. (It was, for the record, *Scatch*erd, and I didn't say anything, even after Mr. Gregory had to correct her for the third time.) And I loved when Lil looked out into the seats to see if I was watching her — which I always was.

In May, Lucas was hired for three stupid jobs.

You can imagine how that felt.

And you can imagine how it felt when he got fired from all three stupid jobs.

The first time was from the Gulf station, and it wasn't his fault. Things started out all right, but then there were three stupid days of stupid rain in a row. When people drove up to get gas, Lucas would wheel out from the garage as quick as he could. He'd come around to the door to find out how much gas they wanted, then wheel around to the pump and pump it, then come back around to the door to get the money, then wheel back to the garage to get their change and their Genuine Crystal Goblet, since Gulf was running a special. By then he was pretty drippy. So when Lucas's boss was driving home and he saw one of his old customers at the Sunoco station instead, he stopped and asked him how come he wasn't at his Gulf station, and the jerk told him he couldn't stand to have a guy with no legs wheel himself out in the rain all that time just to pump gas and so he'd decided to go to the Sunoco station. Lucas got fired the next morning. "We can't be losing our most dependable customers," his stupid ex-boss said.

The second time was from the A&P, when Lucas had to hold on to the edge of a display to shove some oranges high up and the stupid edge broke off in his hand. You can imagine what happened to all the oranges. His boss fired him right there, with all the oranges around him. He wouldn't even give him his salary, because who was going to pay for all those stupid ruined oranges?

The third time was from the Bank of the Catskills, where Lucas was a teller for a whole two and a half hours on a Saturday morning until Mrs. Roethke came in and asked him to deposit three checks and to cash the fourth and he cashed the wrong one—she said. She complained loudly enough that the manager came over and Lucas explained that he had cashed the one she had asked him to cash and he was already fixing the problem and Mrs. Roethke said she wasn't going to be lied about by the likes of him and she had heard what soldiers did in Vietnam and he was probably so drug-addled that he couldn't take proper directions from anyone and how was someone like that to be trusted in a bank and it wasn't a bank's business to take up hard-luck cases like him, at least, not a bank that she would care to put *her* money into.

Lucas didn't even wait. He wheeled himself out of the bank. Christopher was supposed to meet him after work to get him down the stairs out front, but Lucas decided he would take them himself.

At the bottom, he wouldn't let anyone help him back into the chair. He told Christopher it took him half an hour. It was probably longer than that.

I guess he wasn't actually fired from that job. I guess he quit. Sort of.

When I got back from New York City that night, Lucas was alone in the living room watching some John

Wayne Western where John Wayne was riding horses and climbing over fences and walking that way he walks. The television was the only thing on in the room. At the first commercial, I asked him how things were going.

Swell, he said.

I asked him how work was.

He told me.

We left all the lights off so that I couldn't see that he was crying.

If Mrs. Roethke had been there, I would have punched her right in the face.

The play was going to open at the Rose Theater in New York City on the last Friday of May.

That week, you would have thought that Lil was blasting off to the moon, she was that nervous. She had stomachaches almost every day. She missed two of her Advanced Algebra assignments, which had never happened before even once. She forgot to read the first act of *Our Town,* which wasn't missing much, and I'm not lying. And she never even asked how I was doing on the Transcontinental Railroad in the United States, which, if she would have asked, I would have told her was going to get the Golden Spike Award, which she wouldn't have understood because, as you might remember, there's only one of us working on this report.

During classes, she mostly held her stomach and chewed on her pencils.

She bit all the erasers off and ate them.

Then she gnawed on all the metal tips until they came off.

Then she started in on the wood.

There were yellow splinters all around her desk.

Mrs. Verne said it was perfectly normal for an actress. When she played the tragic Jocasta, she had gone through three fountain pens.

On that last Friday, Mr. Ferris set Clarence rocking on the lab table as soon as class started. "This is, if I am not mistaken, the day," he said.

Lil turned red, then white, then red again.

"Lil Spicer," said Mr. Ferris, "what little I know of biology suggests that neither the gum of the eraser, nor the tin of the metal top, nor the wood of the pencil shaft, nor the lead of the interior will do much for your digestive system."

"I can't help it," she said.

Mr. Ferris went over to her desk. He took the pencil from her hand and examined it — and since there wasn't much left, it wasn't a long examination. "Lil Spicer," he said, still looking at the pencil, "perhaps during today's experiment, you should allow Doug Swieteck to handle the more toxic chemicals."

Lil nodded.

Mr. Ferris went back to the front. "A few days ago," he said, "*Apollo Ten* descended to eight-point-four miles above the lunar surface to practice a moon landing. The astronauts described the Earth as a tiny blue, brown, and white basketball suspended in the void of outer space. They said that the moon is pitted with holes, and that it is illumined clearly by Earth's reflected light. They said that some of the craters seemed to glow softly." He threw the pencil stub in the garbage can. "Lil Spicer," he said, "you and Doug Swieteck are doing something extraordinary in an extraordinary time. You are the first Washington Irving Junior High School students to perform in a Broadway play. As far as I know, you are the first citizens from Marysville to perform in a Broadway play. There is no need to be nervous." He leaned forward over the lab table. "The Apollo missions have already descended close to the moon's surface. And you two have already succeeded."

If you could have seen Lil's smile. If you could have seen her relax into her chair.

And if you could have seen my mother, in hat and white gloves, when she got into the Spicers' car to go see a Broadway play that her son was in. If you could have seen her.

We recited Lil's lines together all the way down into New York City that afternoon.

And even though she was so nervous that she had a stomachache again, she got every line right. Except *Scatch*erd.

We stopped at a White Castle on the way down and ate about two dozen hamburgers. Lil gave me her onions, and I scraped my pickles onto her hamburger. But my mother and Mr. and Mrs. Spicer couldn't eat at all. They were too nervous, they said. And even Lil ate only one.

At the theater, Mr. Gregory was, of course, waiting for us. He looked pretty nervous too. He bundled us inside like we were two hours late instead of two hours early. He sent Lil into the dressing room so that she could start becoming Helen Burns. I didn't have to do anything. If you're offstage, you can shriek like an insane woman who has been locked in an attic for a great many years without looking like an insane woman who has been locked in an attic for a great many years.

So I read *Our Town* — terrific — while Lil got ready, and my mother and Mr. and Mrs. Spicer went for a walk in Times Square because they couldn't bear to wait in the theater, they said. And besides, my mother had never seen Times Square.

And that is why they were not around when Mr. Gregory came looking for them.

"They're out for a walk," I said.

His face looked like Disaster.

"What?" I said.

Mrs. Windermere happened to make her theater appearance right then. Blue dress flouncing, a couple of hundred strands of pearls draped around her, an ivory cane that she didn't really need. "Gregory," she said, "this is the night!"

Mr. Gregory looked at her.

"What's happened?" she said.

"Come with me," he said.

"What's going on?" I said.

"Everything's fine," said Mrs. Windermere.

Sure.

They were gone a long time.

While I waited to see how fine everything was, I watched the theater fill up through this little hole in the stage wings. Mrs. Windermere said that she had never had a play open without a packed house, and it looked like she was going to keep her stats perfect. The Rose was filling up pretty fast, and it wasn't filling up with just anybody, I'm not lying. Mayor Lindsay came down the aisle, shaking hands with everyone who could reach him and smiling like this was a parade or something. And a little after him came Jimmy Stewart. Really. Jimmy Stewart, walking down and shaking hands too, with those huge hands he has. Jimmy Stewart!

But you know what? That was nothing.

I saw my mother and Lil's parents come in and sit

in the second row, and then Mr. Gregory going out to
see them, and them all getting up and heading backstage—I guess to wish me and Lil good luck one more
time. And then, right near where their seats were, guess
who came in and sat down. Just sat down, real easy, and
crossed his legs and leaned back and looked up at the ceiling a couple of times and then turned around to someone
and shook his hand and then turned around to someone else and took his program and signed it. You know
who this was?

Joe Pepitone.

I'm not lying. Joe Pepitone was sitting in the second row of the Rose Theater.

Joe Pepitone.

And you know what I was going to do? I was going
to shriek like an insane woman who has been locked in
an attic for a great many years.

In front of Joe Pepitone.

You know what that feels like?

You can't know what that feels like, because no one
has ever had to shriek like an insane woman who has
been locked in an attic for a great many years in front of
Joe Pepitone.

I couldn't do it.

I wouldn't do it.

Not in front of Joe Pepitone.

I looked through the little hole in the stage wings

again. He was reading his program. He was probably getting to the part where it said, *Voice of Bertha Mason: Douglas Swieteck.* Any second now he was going to lean over to someone near him and point to my name. *Isn't that a guy?* he was going to say. *How can a guy play the voice of Bertha Mason?* Then he was going to look at my name again, and he was going to say, *You know, that name sounds familiar.* And then he was going to think about it some more, and he'd say, *That name is so familiar.* And then, then, then he was going to remember.

Terrific.

I looked around wildly.

And suddenly, there were my mother and Mr. and Mrs. Spicer. And Mr. Gregory and Mrs. Windermere. And Lil—who was taking her turn looking like Disaster.

"We've got to get out of here," I said.

Mrs. Spicer nodded. "We know, we know. We're going to take her to the hospital right away."

Her? Hospital?

"We think it might be the pencils," said Mr. Spicer.

Lil smiled, sort of. She was holding on to her parents pretty tight. She had been crying. "Break a leg," she said. She was still crying.

"Break a leg?" I said.

"It's what is said to actors before they go on stage," said Mr. Gregory.

"On stage?" I said.

Lil tried to smile again. "Remember, Doug, it's Scat*cherd*."

I shook my head. "I'm not going onstage."

My mother put both her hands up to her face.

Mrs. Windermere came and stood beside me. She put one hand on my shoulder and another on my elbow. "Who else knows all the lines for Helen Burns?" she said.

I looked at her. I looked at Mr. Gregory. At my mother. Then Mr. and Mrs. Spicer. Then Lil. "Break a leg," she said again, sort of weak.

"He'll be fine," said Mrs. Windermere.

"No," I said.

"We've got to get you to the dressing room," said Mr. Gregory.

"No, no," I said again.

You remember who is sitting in the audience? In the second row?

"You do know the lines, don't you?" said Mr. Gregory.

"No," I said.

"He's lying," said Lil.

"If we were to tie his hair up into a bun . . ."

A bun!

". . . and some baby powder to make his face pale . . ."

Baby powder!

"Did you know that Joe Pepitone is sitting out there?"

"A great many people are sitting out there," said Mr. Gregory.

Lil grimaced, but not because of Joe Pepitone. "I think we'd better..."

The Spicers left. Lil's stomach was hurting so bad, she didn't even look back.

Mr. Gregory and Mrs. Windermere took me to the dressing room. "This is what we have to work with," they said to a whole lot of people who began to smile at me a whole lot — and they weren't the kind of smiles that make you happy.

"Listen," I said, "if this is just because of a stomachache—"

"Remember," Mrs. Windermere said — people were starting to tie my hair up into a bun — "Jane Eyre will walk across the stage and address you. You'll be reading a book on a bench. Jane won't speak to you until you turn the page, so don't forget to turn it. Then she'll say, 'Is your book interesting?' and you say... Skinny Delivery Boy, you say..."

"Nope, it stinks."

"Doug," said Mrs. Windermere.

"I say, 'I like it,' and she says, 'What is it about?' and I hand it to her and say, 'You may look at it.'"

By this time, my hair was tied up in a bun. A tight bun. And someone was powdering the back of my neck.

"Could you go out there and tell Joe Pepitone to go home?" I said.

"And when she says, 'Do you like the teachers here at Lowood Institution?' you say . . ."

"They stink too."

Mrs. Windermere looked at me. Hard.

"They're all criminally insane?"

I think Mr. Gregory was about to start crying right there, even though it wasn't him that was getting his hair tied up in a bun—which, by the way, hurts. "You have to get this right!" Mr. Gregory said.

And I think it was the *have to* that gave me the idea, even as someone told me to raise my arms so she could slip a long Lowood Institution dress over me, which didn't exactly help the bun.

"Mrs. Windermere," I said, "I know the part. But this changes things."

"What do you mean?"

"I mean, Lil and I were getting the Snowy Heron for this, right?"

She nodded, a little suspicious.

"If I'm going to play Helen Burns in front of Joe Pepitone, then I want the Red-Throated Divers too."

Mrs. Windermere opened her eyes wide. I mean, really wide. "I've had those Divers for years," she said.

I waited.

"That wasn't part of our agreement."

I waited.

"They're perfect over the mantel."

"They're perfect back in the book," I said.

She shook her head. "Absolutely not. Do you realize how much that plate costs?"

I waited some more.

"Agreed," said Mr. Gregory.

There it was.

Mrs. Windermere looked at him the way an insane woman who has been locked in an attic for a great many years would look at him. "It's not your decision, Gregory," she said.

"It's my theater, it's my production, it's my reputation, and it's my money," said Mr. Gregory. He held out his hand. I shook it.

"I could use a bowl of lemon ice cream," said Mrs. Windermere.

I'm not lying, I was a killer Helen Burns.

I stepped out on to that stage like I was the Great Esquimaux Curlew. When Jane Eyre came to look at my book — which happened to be *Our Town* — I handed it to her just right. When Miss *Scatch*erd told me I never cleaned my nails, I was about as quiet and innocent as a Large-Billed Puffin. When she hit me a dozen times

with a bunch of twigs, I was the Brown Pelican: I didn't
bat an eye—and you try getting hit a dozen times
with a bunch of twigs. And when I had to die, people
were crying. Really. And you know why? Because I was
the Black-Backed Gull, and so people cried like Helen
Burns was their best friend.

Maybe even Joe Pepitone was crying. Who knows?

And Mr. Gregory was crying too. Probably in relief.
You should have heard the clapping as the curtain came
down on dead Helen Burns. When I got to the wings,
Mr. Gregory picked me up and hugged me and twirled
me around and got baby powder all over himself and I
had to tell him to let me go since I was headed back to
the dressing room because I wasn't going to be Helen
Burns any longer than I had to and was someone going
to help me get this stupid bun untied?

By the way, you can guess what my mother was
doing in the wings.

But the best part was still to come!

Maybe it was because of the Helen Burns applause.
Or maybe it was all the practice. Or maybe it was
because Joe Pepitone was in the second row. But I let
out the Bertha Mason shriek, and by the time the first
echoes finished bouncing back from the mezzanine, I
wasn't the only one in the Rose Theater who was shrieking. It was that good. I bet that everyone there really
did think that there was an insane woman who had been

locked in the attic of the theater for a great many years and they had just heard her.

I guess the rest of the play was all right. I spent some of it reading *Our Town* and some of it working on the Transcontinental Railroad in the United States report, which was almost finished even though a certain someone hadn't written a single word and now she would probably say that she was so sick that she couldn't write a thing.

Terrific.

But I'm not lying, what I was thinking about more was a certain book, and certain missing pages, and bringing those pages back to a certain library, and handing them to a certain librarian, and me and Lil watching him put them back.

I know what the Red-Throated Divers are watching for. I know what the next spectacular thing is.

By the time we got to the "Reader, I married him. A quiet wedding we had: he and I, the parson and clerk, were alone present" part, it was almost eleven o'clock, and Mrs. Windermere still had to drive my mother and me back home, which meant it would be almost one o'clock before I even got close to sleep. But I didn't care. I'd finished laying the last transcontinental rail and pounded in the Golden Spike, and the audience was standing and hollering, and the next day, I'd be handing two Audubon prints to Mr. Powell.

What could be better?

Who cares if Mrs. Windermere was taking forever being The Playwright out in the lobby? Who cares if she was holding my mother beside her like her new best friend?

What could be better?

And about then, Joe Pepitone came backstage.

He really did. Joe Pepitone. Backstage.

"Hey, kid," he said.

I looked at him. Joe Pepitone.

"Doug, right?"

I nodded. Joe Pepitone.

"I threw with you last fall. You still got my cap?"

I nodded. Joe Pepitone.

He laughed. A laugh that only Joe Pepitone could laugh. "I saw your name in the program. So you were the guy who shrieked offstage."

I nodded.

"You know, kid, you almost made me wet my pants."

I laughed. He laughed. I tried to laugh like him.

"And you were Helen Burns too."

My heart stopped. You know what it means when your heart stops? It means that when you think that nothing could be better, right about then, it all falls apart. If you remember, I told you that a long time ago.

I nodded. "Yup," I said.

He shook his head. Big smile. "You were great," he said. "You had me bawling, even though I knew it was you. Bawling, kid." He shook his head again. "Man," he said, "I wish I had your talent. You had the whole house tonight." Then he held out his program.

"I already have one," I said.

He laughed again. "It's not for you, kid. It's for me. I want you to sign it." He opened it up to where my name was. "Right there," he said, and handed me a pen from his inside pocket like he had put it there on purpose just so I could sign a program for him.

So I did.

"And write something for Horace too," he said.

So I did.

Here's what I wrote: *For Joe and Horace. Thanks. Your friend, Doug.*

Joe Pepitone took the program back and looked at it. "Thanks for what?" he said.

"Everything," I said.

Mrs. Windermere drove us back home really late. But you might say that we were both more than a little happy, mostly because Mr. Gregory had called *Jane Eyre* a smash, and told us it was going to have a long run, and so Mrs. Windermere was flying high. I was too, but mostly because Mr. Gregory had promised that if I stayed on as understudy, he would find another actor — actress — to play Helen Burns until Lil came back. Fine by me.

And you know what Mr. Gregory had given me and was now rolled up in a long tube in the back of the car?

My mother and Mrs. Windermere and I sang about living in yellow submarines the whole way back, through Manhattan, across the Whitestone, and all the way up to Marysville. Sometimes when you keep singing the same song again and again and again, it gets really boring. Really, really boring. But not on that drive. It got funnier and funnier, so we finally had to stop singing around Middletown because I thought that Mrs. Windermere was going to drive off the road, that's how hard she was laughing. My mother was about crying.

When we got back home, all the lights were on in the living room. We opened the door, and when we came in, Lucas and Christopher were there, sitting and looking at us.

"How did it go?" Christopher said.

"Fabulous." I told them about Joe Pepitone. I told them about the shrieking. And I even told them about playing Helen Burns, which I hadn't intended to tell them.

"We know about Helen Burns," said Lucas.

"How?" I said.

Lucas looked down.

"Mrs. Spicer called a little while ago," said Christopher. "From a hospital in the city."

"Did she tell you that Lil got a stomachache from eating her pencils?" I said.

My mother took my hand.

"Little brother," Lucas said, "it isn't a stomach-ache."

And the Yellow Shank finally walked into the full dark.

CHAPTER TEN

The Arctic Tern

HERE IS THE STAT that the doctors gave Mr. and Mrs. Spicer:

One in four.

That's the last stat I'm going to give you, because so what? So what? Stats don't mean anything.

Every time Joe Pepitone steps up to the plate, it's new. It doesn't matter if he's hit five hundred home runs or if he's struck out five hundred times. It's a new thing. And no one can predict what's going to happen, except that he's Joe Pepitone, and he's going to try his darnedest, and he's not going to let anything get him down, and he's going to fight his way through no matter what, and he's got all his friends behind him, and if you don't think that matters a whole lot, then you don't know how to get from first base to second.

Because stats don't mean anything.

On the first Saturday of June, I got to Spicer's Deli early, since I figured Mr. Spicer would need my help because Lil wouldn't be there to load the wagons. I was right. When I got there, the first wagon wasn't even close to loaded. Mr. Spicer was standing in the back, one hand holding the orders, the other messing up his hair.

"I can do that," I said.

"Lil usually does it," Mr. Spicer said.

"I know."

I took the lists from his hand.

"Doug," he said, "I'm going to have to let you go. The hospital bills, you can't believe what they're going to be. I don't have enough to pay you anymore."

"I don't have anything else to do on Saturday mornings," I said.

I know. What a chump.

But Mr. Spicer, he looked at me a long time. Then he nodded. Hand back to hair. He went out front.

I loaded the first wagon.

At Mrs. Mason's house, she handed me an envelope with the money for the groceries and another twenty dollars. "For the little girl," she said.

Mr. Loeffler was waiting for me with a glass jar full of yellow tulips. "Will you see the little girl sometime soon?" he said. "Would you mind..." And he handed me the tulips.

All the Daugherty kids were waiting for me when I got to their house, sitting on the front stoop. They were all holding pictures they had drawn—of Lil getting better. In Ben's she was jumping over a fence. In Polly's she was riding her bike with the stupid basket in front of the library. In Joel's she was flying over Washington Irving Junior High School. In Davie's she was reading a huge stack of books under a tree. And in Phronsie's she was kissing someone. "Who is she kissing?" I said. They all started to giggle.

Me, I was almost a chump. Almost bawling in front of kids.

At Mrs. Windermere's, she was waiting too. She opened the door into the kitchen, and we put the groceries away, and I asked how the play was going, and she said it was going fabulous. And I asked about the girl Mr. Gregory got to replace Lil and she said she was fine but not nearly as good as Lil. And I asked about the shrieking, which I wasn't doing anymore since if I was going down to New York City it wasn't to be in a play, and Mrs. Windermere said someone else was doing it now. She wasn't sure who.

Then she asked about Lil.

I was a chump.

When I got back to the deli, Mr. Spicer was bawling beside the cash register. Just bawling, and not even trying to hide behind the flowers that were lined up in pots on the counter. All orchids.

We were both chumps. But you know what? It's not so bad when you're chumps together.

At the library, Mr. Powell had spread one of my sketches of the Arctic Tern out on a table—one of the big sketches, as big as Audubon's. "I thought we might try to work with some watercolors today," he said. "Perhaps we could start with the background."

A box on the table held maybe fifteen, sixteen circles of paint and a bottle of water.

"Mr. Powell," I said.

"We'll mix the colors until we get them right."

"Mr. Powell, we don't have the Arctic Tern plate anymore. How will we know?"

"We have what we remember," he said.

I sat down. I looked across the room to the table where Lil usually was sitting.

"It will be a surprise for her," said Mr. Powell. He dipped the brush into the bottle. "Let's get the color of the water first." He swirled his brush in one of the blues, then handed it to me. "What do you think?" he said.

"It looks like a color from New Zealand," I said.

"Let's see what happens if you start mixing them together, a little bit at a time."

So I tried mixing them together a little bit at a time. And here's what happened: the right color came. We both saw it at the same moment. Exactly the right color of the cold, smooth, frothy deep water below the Arctic Tern. Not at all like New Zealand.

"Now draw your brush evenly along the line. Right. Right. Keep on. Now let the brush up from the paper. Right. Dip your brush again, and start back at the top. Draw down, down—no, it's all right. Let the paint suggest the texture. Down, down. And again."

That afternoon, I painted in two of the waves behind the Arctic Tern.

"How many times did you mess it up?" said Lil.

"None."

"Doug, you are such a liar."

"You'll see it when you get back home."

Then we were quiet, because we didn't know when that was going to be.

And I'm not lying, you wouldn't want to be where Lil was for very long.

If you took the blue paint for the waves and added some green to make it look like puke, that would be the color of the walls. And the tiles on the floor. And the curtains by the window. And the tube that led from a dripping bag into a needle that got stuck in Lil's arm somewhere underneath the tape.

"Does it hurt?" I said.

"How do you think a needle stuck up in your arm would feel?" she said.

"I think I'd start shrieking like an insane woman who has been locked in an attic for a great many years."

"That's what it feels like," she said.

"Do you want me to shriek for you?" I said.

She thought about that. "That might help," she said. "You really do shriek pretty good. But then they might kick you out."

I didn't shriek. She held out her hand, and I took it.

"I loved playing Helen Burns," she said. "I just don't want to *be* Helen Burns. You can sit down on the bed, you know. It's not going to break. At least, not because of a skinny thug like you."

"I thought..."

"I'm not going to break either. One in four, and I'm the one."

I sat down on the bed.

"When all this is over," she said, "we're going to Broadway and see *Jane Eyre*. And then we're going to the top of the Empire State Building. And after that we're going to see the dinosaurs at the Museum of Natural History. And then we're going to walk down Fifth Avenue like we own it."

A nurse came in. "It's time to draw some blood, honey. Just a little poke."

"And afterward we'll go to Central Park and you can sketch people and charge them five dollars a drawing and then we'll take the money and find a French — oh" — she squeezed her eyes shut — "a French restaurant and eat stuff that we can't even pronounce."

"Just a few more minutes," the nurse said to me. "She's tired, so just a few more minutes."

Lil opened her eyes. "Someday I'm going to live in New York City," she said.

"I'm pretty happy in Marysville," I said.

Lil opened her eyes really wide, and maybe I did the same, because it kind of surprised me too. But it was true. It really was. I was happy in Marysville. I didn't even know it until I said it. But it was true.

"We'll find a way to compromise," Lil said.

"No, we won't. We'll live in Marysville."

Her eyes started to close. "You are such a jerk." She yawned. "It's cold in this room. You can lie down if you want and get under the blanket."

That's what I did. She had to scoot over a little, and that wasn't so easy because she was attached to so much stuff. And we had to move the tube going into her arm so that I wouldn't lie down on it. That wasn't so easy either. But we hurried, because we knew we had only a few minutes before the nurse came back. And I lay down next to Lil and I put my arm around her and felt her relax into me. And when she spoke, it was only in a whisper. "Doug," she said, "I sure hope I'm the one in four."

"You are," I said.

"Who says?"

"Me."

A long silence. I thought she was almost asleep.

Then, "All right," she said.

And that's when I knew, I knew, I knew that she was going to be all right. Don't ask me how. But I knew. I'm not lying. Not about this. Not ever about this.

Stats don't mean anything. But some things mean everything.

And that June, those things that mean everything, they kept coming, faster and faster.

On the second Saturday, after my deliveries, Lucas was waiting for me in front of the Marysville Free Public Library. I could tell he'd been out looking for work all morning. He had this tired, beat-up look, and it wasn't hard to figure out what he'd been hearing: "I'm sorry, son." "Nothing for you today." "I don't think you could handle it." "Don't waste my time."

You'd look tired and beat up too, if you'd been hearing that.

"So you want me to pull you up the steps?" I said.

He looked at me, and his face got hard for a second, like the old Lucas. But not exactly like the old Lucas. "You don't think I can do it myself?"

"Lucas."

"You don't think I can handle it?"

"I think you can handle anything," I said.

"Darn right," he said. "Darn right I can handle anything."

He turned around and backed his wheelchair toward the six steps. Then he looked over his shoulder, leaned back, and pulled up on the front of the left wheel. Then he leaned back even more, and I'm not lying, the wheelchair started to go up the first step—kind of crooked, but up—and then he began to fall over.

I started toward him.

But he leaned forward and caught it, and he had the left wheel up on the first step. Then he leaned again, and pulled up on the right wheel, and with a heft, there he was, on the second step, balanced. He looked at me, sweating.

"What do you have that goofy grin on your face for?" he said.

"Do it again," I said.

He backed up to the next step, leaned back, hefted up, sweated.

"Not bad," I said.

The third step, and he almost went over that time, but he caught himself, and leaned forward a little bit more, and then the fourth, and fifth, and then he drew himself back to the sixth, and grunted and pulled, and came back down onto the fifth.

"No. Stay put, little brother."

I did. You would have too.

He backed up again, waited for a moment, leaned to the left and pulled up, squeezing his eyes tight, and brought the chair half up, then leaned to the right, squeezed his eyes again, and so came over the last step of the Marysville Free Public Library. He was breathing a little bit heavily.

So was I.

"Not bad," I said.

"It's all in the balance," Lucas said.

"You were a little slow."

"I'll practice."

That smile.

Then the library door opened and out came—and you're not going to believe this, but it was June, and as true as true—out came Coach Reed. From the library.

I'm not lying.

"Pretty good," he said to Lucas.

"Thanks," said Lucas.

"It would take a lot of strength to pull yourself up like that."

"I guess," said Lucas.

"I guess," said Coach Reed. He looked at me. "Your brother?"

I nodded.

"Jack Reed," he said to Lucas. Then he held the door

of the library open so that Lucas could wheel himself through. Lucas probably didn't want him to, but after a day of trying to fit your wheelchair through the doors of places that didn't want you, he might have been glad to have someone hold the door.

I looked at Coach Reed as I went through.

He looked back at me.

I went on in, and over to the elevator.

"Hey —" Coach Reed.

Lucas stopped and slowly spun himself around. And you know what? He looked like he was going to be okay. He might be tired and beat up, but he was going to be okay. That's what he looked like.

And it was June. I bet Arctic terns fly strong in June.

"I hear you've been looking for a job," said Coach Reed.

"That's right." Old Lucas voice.

"Any luck?"

"Yeah," said Lucas. "Yeah, lots of luck. Everyone around here says that a guy in a wheelchair is just the kind of guy they've been looking for. I'm trying to decide between, I don't know, eight or nine offers."

"Sounds tough."

Lucas started to spin around again.

"Maybe you could come work for me," said Coach Reed.

He really said that. June.

But Lucas didn't believe him.

"Funny," Lucas said. "Really funny. You ought to be on stage. You could make a living telling Guys with Missing Legs jokes. They're not as funny as Guys with Missing Arms jokes, but maybe you could come up with some of those too."

"I'm not kidding."

Lucas wheeled himself closer. Still old Lucas.

"So what do you want me to do? Coach track? Maybe the high jump? Or the pole vault? I'm a heck of a pole vaulter."

Coach Reed looked at me, then back at my brother. "Maybe track. Maybe gymnastics. I saw you come up the stairs. Maybe weight training. I have a feeling you might be able to do a whole lot of things that you don't think you can."

"How do you know?"

Coach Reed looked at me again. "Because I was there too."

Long silence.

"I need an assistant," said Coach Reed.

"Then maybe you better find someone who—"

"Assistant Junior High School Gym Coach. There are two weeks left in this school year. If you started now, you could get your feet wet and be ready for September."

"If you notice, I don't have any — "

"Monday morning. Seven o'clock in the morning. We're beginning the last Basketball Unit. If you're there, the job is yours — that is, if you think you can keep a bunch of junior high kids from pulling any funny business on you."

"I won't be there," said Lucas.

Coach Reed looked at me.

"Yes sirree, buster," I said. "He'll be there."

"All right," Coach Reed said, and went on down the steps.

I think I could have kissed him.

Lucas looked at me. "I'm not going to take a job I can't do."

"You're right," I said. "I don't think you can handle it."

Lucas stared, like the old Lucas was going to say something. But the old Lucas didn't. Instead, Lucas nodded, and his face got all set and determined. And then he started to smile. He spun his chair around.

Mrs. Merriam walked up. She had her glasses on, so she didn't look so loopy.

Lucas laughed. He laughed!

"Can I help you?" she said to him.

"I think I'm fine," he said.

We took the elevator upstairs.

Lucas didn't mind the steel gate that we had to draw

across. And he didn't mind the way the elevator rattled around on its way up. And he didn't mind the sound of the pulleys straining themselves. And he didn't mind that at the top, the elevator stopped a couple of inches below the floor. He jerked his chair up and pulled himself over the lip.

At the table where Lil usually worked, Mr. Powell was mixing watercolors. "You're late," he said.

"Lucas had a job interview," I said.

"For what position?"

"Assistant Junior High School Gym Coach," said Lucas. "We start a Basketball Unit on Monday."

And you know what? I'm not lying. Mr. Powell didn't seem surprised at all. "Make them do free throws," he said. "Free throws discipline the mind and the eye and the hand. There's nothing like them."

Lucas laughed. So good. "It sounds like you know what you're talking about."

Mr. Powell raised an eyebrow. "I'm a librarian," he said. "I always know what I'm talking about. Mr. Swieteck, does this gray look right?"

We went over to the table which, you might remember, my Arctic Tern was on top of. "Who drew this?" Lucas said. He didn't need to lean down so close anymore.

"Your brother," said Mr. Powell.

Lucas touched the edge of the paper.

"It's a copy," I said.

"My brother?" said Lucas. He leaned forward. "It looks like he's flying off the page."

"He's falling into the water," I said.

Lucas shook his head. "No, he's not. He's going wherever he wants to go."

"Exactly right," said Mr. Powell, and he handed me a paintbrush.

You know what it feels like to stroke color onto an Arctic Tern flying off the page, going wherever he wants to go?

Terrific.

It was June, you remember.

On Monday, Lucas left the house before I did. By himself. Heading to Washington Irving Junior High School. I went down to the gym between periods to watch him practice free throws from his chair. (The stats weren't so good, but if you remember, stats don't mean anything.) During lunch — which I had again — I watched Lucas run basketball drills. And at the end of the day, he was gathering up loose basketballs when I came in, and James Russell was calling out, "Coach Swieteck!"

You think Lucas wasn't smiling when he heard that?

You think I wasn't smiling when I heard that?

I waved, and Lucas waved, and I went into Coach

Reed's office. He had the Presidential Physical Fitness charts spread out, and he was going through each one with his finger on the lines. He paused and looked up at me.

"Thanks," I said.

"Go home," he said.

June.

Somehow the message had gone out to all the teachers that the last two weeks of school were the last opportunity to bury the students of Washington Irving Junior High in work. Every other school in the country was getting ready for campouts and parties to celebrate the end of the year. But not us.

In world history, Mr. McElroy was starting the Causes of World War I. You know how many Causes there were for World War I? No wonder they fought.

In English, Miss Cowper said we were going to finish the year with selections from John Steinbeck's *Travels with Charley,* which didn't sound bad because Charley is a dog and how bad could a dog story get? And it wasn't bad, except we had to keep notes about Steinbeck's technique because we were going to be writing our own travel accounts — fictional or nonfictional — for the year's final composition.

Doesn't that sound all-fired exciting?

In Advanced Algebra, Mrs. Verne told us that

she was going to end the year with an Introduction to Geometry, and when we pointed out that Geometry wasn't taught until tenth grade, she congratulated us on our powers of observation and told us all to be sure to bring protractors the next day.

In PE, we were practicing free throws. Every day. Lots of free throws. Because they were supposed to discipline the mind and the eye and the hand.

I didn't complain to the coach.

In physical science, Mr. Ferris announced that NASA had given the go-ahead and in just a month, Apollo 11 would blast off to the moon. This is what happens when you dream dreams, he said. He couldn't stop smiling, not even when he was describing the thermodynamics of the fuel for the Saturn rocket that would carry the command capsule and the LEM. Otis Bottom asked if we were going to make some fuel to see if it would explode. Even then, Mr. Ferris could not stop smiling.

In geography, we had gotten all the way over to France, and Mr. Barber started us on Maps of France Under Louis the Fourteenth—or maybe it was the Fifteenth—and we were supposed to copy all the important rivers and mountains and cities and towns and underline places that Louis the Fourteenth or Fifteenth had visited according to *Geography: The Story of the World.*

I'm not lying, the map that I drew was something that you would stop to look at. Audubon himself would have stopped and whistled, which is just what Mr. Barber did. Then he crouched next to me, and the scent of his coffee steamed up.

"Douglas, did you trace that?"

"Nope."

"And those seagulls?"

"I thought they would add realism."

"They're fantastic," Mr. Barber said.

"Thanks," I said.

He whistled again. Then he stood up and took a step.

You know one thing that Mr. Powell taught me? He taught me that sometimes, art can make you forget everything else all around you. That's what art can do. And I guess that's what happened to Mr. Barber, who forgot that his left foot was behind the back leg of my chair. Who took a step without remembering to take his foot away from the back of my chair. Who tripped, but caught himself. But who couldn't catch the coffee that flew out of his cup, swirled around in the air for a second, and finally splashed down all over my *Geography: The Story of the World* and started to soak into the pages as fast as it could.

I won't tell you the sound that Mr. Barber made. It was something like the shriek an insane woman who has been locked in an attic for a great many years would make.

* * *

My father hadn't said a word to me — or much to anyone — since I'd seen Ernie Eco wearing Joe Pepitone's jacket. He wouldn't even look at me during supper. Which was fine, just fine. My mother covered the silence with talk about orchids, and Lucas couldn't stop talking about his job if someone had threatened to bloody, bloody murder him if he said another word. "They call me Coach Swieteck," he said. "Can you believe that? Coach Swieteck."

"Even if you can't shoot a free throw worth diddly?" said Christopher.

"Seventy-five percent from the free-throw line," Coach Swieteck said, which is a stat that he was probably stretching really far. I mean, really far.

"That's something you dreamed, you mean," said Christopher.

"Chris, why don't you open your mouth, look up to the ceiling, and we'll see how many of these carrots I can make from here?"

"Lucas," said my mother.

"It's all right," said Christopher. "I'm not going to do it. He'd probably get them all in, just for spite. Isn't that right, Coach?"

"Absolutely."

My mother started laughing. You know how good it is to see my mother laugh?

My father left the table.

My mother stopped laughing.

Lucas began eating his carrots.

Christopher held his fork still over his plate.

"Isn't the orchid delicate in this light?" said my mother.

June.

A week before Christopher's hearing — which the Town of Marysville was taking its time setting up, probably to make him sweat — my father stopped eating supper with us. He'd fill a plate in the kitchen before we started and then go into the bedroom. He didn't come out afterward. So what? So what? No one cared. Except maybe my mother.

None of us talked about the hearing. None of us talked about what might happen. None of us used the word *jail*. Would you?

Except at the hospital. At the hospital, I could talk about it.

"You know that your brother didn't break into the stores, right?" said Lil.

I nodded.

"You're sure?"

"I'm sure."

Lil looked at me kind of slantwise. "Then he didn't do it, and everything will be okay."

"Thank you, Judge Spicer."

"You're very welcome. So get out of your funk before I throw my bedpan at your head."

Lil.

But back at home, none of us talked about it.

And meanwhile, I saw my father less and less. And whenever I did see him, he was sort of . . . unstable. It's hard to say how exactly he looked like this. Maybe because of the way he stood, with his hands in his pockets, his eyes looking anywhere but at you, and bent over, like he was hurting.

Until the day before the hearing, when he came home from work late. He opened the door—I was helping Lucas with his weights in the living room—and he came in.

He was carrying Joe Pepitone's jacket.

It looked about as heavy as Lucas's weights.

My mother came out from the kitchen.

My father handed Joe Pepitone's jacket to me, his eyes looking away.

Then he went into the bedroom.

My mother followed him.

When they came out, they went into the kitchen and they put food on the table together, my father looking so out of place carrying a bowl of mashed potatoes. Then my mother sat down in her chair, and he sat down in his. And when my mother didn't speak, Lucas started to talk about this new drill he had come up with for dribbling around cones and then going to a lay-up. And my mother and father and all of us filled our plates with mashed potatoes and green beans and a pork chop each, and Lucas and Christopher and me, we started to eat. But my father sat in front of his full plate, and my mother sat in front of hers, and they didn't eat. Not a bite. And Lucas talking about dribbling, and my mother and father looking at their full plates.

The whole meal, they never said a word.

Everything was quiet — except for Lucas.

Then someone knocked at the door.

My father looked at my mother. And my mother looked at my father.

"Could you answer that, Chris?" said my mother. And when Christopher got up to answer the door, my mother stood and walked over to his seat, sat down, and took my father's hand.

Christopher came back in. Behind him, Mr. Daugherty. In uniform.

"Evening, folks," he said. "Sorry to bother you at dinner."

He seemed huge in the house. Or maybe it was his uniform that seemed huge. If he sat down in one of our kitchen chairs, he would probably have broken it into pieces, he was that huge.

"Hello," said my mother, and stood up.

"Hello, Mrs. Swieteck," said Mr. Daugherty, and he nodded his head. He looked at me. "The kids all say hello, Doug."

"Tell them I said hi," I said.

"I'll do that." He turned to Lucas. "I heard about the job, Coach."

Can you guess what Lucas looked like when huge Mr. Daugherty called him Coach?

Then Mr. Daugherty looked at my father, and nodded. "Mr. Swieteck," he said.

My father nodded back. Looking at my mother. Never taking his eyes off my mother.

Can you tell that not a single one of us knew what to say?

My mother coughed a little bit. "Would you like a pork chop?" she asked.

Can you tell that my mother really did not know what to say?

"They look good, but I'd better not," said Mr. Daugherty. "I'm late for supper as it is, and you know what the missus will say if I can't eat a bite of what she's been cooking." He cleared his throat. Twice. "Christopher . . ." he said.

"The hearing isn't till tomorrow," said Lucas. "You shouldn't —"

"There isn't going to be any hearing," said Mr. Daugherty.

There is no noise in space. Did you know that? If one of the *Apollo 11* astronauts decides to go for a walk around the space capsule, he won't hear a thing. There's no sound at all — sort of like in our house for about the next minute.

Then my father stood up. "Chris," he said, and stopped. Tried again. "Chris..."

"We got an anonymous tip," said Mr. Daugherty. "We found all the stuff from the hardware store. Everything. And the guy confessed. To that, and to the break-in at Spicer's Deli last fall."

My mother got up and stood close to my father.

"The Marysville Police Department would like to apologize to you, Christopher," said Mr. Daugherty.

"Chris..." said my father.

"The tip was anonymous, and as far as the investigating officer — who is me — is concerned, the case is closed. There won't be any more charges."

My mother took my father's hand again.

"And I'm sure," said Mr. Daugherty, "I'm really very, very sure that the person who phoned in the tip knows now that getting involved with something like this could wreck a whole lot of people's lives — not only his."

"I'm sure he does," said my mother. She went behind my father and put her arms around his chest. My father reached up and held on to her hands.

"And I'm sure he has a terrific family and he never meant to hurt them. I'm sure he knows now that they're all he really needs."

"He knows that too," said my father.

Mr. Daugherty nodded. "I'm sorry again, Christopher. If there's ever anything I can do for you..."

"Thanks," said Christopher.

"See you Saturday, Doug."

"See you then."

He turned and was gone. And you know what? The house was bigger. I'm not lying. It was like he left his hugeness behind him, and we had more room.

And you know what else? It wasn't The Dump anymore. It seemed...I don't know. Maybe I'm just a chump.

We all sat back down. We all looked at our cold mashed potatoes and cold pork chops. And we were all hungry. We started digging in like we hadn't eaten for a week. Christopher especially—and you can probably figure out why. Everyone eating and laughing at how fast we were eating and eating even faster, mashed potatoes flying, Lucas belching, and Christopher belching, and me belching, and my father belching.

My father, who sat back in his chair when there was no more food on the table, who looked around at us, and who said, "Isn't that orchid the most beautiful sight you ever saw?"

I looked at my mother.

That smile.

That June smile.

And then my father looked across at my mother. "I mean," he said, "the second most beautiful sight you ever saw."

* * *

The next morning, Principal Peattie was waiting for me when I came into Washington Irving Junior High School. He told me to come by his office after Mr. Barber's class — Mr. McElroy already knew I'd be late for world history. "And you'd better not try to get out of this," he said.

He was smiling when he said it.

When I got to his office, I didn't have to wait a half hour, like usual. His door was propped open and he was standing beside it, waiting for me. Guess what was off his wall and leaning up against his desk. Just guess.

But the first thing that Principal Peattie said was "I'm sorry. I was wrong. I was wrong about a great many things, and I'm sorry." He held out his hand. I took it, and we shook. Then he pointed to the Brown Pelican. "That's yours now," he said.

I nodded.

"I always thought he looked sort of..."

"Noble," I said.

"That's not the word I was thinking of, but now that you say it..." He considered the Brown Pelican. "Maybe so."

"Definitely noble," I said.

"If you want, I'll drive it over to the library," he said.

"I'd like to take it myself," I said.

He nodded. He studied the Brown Pelican for a long

moment. "You know, Mr. Swieteck," he said, "I haven't told this to many students, but I'll tell it to you. I think that you're going to go wherever you want to go."

That pelican. As sturdy as if all he had to do was watch the world.

"Thanks," I said.

"Now you'd better get on to Mr. McElroy's class. The bird will be waiting right here for you."

I turned toward the door.

"And Mr. Swieteck," Principal Peattie said.

I looked back.

"Thank you for what you did for Coach Reed."

"I don't know —"

"Principal Peattie thanks you," he said. "Now get on."

I got on.

Do you know what it feels like, leaving the principal's office knowing you're going to put a piece of something back, and the principal just said thanks?

Do you know what it feels like when the principal has just told you that you're going to go wherever you want to go?

Do you know what it feels like when you think you know just where you want to go and maybe you're already there?

It feels like you're on *Apollo 11*, and the moon is in your sights.

That's what it feels like.

* * *

I brought the Brown Pelican to the library after the Saturday deliveries. I was a little late because Mrs. Mason had loaded me down with three hostas and five tall ferns "for your mother's perennial garden." When I told her she didn't have one, she said, "Oh, she will, dearie — it's June."

Mr. Loeffler had the same idea. He loaded me down with three pots of sweet marjoram, which he said everyone needs in his or her garden.

Even Mrs. Daugherty figured that my mother needed a perennial garden. She had dug up a bridal wreath as tall as Ben and wrapped it in burlap.

And Mrs. Windermere. She had heard too, I guess. Five yellow rosebushes.

You know how long it takes to wheel all that stuff back home?

You know how happy my mother was?

I'm not lying, she had the hostas, the ferns, and the sweet marjoram planted before I got back with the bridal wreath, and the bridal wreath planted before I got back with the roses.

So I was late to the library.

But Mr. Powell didn't care. Somehow he knew about the Brown Pelican. He had *Birds of America* open to the right place. We put it in together.

"Just one more," Mr. Powell said.

But I knew we'd never get it. An anonymous collector from overseas.

I shook my head. "The book will always be missing one bird," I said.

Mr. Powell shook his head. "Not exactly," he said.

"How not exactly?" I said.

That Saturday afternoon, I finished my Arctic Tern. He was beautiful. He was diving into the water because there was so much for him to find. The waves rolled all around him and were already starting to break, but he was going to be fine. He had so much to do. He had so much to see. He was going to go wherever he wanted to go. And he wasn't alone, you know. If you could see the picture like I saw it, there was a whole flock of Arctic terns all around him, all flying above the waves. And I'm not lying, they were a sight.

And after I finished, Mr. Powell opened *Birds of America* again. He laid my painting in at the place where Audubon's tern was missing. "Nothing is ever perfect," he said. "But this comes pretty close."

On the last day of school, Mr. Barber collected his *Geography: The Story of the World*s. He paused for a moment when I handed him mine. It was stained a dark brown. It still smelled of coffee. I think Mr. Barber wanted to cry.

On the last day in world history, Mr. McElroy asked us to pass in our final map, which we could make of any place we wanted in the whole world. Do you know what my map was of? Marysville.

On the last day in English, we finished selections from *Travels with Charley* and I turned in my Travelogue assignment. Do you know what I did my Travelogue assignment on? Let's just say it started at Cape Kennedy and headed up into the sky. And by the way, if I ever do meet Percy Bysshe Shelley, I'm still going to punch him right in the face.

On the last day in Advanced Algebra, Mrs. Verne told us that we had made great progress and that we were far in advance of most eighth-grade mathematicians in the state of New York. If we kept up our studies, we would all find next year's algebra Regents exams to be well within our abilities, and we would fare quite well against all the other algebra students in the great State of New York.

Terrific.

On the last day of physical science, we watched a filmstrip about the Project Mercury space missions — six manned flights from 1961 to 1963 — and about the Project Gemini space missions after them — ten manned flights from 1965 to 1966. There was a ping before every frame, which was enough to make you wish we had never gone into space at all. But when it was finally over, Mr. Ferris turned on the lights and said, "Everything you have just seen is changing. With the flight of *Apollo 11,* scientific discovery is about to make a giant leap, and those leaps are going to come faster and faster." He held up his slide rule. "Someday, people will be buying these in antique shops, and they'll have tiny computers that they carry around with them"—which I think he probably meant as a joke, except he didn't laugh.

On the last day of PE, Coach Swieteck made us run the mile and he gave everyone heck if they couldn't do it in under seven minutes and forty-three seconds. He told us that we'd better be running over the summer because they didn't fool around in high school PE. No sirree, buster.

"How about you, Coach?" Otis Bottom hollered.

Coach Swieteck wheeled around. "If you guys can't cross the line in under six minutes, you won't be able to touch me."

"Is that a bet?"

"Mr. Bottom, that is a bet."

Now you know what Lucas will be doing all summer.

There was only one more thing that needed to happen for June to be perfect—and it did. For a little while. The last week of the month, when everything was warm and green, when there were hawks gliding on the high breezes, Lil came home. On the first Saturday back, we went to the library together and I showed her the Arctic Tern in John James Audubon's *Birds of America*. She looked at it and started to cry.

I told you what art can do to some people.

June.

But Lil was only home for a couple of weeks, and then she went to Middletown Community Hospital. I think she kept her eyes closed the whole way there.

Mr. Spicer took me to see her the morning that *Apollo 11* blasted off.

You remember how Mr. Daugherty seemed so big in our house? You remember that? Lil's room was filled with huge machines, and they made the room tiny. There were pictures of birds on the walls, not even close to good. There were two windows, but they were small and so high up that you could only see the sky, and you could only see the sky if you angled your head just right.

More tubes. Stuff dripping into the tubes. Into Lil.

Lil with a kerchief on when I came in, which she pressed down, dragging her tubes up with her arms, pressing down the kerchief so that I couldn't see that she had no hair. Crying.

I turned the television on and then lay down on the bed beside her—which took a lot of figuring out.

And we watched *Apollo 11* blast off to the moon. It was something. First, this flash of light leaps out everywhere, all this fire behind it. And then big clouds of smoke right behind the fire, and then slowly, like it is barely moving at all, this huge tower of a rocket starts to go up, and you can't believe it's really going up, but it is. And then it starts to tilt a little bit, and then it heads up with the fire beneath it, and up, and suddenly it's hurtling through the blue, flying faster than Audubon could ever imagine. And then it gets smaller, and smaller, and you hear people at Mission Control clapping, laughing—and you want to clap and laugh too.

Which Lil and I did together.

"It was beautiful," she said.

I looked at her. "Beautiful," I said.

We watched as the flickering light of the fire beneath the Saturn rocket—and I could tell you about the thermodynamics of the fuel if you want to know—we watched as the rocket moved farther and farther up into the sky, heading to the moon. To the moon!

To the moon!

I held Lil's hand.

It was trembling a little. The needle.

And when I looked at her, I could tell she was thinking of stats, even though they don't mean a thing.

"You know," she said, "if I close my eyes, I could almost be an Arctic tern flying over the water."

"Close them," I said.

She did.

"Imagine a whole lot of Arctic terns flying around you. A whole lot."

She smiled.

"Now imagine one coming down to fly right next to you to show you the next spectacular thing that's going to come into your life."

Bigger smile.

"Like landing on the moon?" she said.

"Like landing on the moon."

Even bigger smile. Her eyes still closed.

"Will he stay next to me?" she said.

"Always," I said. "You think the moon's all there is? There's a whole lot more for us to see. Haven't you ever heard of New Zealand?"

She snuggled closer, over the tubes.

"Always," she said.

"Always," I said.

And I'm not lying, I heard, all around us, over the sounds of the huge machines in the room, over the sounds of *Apollo 11* heading to the moon, I heard, all around us, the beating of strong wings.

Meet another remarkable hero in
Pay Attention, Carter Jones by Gary D. Schmidt

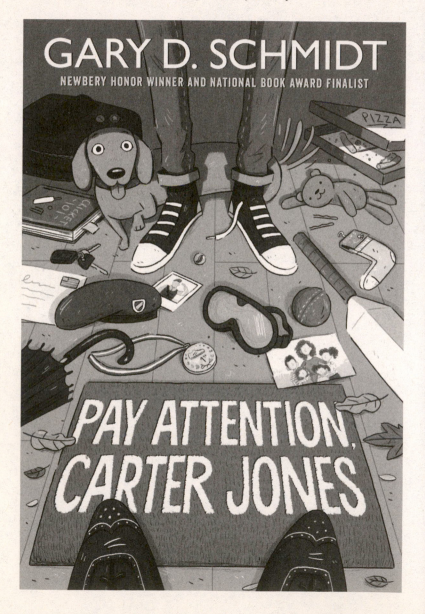

• 1 •

THE PLAYERS

Cricket teams, both batting and fielding, may have up to eleven players each. The captain of the batting team determines the order of the batsmen; the captain of the fielding team sets players in positions determined by the style and pace of the bowler.

IF IT HADN'T been the first day of school, and if my mother hadn't been crying her eyes out the night before, and if the fuel pump on the Jeep had been doing what a fuel pump on a Jeep is supposed to be doing, and if it hadn't been raining like an Australian tropical thunderstorm—and I've been in one, so I know what it's like—and if the very last quart of one percent milk hadn't gone sour and clumped up, then probably my mother would never have let the Butler into our house.

But that's what the day had been like so far, and it was only 7:15 in the morning.

7:15 in the morning on the first day of school, when the Butler rang our doorbell.

I answered it.

I looked at the guy standing on our front stoop.

"Are you kidding?" I said.

That's what you would have said too. He was tall and big around the belly and wearing the kind of suit you'd wear to a funeral—I've been to one of those too, so I know what a funeral suit looks like—and he had a bowler on his head. A bowler! Which nobody has worn since, like, horses and carriages went out of business. And everything—the big belly, the funeral suit, the bowler—everything was completely dry even though it was an Australian tropical thunderstorm outside because he stood underneath an umbrella as big as a satellite disk.

The guy looked down at me. "I assure you, young man, I am never kidding."

I closed the door.

I went to the kitchen. Mom was tying back Emily's hair, which explains why the dry Ace Robotroid Sugar Stars Emily was eating were dribbling out both sides of her mouth. Charlie was still looking for her other yellow sock because she couldn't start fourth grade without it—she couldn't she couldn't she couldn't—and Annie was telling her what a baby she was, and Charlie was saying she was not she was not she was not, and just because Annie was going into fifth grade that didn't make Annie the boss of her. Then Charlie looked at me and said, "Does it?" and I said, "You think I care?"

"Carter," my mom said, "your oatmeal is on the stove and you'll have to mix in your own raisins and there's some walnuts too but no more brown sugar. And, Carter, before you do that, I need you to run down to the deli and—"

"There's a guy out on our front stoop," I said.

"What?"

"There's a guy out on our front stoop."

My mother stopped tying back Emily's hair.

"Is he from the army?" she said.

I shrugged.

"Is he or isn't he?"

"He's not wearing a uniform."

"Are you sure?"

"Pretty sure."

My mother started tying back Emily's hair again. "Tell him it's the first day of school and he should go find someone else to buy whatever he's selling at seven fifteen in the morning."

"Annie can do it."

My mother gave me That Look, so I went back to the front door and opened it. "My mom says it's the first day of school and you should go find someone else to buy whatever you're selling at seven fifteen in the morning."

He shook his umbrella.

"Young Master Jones," he said, "please inform your mother that I would very much like to speak with her."

I closed the door.

I went back to the kitchen.

"Did you tell him to go away?" said my mother. I think this is what she said. She had a bunch of bobby pins in her mouth and she was sticking them around Emily's head and Emily was hollering and spitting out Ace Robotroid Sugar Stars at every poke, so it was hard to understand what my mother was saying.

"He wants to talk to you," I said.

"He's not going to—"

A sudden wail from Charlie, who held up her other yellow sock, which Ned had thrown up on. Ned is our dachshund and dachshunds throw up a lot.

"Carter, go get some milk," said my mother. "Charlie, stop crying. Annie, it doesn't help to make faces at Charlie. Emily, if you move your head again I'm going to bobby-pin your bangs to your eyebrows."

I went back to the front and opened the door.

The guy was still standing on the stoop, but the Australian tropical thunderstorm was starting to get in under the umbrella.

"Listen," I said, "my mom's going crazy in there. I have to go to the deli and get milk so we can eat breakfast. And Charlie's crying because Ned threw up on her other yellow sock, and Annie's being a pain in the glutes, and Emily's bangs are about to get pinned to her eyebrows, and I haven't even packed my backpack yet—and that takes a while, you know—and we have to leave soon since we have to walk to school because the fuel pump on the Jeep isn't working, and we only have one umbrella. So just go away."

The guy leaned down.

"Young Master Jones," he said, "if you were able to sprint between wickets with the speed of your run-on sentences, you would be welcome in any test match in the world. For now, though, go back inside. In your room, gather what is needed for your backpack. When you have completed that task, find your mother and do whatever is necessary to insure that she is no longer"—he paused—"going crazy." He angled the umbrella a little to keep off the Australian tropical thunderstorm. "While you are doing whatever is necessary, I will purchase the milk."

I looked at the guy. He was wet up to his knees now.

"Do you always talk like that?" I said.

"If you are inquiring whether I always speak the Queen's English, the answer is, of course, yes."

"I mean the way you say everything like you want it to smell good."

The guy shook the rain off his umbrella. I sort of think he meant to shake it all over me.

"Young Master Jones—"

"And that: 'Young Master Jones.' No one talks like that."

"Obviously, some do."

"And that: 'Ob—vi—ous—ly.' It takes you a whole minute to say it. 'Ob—vi—ous—ly.'"

The guy leaned down. "I am going to purchase the milk now," he said. "You shall pack your backpack. Do it properly, then attend to your mother."

He turned to go.

"Are you trying to convert me or something?" I said.

"Yes," he said, without turning back. "Now, to your appointed tasks."

So I went upstairs and packed the new notebooks and old pens and old pencils and my father's old science calculator in my backpack, and I put the green marble in my front pocket—all this did take a while, you know—and then I went down to the kitchen where my mother was braiding Annie's hair and Charlie was sniffing with her arms crossed and Emily was finishing her dry Ace Robotroid Sugar Stars. My mother said, "Where's the milk?" and then the doorbell rang again.

"I'll get it," I said.

Guess who it was.

His pants were wet most of the way up when he handed me a bag.

"I have procured the milk," he said.

"Obviously," I said. "Is it one percent?"

"Certainly not—and mockery is the lowest form of discourse."

He handed me another bag.

"What's this?" I said.

"The package is for Miss Charlotte," he said. "Tell her we are most fortunate that American delicatessens are, though parsimonious in their selection of food items that have seen the light of the sun, at least eclectic."

"She won't know what *eclectic* means."

"Copious."

"That either."

The guy sighed. "The contents are self-explanatory."

I took the bags and closed the door. I carried the milk to the kitchen and set it on the table. Then I gave Charlie the other bag.

"What's this?" she said.

"How should I know?"

"Because you're handing it to me. That's how you should know."

"It's something electric," I said.

"Something electric?"

"I don't know. It's from the guy standing on our front stoop."

My mother looked up from Annie's braids. "The guy standing on our front stoop? He's still there?"

Charlie opened her bag and took out—I know this is hard to believe—brand-new bright yellow socks. She screamed her happy scream. That's the scream she makes that could stop a planet from spinning.

My mother looked at the bright yellow socks, then at the milk.

"It's not one percent," she said.

"Certainly not," I said.

My mother dropped Annie's braids and headed out of the kitchen.

• 2 •

THE WICKET

The wicket may refer to the stumps and bails placed at either end of the playing surface or to the playing surface itself.

WE WERE ALL behind my mother when she opened the front door.

The guy was still standing there, underneath his satellite-disk umbrella, which wasn't doing much anymore since the Australian tropical thunderstorm was blowing sideways now.

"Who are you?" said my mother.

He gave a little bow and rain waterfalled off the front of his umbrella, just like in an Australian rainforest. "Mrs. Jones, I am an acquaintance of your father-in-law and husband, having served the first for many years and attended the childhood of the second."

"Is he all right?"

"I assume you speak of the second."

My mother put her hands on her hips. She still had a bobby pin tucked in the corner of her mouth, and she put on That Look, so she came off pretty tough.

"Captain Jones was, during our last connection, well enough. I called him ten days ago by telephone to inform him that his father, Mr. Seymour Jones, had passed away."

"Passed away?" said Emily.

The guy leaned down. "I am so very sorry to tell you, Miss Emily, that your grandfather has died."

"She never knew him," said my mother. "None of us did. You better come in."

"Thank you, madam. Dripping might pose a problem."

"It's only water," said my mother.

"Thank you, madam."

Together we all moved back, and the guy stood in our front hall, and dripping was a problem.

"So you're here to tell us about my husband's father?" said my mother. "You could have just written."

"Your father-in-law's passing is only part of my message, madam. I am to inform you as well that Mr. Seymour Jones has left a most generous endowment to support my continuing service to his family."

"I don't understand," said my mother.

"It seems reasonable to consider that a family with four young children and a father currently deployed in Germany might well stand in need of some aid suited to my occupation."

"You're here to help out?"

The guy gave another little bow. Really.

"While Jack's deployed?"

He nodded.

"Jack," she said. "Jack sent you."

"In a manner of speaking," said the guy.

My mother dropped That Look. She smiled. She started to bite her lip like she does when she's about to . . . Never mind.

"I can assure you, madam, my service in this capacity is exemplary, and I would gladly furnish names and addresses for reference, should you desire them."

"Wait," I said. "You mean my grandfather, like, left you to us in his will?"

"Crudely articulated, but true in the most generous sense."

"Like, we own you?"

The guy carefully tied shut the folds of his umbrella. "Young Master Jones, indentured servanthood having been abolished even in your country, no. You do not, like, own me."

"So," said Charlie, "you're a nanny?"

The guy's eyes opened wide.

"No, moron. He's not a nanny," I said.

"Jack sent a butler," my mother said, mostly to herself.

The guy cleared his throat. "I am most conservative about

such matters," he said. "I would very much prefer to be known as a gentleman's gentleman."

My mother shook her head.

"A gentleman's gentleman," she said. "Jack sent a gentleman's gentleman."

The guy bowed his little bow again.

"There's just one problem," she said. "There's no gentleman here."

Then the guy looked straight at me. Really. Straight at me. "Perhaps not yet," he said, and he handed me the satellite-disk umbrella.

That was how the Butler came into our house.

Can I just say, I wasn't so sure about this. I mean, he *said* he was a gentleman's gentleman — which, obviously, is a dumb way to say "butler" — but he could have been some kind of missionary in disguise. Or someone selling satellite-disk umbrellas. Or someone casing out our place for a burglary. Or a serial killer. Anything.

I could tell my mother wasn't so sure about him either.

That's why she thought for a long time when the Butler offered to drive us to school. When he asked, I whispered "Serial killer" to my mother, and she whispered "The fuel pump in the Jeep," and I whispered "Probably no ID," and she whispered "Raining hard" — and it was still raining like an Australian tropical thunderstorm — but I shrugged and whispered, "Does it matter to you if you never see us alive again?"

and that was really stupid because now she bit her lip hard and it was so really stupid because it was like I had forgotten that funeral.

So really stupid.

She closed her eyes for, like, a minute and then she opened them again and said she'd decided to go along with us to school, and the Butler nodded. My mother gave me a look—not That Look, but a look that said, "Don't let this guy out of your sight because maybe you're right and he really could be a serial killer," and then she went upstairs to get dressed.

So I was all over him when he opened up the four lunch bags and folded napkins into them—just to be sure he was putting in only napkins and not tracts or poison powder or anything like that. And I was still all over him when he finished Annie's hair and got the staples out of Charlie's new socks and pinned back Emily's bangs again because they had already come out.

You never know what a serial killer might do to throw you off-guard.

Ned would have been all over him too, but he was pretty excited, and like I told you, dachshunds throw up a lot—which he did again underneath the kitchen table after he sniffed the Butler's wet cuffs. The Butler started to wipe it up—I didn't need to be all over him while he was doing that—and when my mother came down and saw him under the kitchen table, she said he didn't come across the Atlantic to clean up after a dog, and he said, "Madam, the parameters of my duties are wide-ranging"—so my mother let him take care of Ned's throw-up and then we all went outside, sort of crowded together under the satellite-disk umbrella, which I was still holding.

My mother got in front and the four of us squeezed in the back, and we drove to school in the Butler's car, which was big and long and purple—like an eggplant. It had white-rimmed tires. It had running boards. On the front it had a chrome statue of someone who looked like she would be pretty cold in a stiff wind. It had pale yellow seats made of soft leather. And it also had, according to the Butler, "a properly placed steering mechanism"—even though it sure looked wrong to me.

So that's what we drove in to school instead of the Jeep.

When we dropped Annie off at the fifth-grade door, the Butler got out of the car, came around in the Australian tropical thunderstorm with his satellite-disk umbrella, opened the passenger door, and said, "Miss Anne, make good decisions and remember who you are."

"I will," she said.

My mother watched her run into the building. "I could have sworn I put her hair in two braids," she said.

"She preferred the one," said the Butler.

When we dropped Charlie off, the Butler opened the door and said, "Miss Charlotte, make good decisions and remember who you are," and Charlie held up her foot to show the Butler she was wearing her new bright yellow socks.

My mother told her to cut it out and get inside before she got soaked.

When we dropped Emily off, the Butler opened the door and said, "Miss Emily, make good decisions and remember who you are," and Emily asked if the Butler was going to pick us up in his purple car after school.

"No," I said.

My mother said, "Watch for the Jeep."

Then we drove to the middle school building, and while the Butler got out of the car, I got out too — before he could open my door. But he stood at the curb with his satellite-disk umbrella in the Australian tropical thunderstorm — the rain was splashing off the running boards — and he took off his bowler and said, "Make good decisions and remember who you are, young Master Jones." He put his bowler back on.

"You think I'm going to forget who I am?" I said.

"You are entering middle school now," he said. "I think it quite likely." Then he opened his door, folded his umbrella, and got inside again.

He drove off with my mother in the seat beside him. For a moment, I wondered if I would ever see her again.

I checked my front pocket for the green marble.

Then Billy Colt came up behind me, and he said, "Who was that?"

"Our butler," I said.

"You have a butler?"

The marble was there. "So?" I said.

We watched the purple car pull in front of a bus and drive away in the rain.

"His car looks like an eggplant," said Billy Colt.

"Yup."

"And he looks like a missionary."

"Yup," I said.

"Or a serial killer."

"That too."

Then we went inside to start our first day of sixth grade.